The W

Sadie turned around and took a step—and went right through Trudy Toth.

"Eww, yuck!" Sadie shuddered and goose bumps popped out on her arms. "I *hate* when that happens!" She wagged a finger at Trudy. "Don't sneak up on me!"

Trudy's dark eyes were sad and filled with a pleading insistence that Sadie wanted no part of. Still, she felt her anger dissipate.

"It's okay to talk to me," Sadie said gently. "I can hear you, so go ahead and say whatever's on your mind. Just let it out. I promise you'll feel much better if you do."

Trudy looked around the room; then her eyes fixed on the huge red stain on the sofa. There was a good chance the woman didn't even know that her husband was dead. Sadie watched as Trudy walked around and around the room, clearly mystified.

"This is great. I've got a ghost in shock." As if the job wasn't hard enough already.

"Okay, listen up," Sadie began. She cleared her throat and spoke loudly. "Trudy, I'm sorry to have to tell you this, but you're dead. Your spirit is stuck here because, well, I don't know exactly why. Anyway, Grant is gone too, but I don't see him. I guess suicides don't hesitate. Look, you just need to let go. Your time here is over and—"

Trudy walked to the sofa that Grant had chosen as his final stop. She rubbed her finger into the stain.

"What the hell are you doing?" Sadie asked.

Trudy walked to the wall and began to print, using the blood on her finger. When she was done, the macabre message read *Not Grant.*

THE REMAINS
OF THE DEAD

A Ghost Dusters Mystery

WENDY ROBERTS

AN OBSIDIAN MYSTERY

OBSIDIAN
Published by New American Library, a division of
Penguin Group (USA) Inc., 375 Hudson Street,
New York, New York 10014, USA
Penguin Group (Canada), 90 Eglinton Avenue East, Suite 700, Toronto,
Ontario M4P 2Y3, Canada (a division of Pearson Penguin Canada Inc.)
Penguin Books Ltd., 80 Strand, London WC2R 0RL, England
Penguin Ireland, 25 St. Stephen's Green, Dublin 2,
Ireland (a division of Penguin Books Ltd.)
Penguin Group (Australia), 250 Camberwell Road, Camberwell, Victoria 3124,
Australia (a division of Pearson Australia Group Pty. Ltd.)
Penguin Books India Pvt. Ltd., 11 Community Centre, Panchsheel Park,
New Delhi - 110 017, India
Penguin Group (NZ), 67 Apollo Drive, Rosedale, North Shore 0632,
New Zealand (a division of Pearson New Zealand Ltd.)
Penguin Books (South Africa) (Pty.) Ltd., 24 Sturdee Avenue,
Rosebank, Johannesburg 2196, South Africa

Penguin Books Ltd., Registered Offices:
80 Strand, London WC2R 0RL, England

First published by Obsidian, an imprint of New American Library,
a division of Penguin Group (USA) Inc.

First Printing, December 2007
10 9 8 7 6 5 4 3 2 1

ACKNOWLEDGMENTS

I'd like to gratefully acknowledge Theresa Borst of Bio Clean Inc., who answered my countless questions regarding bio-recovery. She is a compassionate professional in her field. Any and all errors are my own.

Hugs to friend and author Mary J. Forbes, who is never too busy to consume huge amounts of coffee while brainstorming. A debt of appreciation goes out to the Non-Bombs—Colleen Gleason, Diana Peterfreund, Jana DeLeon, and Elly Snyder—for their huge support. Additional thanks to my fabulous agent, Miriam Kriss, for believing in this story and to Kristen Weber for her superb editiorial skills.

Most important acknowledgments go to my husband, Brent, and our four brilliant children, who endure countless boring meals and a lack of clean socks whenever I'm held prisoner by my muse.

Dying is the most embarrassing thing that can ever happen to you, because someone's got to take care of all your details.

—Andy Warhol

1

She dipped a scrub brush into the cleaning fluid and stroked the bedroom wall in wide, arched swipes. Although concentrating on the task at hand, Sadie tried not to ignore the person behind her.

"It's just not fair," he whined.

"Jacob, we've been over this a dozen times since yesterday," Sadie stated evenly as she brought the dripping brush up once more. "Talking about it won't change what happened. What you created. You made your bed and now you must lie in it, so to speak."

"That's not funny."

"Sorry." But Sadie laughed just the same, then took a step back to examine her work. Sometimes a little distance was necessary to see if you got it all.

"There should be another way," he griped.

"Jacob, I'll be blunt. You're dead. You sat on your bed and blew your brains out all over this wall." She strode toward him with a look of determination. "I'm sorry, but there's just no coming back from that kind of decision."

He looked pained—and not just because the entire left side of his head was missing. Sadie didn't blame him for hanging back—it was natural to be afraid to move beyond this life—but someone had to give him the kick in the ass he needed.

"But it was an accident," he said. "I didn't know it was loaded."

Sadie knew that was true. She felt Jacob's one good eye watching her intently.

"You believe me. I can tell."

"Fact is, we wouldn't be having this conversation if you'd committed suicide. I don't know why, but those who've intentionally pulled their own plugs have been immune to my abilities."

"Your family must be very proud," he said sarcastically. "Or is your whole family nuts?"

"I don't know anyone else cursed with the same power," Sadie said truthfully. "My parents don't know, my sister is still adjusting to the idea, and my best friend would like me to go on *Oprah*. But enough about me." She pinned him with a firm glare. "You can't hang out here. It's time to move on."

Jacob slumped down in the center of the room, in the exact place where his bed would have been if she hadn't already had the blood-soaked mattress hauled off to her warehouse to be kept in a secure biohazard room until it was picked up by the medical waste company. He sat there suspended, as if the bed were merely invisible.

"So, then what do I do?" he asked pitifully.

Sadie sighed. "Just relax and let it happen. Stop fighting and let go." She reached out to put her hand on his shoulder, but it dropped straight through because, of course, he wasn't physically there. A shiver of revulsion coursed through her, as it always did when she attempted physical contact with a spirit.

"I *am* tired," he admitted. "Okay, I'll try." Bravely closing his eyes, he let out a long, slow breath of surrender.

Jacob, or the apparition of Jacob, shimmered first, then gradually dissipated until it was totally gone.

"Finally."

Sadie blew out an exasperated breath. Sometimes

dealing with the dead was frustrating. Although it was gratifying to help them go over, she wished they'd do more listening and less talking. She knew, though, that the dead just wanted to be heard, and she was the only one who could listen.

She returned to the wall to scrub off the remaining brain matter that clung like petrified oatmeal.

"You're doing it again." Zack's voice was muffled from behind his disposable paper respirator. He walked closer to Sadie to make it easier to communicate. "I'm carrying supplies into the next room and I can hear you talking."

"Sorry," Sadie said over her shoulder. But she wasn't.

"If you're going to talk to the dead, at least do it when I'm not around." Zack stood with his hands on his hips. His blue disposable Tyvek suit, respirator, and booties matched her own.

"I can wait, but sometimes they can't," Sadie replied. She was sure that behind Zack's goggles he rolled his eyes.

"I'm bringing another load of bins to the warehouse," he said.

"That's fine." Sadie had already returned to her task. "I'll do a bit more here and we can finish the last of it in the morning."

"Don't stay too late or you'll miss Dawn's party."

"Oh, damn." Sadie sighed. "Guess I don't have much time."

"Not unless you want to go to your sister's thirtieth birthday party smelling of decomp." He chuckled and offered her a wink.

Zack was right. Washing away the smell of body decomposition took longer than a five-minute shower. Reluctantly, Sadie wrapped things up at the scene early and hurried home. She spent a lot of extra time in the shower and cringed when she glimpsed her watch as she dressed and rushed out the door.

It was only a couple miles to Dawn's Ballard-area home, but the misty drizzle made the roads slick. Sadie carefully cornered onto Midvale and then turned up the radio volume to cover the *thump thump* of the wipers.

A few minutes later she parked at the curb on Dawn's street, flung open the car door, and ran toward the house, dodging the branches of an overgrown cedar hogging the sidewalk. At the door, she could already hear the loud chorus of "Happy Birthday" being sung within, so she didn't bother with knocking, but just let herself inside. She quickly joined the back of the crowd of forty or so people in time for the finale. Dawn dramatically closed her eyes for her wish and blew out the candles to a crescendo of applause.

"By the skin of your teeth," Zack said in Sadie's ear.

"Has she noticed I'm late?"

"I don't think so. She's had a few."

Sadie looked at Dawn. Her face was flushed with liquor, and she was giddy from being the center of attention. Her long brown hair was clipped up in the back, and she wore a red sweater with a plunging neckline. Sadie slipped her arms out of her jacket and tossed it on the back of a chair, then made her way through the crowd to the dining room table.

"Sadie!" shouted Dawn's boyfriend, Noel, grabbing her by the arm and pulling her into an awkward hug. "You made it!"

"I wouldn't miss my baby sister's birthday," she said, forcing a smile.

"Better late than never," Dawn quipped, dipping her finger into the thick chocolate icing on the cake and then licking it off.

"Sorry I'm late." Sadie bent and kissed her sister's heavily rouged cheek. "Wow, so you're thirty, huh?" She pretended to look Dawn over critically. "You're officially old, then, and I guess that means I'm old as dirt."

"Thirty-two isn't dirt. You've got a little time before I put you in a home," Dawn teased. "You got your hair done. It looks nice."

"You think?" Sadie's hand went instinctively to her bobbed hair. She'd added blond highlights too, at the stylist's insistence. It still surprised her every time she looked in the mirror.

"I thought you liked it long. What made you cut it?"

"Just felt like it." Sadie shrugged. There was no way Dawn wanted to hear the truth—that it was difficult to get the smell of body decomp out of her hair when it was long.

"Help me hand out the cake. And don't sneak out early. We got a surprise for later."

Carrying as many cake-loaded paper plates as she could manage, Sadie served and smiled until her face hurt. Then her mouth curved down and she frowned at Dawn sucking face with Noel in the corner. Damn, if they didn't look happy. Too happy.

Snagging the last two pieces of cake, Sadie went in search of Zack. She found him in the living room, drink in hand, talking to a pretty redhead. He looked good out of a hazmat suit. He wore snug Levi's and a green long-sleeved T that brought out the olive in his complexion and clung nicely to his broad shoulders. He'd let his dark hair grow out a bit lately and it softened the determined look of his square jaw. He had no trouble attracting the ladies. His trouble was keeping them, although Sadie sensed he was not the relationship kind.

So as not to interrupt his chances with the young woman, Sadie hung back and perched on the arm of an overstuffed sofa. Carefully balancing the two plates of cake, she pretended to be interested in the conversation between two women nearby.

"So, what do you do?" the redhead asked Zack, tossing her hair flirtatiously.

This should be good. Sadie leaned in just a little. She couldn't help herself.

"I'm involved with a niche cleaning company," Zack replied, straightening to his full height, just shy of six feet.

Not a bad line, Sadie thought. She'd used that one herself. All would be hunky-dory now if the redhead let it go.

"How about you?" Zack asked. "Let me guess— you're a model."

Sadie rolled her eyes.

"I'm a dental hygienist." She smiled, pleased with the compliment, and sipped her drink daintily. "What exactly is a niche cleaning company?"

"Nothing too interesting," Zack replied smoothly. "How do you know the birthday girl?"

"We're neighbors. I live just a few doors down." She reached out and picked invisible lint from Zack's shirt. "So what kind of things does a niche cleaning company clean?"

Time to attempt a rescue.

"Cake, anyone?" Sadie asked. Getting to her feet, she thrust the two plates of cake toward Zack and his potential lover.

"Just what I was waiting for," Zack said, his black eyes locked in a serious gaze with Sadie's.

She smiled back. She was pretty damn sure Zack wasn't talking about the cake. He looked relieved to be momentarily rescued. Taking both plates, he offered one to the redhead. She looked the type to be on a perpetual diet, and sure enough, she refused the cake, so it was returned to Sadie.

"You don't know what you're missing," Sadie remarked to the model-type hygienist as she dug a fork down through the layers of the cake and brought a bite to her mouth. Between the chocolate layers was custard filling. The gooey texture and color reminded her of the bodily fluids they sponged up after a death that had been left unattended, but it didn't faze her. Sadie eyed Zack. He was looking at the custard too and possibly thinking the same thing.

"I heard you mention that you're a dental hygienist," Sadie said around a mouthful of cake. "That sounds really interesting. Doesn't it, Zack? I bet you meet all kinds of different people, from all walks of life."

"Not really," she said with a smirk. "You've seen one mouth, you've seen 'em all."

We laughed politely.

"I bet your niche cleaning company involves something like toxic waste, right?"

"Sort of," Zack replied. "There is definitely bio-recovery involved."

Well, I tried, Sadie thought, and she made her way back across the room to where one of Dawn's girlfriends was liberally pouring drinks from a makeshift bar. The friend fixed Sadie a very strong gin and tonic and tossed in a large wedge of lime to bob amongst the ice cubes. Sadie sipped her drink, then turned to look across the crowded living room to see if Zack had managed to extricate himself from the woman's career-directed questions.

Sadie could tell the *exact* moment when the redhead got it. First, a look of wide-eyed, jaw-dropping surprise crossed her face. It was followed immediately by pure, unadulterated revulsion.

Sadie managed to hide her bemused grin behind her drink. Being a social leper was a by-product of their line of work. Her enjoyment of Zack's discomfort faltered when her mother and father walked through Dawn's front door. She hadn't expected them to show, since Dawn had mentioned she'd already shared a birthday lunch with the parental unit earlier in the day.

Noel walked up to Mom and Dad and dragged them over to the front of the room, where Dawn appeared to be waiting.

"Okay, everyone. Can I have your attention, please?" Noel was standing on a chair over by the fireplace, waving his hands in the air and just generally looking ridiculous.

Dawn giggled and pulled him off the chair so they were standing side by side. Once the chatter in the room subsided, he cleared his throat loudly.

"It's great to see so many of our closest friends here as well as family. Dawn and I thought there'd be no better time to make an important announcement." He paused for effect. "Earlier this evening I asked Dawn to be my bride, and she said yes."

There were raucous cheers, and the crowd tightened around the couple in congratulatory hugs. Mom's eyes shone with happy tears, and Dad's chest puffed proudly as he moved forward and pumped Noel's hand in an enthusiastic shake.

"Don't look so thrilled," Zack whispered in Sadie's ear.

"You wouldn't get it," she mumbled into her glass before quickly downing the rest.

"Sure I would. It's simple. You hate the guy. It's written all over your face. Oh, and if you grip your glass any tighter, it'll break and you'll be bleeding all over your sister's floor."

Sadie put her glass down on a side table and shook her head vehemently. "Noel is a nice guy. I don't hate him."

"Then why—"

But Sadie had turned away and was making her way through the crowd to disappear down the hall, where it was quieter. She wasn't at all surprised to see that Zack had followed her.

"Sorry. It's none of my business," he said.

"Right," she agreed. "It's not." At the hurt look on

his face, she lightened the moment with a quick smile and added, "Hey, it's just the ex-cop in you that makes you nosy."

"Not being nosy. Just worried. I care about you, Sadie."

She shifted uncomfortably from one foot to the other.

"Sure. We're friends, right?" She looked over his shoulder, instead of up into his serious gaze.

"You hired me when no one else would touch me, so yeah, we're friends. Except a real friend would probably tell me what's going on."

"Look, there's nobody I'd rather mop guts with, but some stuff I don't talk about. With anyone."

He nodded and turned to walk away. Feeling the need to offer an olive branch, Sadie tugged at his sleeve.

"C'mon." She pulled him into the master bedroom and shut the door behind them.

"Look at this," she said, lifting a heavy pewter frame from Dawn's dresser and thrusting it into Zack's face. "You know who this is, right?"

"Sure." Taking the picture from her hands, Zack frowned uneasily. "It's your brother, Brian."

"And?"

"And what?"

"Look at him," she insisted, stabbing at the photo with her finger.

The photo had been taken when Brian was in his late twenties. He was leaning against the hood of an old Mustang, his pride and joy. The smile on his face didn't offer a single hint that he would blow his head off in the bathroom of his home a year later.

"Can't you see it?" Sadie demanded impatiently. "Noel looks *just* like him. The nose, the hair, the eyes—they could be twins, for God's sake!"

"Really?" Zack pulled the picture close and squinted at it for a moment before handing it back.

He combed his fingers through his thick dark hair and shrugged. "I don't see it."

"Really? Sheesh, open your eyes! Noel and Brian are both tall, skinny guys, and they have blond hair that they wear a little long."

"Sadie, you just described thousands of guys in Seattle and probably at least ten at this party."

She ignored his remark as she dusted the frame lovingly with her sleeve.

"Brian was the oldest. He looked out for us. Sometimes he was a pain in the ass because he'd scare off any boyfriends we happened to bring around." She smiled tightly at the memory. "He said if they weren't tough enough to deal with him, they weren't good enough for us." She put the picture frame back on the dresser. "Dawn took it hard when he died. We both did. I thought she was handling it okay until she hooked up with Noel. Then within two months they're living together and now they're getting married." She frowned. "I've seen the way she looks at Noel and how they joke around. It reminds me so much of her and Brian together that it's practically incestuous. I just don't want to see her get hurt."

Zack was quiet for a minute, then said, "We should get back. They're probably opening the gifts by now."

"Damn. I left mine in the car."

Zack joined the rest of the crowd in the living room while Sadie snagged her jacket.

"You're not sneaking out, are you?" her mother asked, stepping forward to block the door.

"I'm just going to the car to get Dawn's gift."

"We'll need to discuss the wedding shower."

"Mom, they've been engaged for mere seconds. There's no need to rush out and buy invitations."

"You don't look happy." Her mather frowned and put a hand on Sadie's shoulder. "And you're too skinny."

Just then a few *ooh*s and *ah*s erupted from the living room as Dawn opened her first gift.

"I've got to get Dawn's present," Sadie said and zipped around her mother and outside into the cool February drizzle.

She walked to her Honda Accord, then reached in through the passenger-side door to retrieve the envelope with a tiny red bow on it. It began raining harder, so she quickly tucked it into her coat pocket so it wouldn't get wet. She'd gotten Dawn a gift certificate for a manicure and pedicure. She planned to suggest they go together, do lunch, and make it a sister day. Now visions of that time being filled with wedding discussions turned her stomach.

As she headed back up the walk, she saw Zack leaving the house.

"Going so soon?" she asked.

He nodded. "Yeah. I want to finish the Carson place early tomorrow."

Her cell phone rang and she dug it from her pocket. "Scene-2-Clean," she answered.

"Hello, my name is Sylvia Toth. I got your number from Detective Petrovich with the Seattle Police Department. He said that you do cleaning. Well, not regular cleaning but, um, crime-scene cleaning?" Her voice trembled with emotion as she got the last words out.

Sadie lifted a hand to stop Zack from walking any farther.

"Yes, Mrs. Toth, my company specializes in cleaning crime scenes. Are you in need of our services?" A silly question—there would be no other reason for Petrovich to give out Sadie's number.

"It's my son's place," she whispered. "His house is on Taylor Avenue in Queen Anne. The police said they wouldn't do it. They told me that once they take their evidence, they're done. I can't believe that they

just leave the place like that and it's up to the family.
I looked up cleaners in the phone book, but they don't
handle this kind of work." She paused. "I didn't want
to . . . I mean, I just can't do it myself."

"Of course not," Sadie said soothingly. "This is exactly why we're here, Mrs. Toth. Could you hold on
just one moment?" Sadie held the cell phone to her
leg so she could mute her voice and whispered to
Zack, "Next of kin calling regarding a situation in
Queen Anne. Have you heard of it? Last name is
Toth?"

"Toth. Toth," he repeated with a frown. Then realization dawned. "Right. M.S. case." "M.S." was their
code for a murder-suicide. "It was in the *Times* a couple weeks ago."

The scene had probably only recently been released
by the police.

"It was harsh," he said, shielding his eyes from the
rain, which was coming down harder now. "Husband
stabbed his wife upstairs, then shot himself downstairs.
There'll be two scenes to clean up in that house."

Sadie returned the phone to her ear. "Mrs. Toth?
We'd be pleased to assist you in cleaning your son's
home. If it's okay with you, I'll contact Detective Petrovich to see if I have his permission to enter the
home. Then I'll go in and look for the insurance papers in order to make the claim—unless you already
have those?"

"Oh no, they'd be inside the house. Do I, will I
need to . . ."

Her voice trailed off.

"No, Mrs. Toth, you won't need to enter the home,"
Sadie said gently. "Just leave it all to me."

"Thank you," she whispered, her relief evident.

Sadie got the woman's phone number, then disconnected with a promise to call her back in the morning.

"Tell me about this one," Sadie said to Zack. "How
long till discovery?"

"I think the paper said it was three days before the bodies were found. The husband owned a sportswear store and the employees thought it was weird that he didn't show up at the store. Guess they called it in."

She nodded. Three days. The decomp might not be too bad, then, unless they had the heat cranked high in the house. Still, there would be the usual flies and maggots mingling with blood spatter and tissue.

"Are you going to head over there tomorrow?" Zack asked. "Do you want me to come along while you do the initial walk-through?"

"Nah, that's okay. We're almost through at the Carson house. Go ahead and finish up that one. There'll be time enough for you to meet me at the new scene later tomorrow, after I've met with Mrs. Toth to get the contract signed. Provided she wants to go ahead—"

"She will. Her only other choice is to do it herself," he said dryly.

"Right, so if she wants us to proceed," Sadie continued, "we'll start on it after lunch and go late."

"Why the rush?"

"Didn't your mom teach you to never put off to tomorrow what you can clean today?"

"Yeah, but she was talking about cleaning my bedroom, not mopping body decomp fluids."

2

Detective Petrovich didn't sound at all surprised to hear from Sadie on Saturday morning.

"Figured you'd end up getting the job," he said.

Seattle detectives would send clients her way, but even if they didn't, sometimes people would find her company listed in the Yellow Pages under *Trauma Clean*. Scene-2-Clean was listed with only one other company, Scour Power. Scour took care of drug lab cleans and squalor, while Sadie's company handled the blood and guts. Advertising in her line of work was a little difficult. She couldn't exactly send out coupons in the mail.

"So SPD's all done? The house is cleared for entry?" Sadie asked.

"For all those willing." He paused. "And the only ones willing would be you and your partner."

Technically, Zack wasn't Sadie's partner. She was the boss and he the employee, but frequently people thought it was the other way around. Apparently, the public felt that if trauma cleanup had a gender, it was male.

Having picked up the keys earlier, Sadie headed her Scene-2-Clean van toward Queen Anne, veering away from the Space Needle, which at the moment was cut in half by low clouds. It was just after nine, and she hadn't had coffee yet, so she stopped by Coffee Ladro in Lower Queen Anne, where the barista happily made her a latte to go. Sadie warmed her hands on the cup as she stepped outside. Even though the pregnant clouds overhead promised another damp day, all the chairs outside the café were occupied by customers.

Sadie hopped back into her van and drove deeper into the affluent neighborhood. As she sipped her coffee, she slowed, alternately checking her map and admiring the stylish architecture of the older, well-maintained homes in the area. She picked up speed down the tree-lined streets and turned onto Taylor. Sculpted hedges were pruned carefully so as not to block the views. Sadie looked closely at the house numbers as she drove and finally found the right place. She parked in front of a turn-of-the-century home, taking a moment to whistle appreciatively at the view of Mount Rainier, majestic in the distance.

It wasn't often that she got to work in a home with such a nice view. Of course, the inside wouldn't be nearly as pleasant.

Sadie grabbed her gear—disposable Tyvek hazmat suit, respirator, gloves, booties, and camera—from the back of the vehicle, then walked around the house to the back door. She geared up on the back deck before entering the house for the first time.

A huge part of the job involved protection from blood-borne pathogens, and it wasn't something she took lightly. She now completely understood why some men were reluctant to wear condoms. It was difficult for her to feel her way around a crime scene when she was so thoroughly protected. However, she was in no hurry to pick up HIV, hepatitis C, or any of the other dozen possible diseases that could be floating about at a scene, so she wouldn't cut corners on protection.

From what she knew, the kitchen hadn't been touched by the crime, so it would be an area they could designate as a safe zone for donning and doffing gear. If possible, she and Zack always liked to have a room at a scene where they could change and have space to store the supplies they needed.

Fully dressed, she felt like an astronaut ready to step onto a new planet (one small step for Sadie Novak, a giant, nasty stride for womankind). She headed for the back door.

The faint coppery scent of blood reached her a few steps away. When she slid the key into the dead bolt, she donned her inner protective gear and slammed shut the gates of her emotions.

The back entrance of the turn-of-the-century renovated Craftsman home swung open into a newly updated eat-in kitchen. Black-and-white checkerboard tiles glistened beneath her feet. Yes, the room would be a perfect safe zone, particularly since a heavy wooden door separated it from the rest of the house. That door was closed, so with camera in hand, Sadie walked through the kitchen and pushed it open, stepping into a formal living room. She spent a moment admiring the sleek hardwood and tasteful antiques. The large granite coffee table in the center of the room probably weighed a ton.

What had once been a stunning ivory brocade sofa trimmed in maple was now part of a macabre death scene. It was a real shame that she would have to cut up that blood-soaked couch and stuff it piece by piece into the large rubber tubs used to dispose of contaminated waste.

The house had two scenes to be dealt with. This one, where the husband had taken his own life, and one upstairs, where he'd slaughtered his wife. Those were all the details Sadie needed—or wanted—to get the job done.

She focused her camera, angled her head, and snapped one picture, then turned and snapped another. She needed the photos both for insurance purposes and for her own personal files. Slowly she walked around the circumference of the living room, taking in the entire main-floor scene and snapping photos from different angles, zooming close on spatter that covered a floor-to-ceiling bookshelf against the wall.

Flies buzzed around her head and she nonchalantly swatted them away. She didn't need to be told that the husband had sat on the sofa and used a high-powered rifle to end his life. The room told the complete story through its horrific display of blood spatter, dried tissue, and bone fragments.

With detached reason, Sadie examined the blood-soaked sofa. She bent close to the congealed puddle on the hardwood beneath it, where a few maggots still attempted to survive even though their main food source, the body, had been removed.

Sadie snapped close-ups as well as wide shots to take in the entire scene. After a few minutes more, she moved upstairs, pausing briefly to note the scenic view from a window on the top landing. Once cleaned, this house would sell. Maybe not quickly, due to the circumstances, but it would eventually fetch a hefty price tag in today's hot real estate market.

Sadie made her way to the master bedroom, the next trauma scene. Later, she would check all the other rooms to be sure she hadn't missed anything. The bedroom walls had high arcs of blood spatter, small flecks of tissue, and a final wide expanse of sticky red in the corner between the bed and the dresser. There would be no saving the wall-to-wall Berber carpeting.

After snapping half a dozen photos of the room, she folded her arms across her chest thoughtfully, calculating how many forty-gallon bins she would need for hauling out all the contaminated waste, as well as the cleaning supplies and man-hours. She preferred to estimate high to be sure she allowed enough time to get the job done. When she was confident she had a handle on what would be required, she turned to leave.

A scream burned her throat but was muffled by her respirator and mask. There was a man casually leaning against the door frame.

"Sorry. I didn't mean to scare you," he said through a hesitant smile of perfect teeth.

"You didn't scare me. Just gave me a start." Sadie shouted to be heard through her disposable respirator and placed a hand over her heart in startled annoyance.

Sheesh, why couldn't the dead ever knock?

"You get the job of cleaning up, huh?" he asked. "I wondered who'd be doing that." He shifted nervously from one foot to the other.

He was a gorgeous man—blond, blue-eyed, and buff. Dawn would've called him eye candy. He also appeared to be intact. Usually spirits appeared to her in the same bodily condition and clothing they had died in, but occasionally they appeared as they remembered themselves. Maybe it was a last-ditch attempt at denial or vanity.

"The place is a real mess," Sadie said flatly. She couldn't pick and choose who visited her, but she was in no mood to make polite conversation with a murderer.

"A dirty job, but someone has to do it, I guess," he said dryly. "I don't envy you."

He's certainly casual enough about it, Sadie thought with distaste. Annoyance pricked at her. The souls that visited her were usually contrite and frequently remorseful, particularly in a murder-suicide. This guy looked neither. Then again, he could've been crazy, probably *was* to do this to his wife and himself. Sadie believed that crazy didn't fade much, even in death.

"You're probably wondering who I am and why I'm here," he said.

"Not particularly," Sadie replied, fiddling with her camera.

She suddenly realized she'd yet to check the bedroom's powder room to see if her services were also required there.

"I've got work to do."

Turning her back on the specter, she opened a nearby pocket door and walked into the bathroom. It appeared clean, but to be sure, she pulled up the window blinds and allowed in some natural sunlight before examining the area more closely.

A couple of minutes later Sadie stiffened with a potent realization. If the guy she had just seen was the one who blew his brains out downstairs after killing his wife, she shouldn't have been able to see him. Suicides didn't appear to her. She stepped back into the bedroom to confront her visitor, but he was gone.

Something about the situation made her uncomfortable. Still, she pushed her uneasy thoughts aside and began her thorough search of the rest of the house. All the other rooms seemed fine. No more visitors appeared, and the scenes to be dealt with were confined to the master bedroom and living room. An upstairs spare room had been converted to an office, and after looking through an already opened file cabinet, she located the insurance paperwork for the house.

Usually Sadie would file the claim herself. If the insurance company balked, she occasionally had to get the next of kin to do it. The more responsibility she took on, the less traumatized the families would feel. She got satisfaction in making sure the families didn't have to suffer through the cleaning. Easing spirits over to the next dimension also gave her a surreal boost, something she hadn't experienced while teaching math to second graders.

With the necessary documents in hand, she headed

back downstairs and into the kitchen. She made a mental note to ask Mrs. Toth if she wanted all food items in the fridge and pantry disposed of. That wasn't something the families often thought about and it wasn't a service the insurance company would pay Sadie's company for, but she usually offered to take care of it regardless.

From the corner of her eye, she noticed that the dead bolt on the back door was unlocked. She cursed under her breath. It was unlike her not to secure the place when she was inside, particularly if she was alone.

After doffing her gear and stuffing it into a medical waste bin, Sadie locked up the house and returned to her van.

When Sadie arrived at Mrs. Toth's small condo in Bellevue after lunch, the woman insisted on making a large pot of tea. Sadie hated tea, being more of a Starbucks coffee girl. Still, she realized that Mrs. Toth wanted to sit in her cozy kitchen in her pleasant apartment to discuss this unpleasant business, and she was willing to grant the woman that dignity. Having a sit-down with the client was the polite thing to do. Particularly since her clients tended to sob, wail, and occasionally be heavily medicated.

Mrs. Toth did not cry, but she wrung her hands incessantly when she didn't have them wrapped tightly around her delicate china teacup.

"I just didn't know what to do about the house. If my husband was alive, he would've handled it, but I didn't know where to turn. It was a relief to find someone who actually does this kind of thing. Thank you," Mrs. Toth repeated for the fourth time.

"You don't need to thank me, Mrs. Toth. This is what I do. It's my job," Sadie said softly. "I'm glad to save families from the ordeal."

Mrs. Toth nodded, picked up the pretty flowered

teapot on the table, and topped off her tea. Sadie covered her own cup to indicate she didn't want a refill.

"You can call me Sylvia," Mrs. Toth said. "I guess you're used to this kind of thing since it's your job." Her face slipped into a bewildered, mournful gaze. "I just don't know what happened." Her eyes met Sadie's. "They were so happy. I even thought they'd start a family soon. Grant had been hinting about filling the house with the pitter-patter of little feet. They'd finally finished renovating that old place, and Grant's business was doing so well that he'd expanded to a second store in Portland."

Damn. Sadie hated knowing too many details about the victims. It made it difficult for her to remain detached about her work.

"Look how happy they were." Sylvia pulled a photo out of her purse.

Sadie was about to stop her. She really didn't like to look at photos of people when she was working a trauma clean. But now, when she caught a glimpse of the couple, she took the picture from Sylvia's hand.

"How odd. I actually thought he was blond," Sadie murmured.

"Grant? No, he's always been a brunette, like me. At least, like I was before the gray." Sylvia frowned. "Why would you think he was blond?"

Oh, just because some blond ghost visited me at Grant's house. She frowned at the picture. Guess that explained why she was able to see her ghostly visitor. Wrong ghost. The house was old. She must've been visited by a spirit unrelated to the scene she was working.

Sadie handed the photo back and said, "The house was beautifully remodeled, but it has to be nearly a hundred years old, right? Possibly many owners have lived there?"

"Oh yes," Sylvia replied. "Grant and Trudy were quite proud that they'd kept some of the original character of the home. They were constantly scanning antique dealers for unique odds and ends. Just last month Trudy found some perfect glass doorknobs."

Sadie wasn't listening to most of what Mrs. Toth said. She just kept thinking, *Lord, I hope a half dozen people haven't died in that house. If all the other spirits haven't found their way to the other side by now, I'm never going to be able to get any work done there.*

As Sylvia looked sadly at the photograph, the sorrow on her face appeared to age the sixty-something woman another ten years.

"I should've known something was wrong. I should have seen it." Her shoulders fell.

"There's no way you could have known."

It was what families wanted to hear, and more often than not, Sadie believed, it was the truth.

"It really doesn't make any sense. They were happy and finally settled. They moved down to Portland for a few months to get Grant's new sportswear store up and running, but Grant couldn't wait to get Trudy back to Seattle. She hated Portland and he loved her with all his heart. He wanted her to be happy." Her lower lip began to tremble. "He loved her so much, he would never . . ."

She fumbled then, because of course there was no *he would never*—Grant *had* killed his wife, and that was the sickening truth. Poor Mrs. Toth would probably never be able to align the son she knew with the man who had committed such a horrific act.

Sylvia's sobs grew louder, and Sadie decided it was time to call in the big artillery.

"Five years ago my brother killed himself," she began.

It was something she seldom discussed with anyone except her clients. They knew her loss. Could feel her pain.

"Brian was twenty-nine, healthy, had just been promoted, and was engaged to be married. He loved to rock climb and hike. Mr. Outdoors." She smiled at the memory. "Nobody in my family suspected anything was wrong. He shot himself. It's still hard for us to accept." Truth. "But time does lessen the pain." Big fat lie.

Sylvia sniffed and dabbed at her eyes with a napkin. "And that is why you chose this line of work?"

Sadie nodded. "I like to think that this line of work chose me. My brother was an unattended death, meaning nobody discovered his body for weeks." Uhoh. Too much information. Sadie rushed on. "We actually thought he was away on vacation." She bit down on the inside of her cheek. She wouldn't drag out any of the details that still haunted her dreams at night. "I had to do the cleanup because I didn't want the job to fall to my parents. At that time, one of the police officers told me that many big cities had independent bio-recovery technicians who were trained to perform this kind of cleaning service, but unfortunately Seattle wasn't one of them at that time."

"It must've been horrible for you."

"It was," Sadie said. "But afterward, I left my job as a second-grade teacher and took the training I needed to start this business." She paused and added with conviction, "Families of victims should never have to see what I've seen."

Sylvia Toth nodded and reached out to gently squeeze Sadie's fingers.

Misery loves company, Sadie thought. *And people sure bond quick over tragedy.*

Without further delay, Sadie brought out her contract and had Mrs. Toth sign for the work to be done.

After leaving the Toth residence, Sadie met Zack at the Carson place and was pleasantly surprised to find that the clean had been completed.

"You must've worked your ass off this morning," she remarked.

Zack looked over his shoulder and said with mock alarm, "You're right! It's gone!"

"Oh, it's still there." Sadie was tempted to pinch his butt good-naturedly, but she didn't.

There were always lighthearted moments when a job was finished. Sadie felt particularly good when she'd helped a spirit like Jacob's to go over. It was an endorphin-fueled rush that pooled with relief that she was able to help another soul.

They busily loaded the balance of the supplies from this job into the Scene-2-Clean van. If they hadn't had the Toth scene waiting, they would have headed to a pub to obliterate death with a few beers. Instead, they left Zack's Mustang and drove together to the Blue Onion Bistro for sandwiches. The bright blue and yellow interior of the cozy café offered a cheery contrast to the dreary day outside. While they sat, they talked about the crappy weather, agreeing that rain was still better than snow, and they moved on to discuss the Seahawks' chances for the Super Bowl. The conversation covered pretty much anything except work.

They each ordered the turkey club, which came with the best potato salad in the world, but neither of them ate much. Zack didn't like having a full belly when they started a new job, and though Sadie possessed a cast-iron stomach that wasn't affected by the gross-out factor, she hadn't felt a burning appetite for food in months. Not since the fifth anniversary of Brian's suicide, when her mother had deemed it appropriate to have a massive banquet to honor his life. Every bite of food had tasted like failure, a reminder that Sadie would never know why he did it.

Sadie ate a few bites of her sandwich and asked the waitress to wrap it up to go as she got up and slipped her arms into her Gore-Tex jacket.

"You feel like driving?" she asked.

"Sure."

Sadie tossed him the keys and they walked out the

door and quick-stepped through the drizzle toward the van. Once buckled up, Sadie started to give Zack directions to the Toth house, but he stopped her.

"Give me the address and I'll find it on my own. I don't trust you," he said.

"Sheesh, I give bad directions one time—"

"Yeah, and that one time landed me asking for directions at a gay nightclub on a clothing-optional night," he growled.

"And yet your masculinity remained intact," Sadie said with a smirk.

"No thanks to you."

They drove the few miles to the Toth house in easy silence. When they arrived, Zack hopped out and Sadie got behind the wheel and drove back home to stock up on a few extra things they might need for the large job. Her errand would give Zack the couple moments alone that he always preferred when adjusting to a new job.

While she was at home, her best friend dropped in for a visit.

"You have to see it to believe it!" Pam gushed. "I ran into Marge—remember her from school? She looks years younger. I bet she's had work done. I've been thinking of going for Botox. What do you think?"

Sadie looked over at her friend. Her pale complexion needed something, but it wasn't Botox.

"You look great, like always." Sadie turned away and resumed loading supplies into the van. Pam quickly got the message.

"You're busy. Let's have a drink later."

"I don't think so. This is a new scene, and I'll probably be working late because—"

"Ugh. No details, please."

Sadie glanced sideway at Pam's sour face. She hated Sadie's job and anything related to blood or gore.

"I have no idea how late we'll go today, but you can always try me later."

"Sounds good," Pam said. "Ciao for now."

Sadie had finished packing up while they talked, and now she drove back to the Toth house and joined Zack inside.

She greeted him with a wave. There wouldn't be a lot of chitchat between them at this point, not until they got into the next stage of cleaning, when most of the grisly remains were cleaned and respirators were no longer required.

Sadie moved closer so Zack could hear her through the respirator.

"Why don't you work the upstairs scene and I'll take the main floor?"

Zack gave her a thumbs-up, grabbed the supplies he needed, and disappeared up the stairs.

Sadie liked to begin on the edges of a scene and move in an ever-tightening circle toward ground zero. With a red rubber bin in one hand and cleansers in the other, she headed for the farthest wall, toward the floor-to-ceiling bookshelf. Using a step stool she'd brought, she systematically took everything off the top shelf and scrubbed away spatter with powerful disinfectant. It wasn't enough to simply swab off the blood; absolutely everything had to also be decontaminated. It was slow, exacting work.

As she neared the middle of the eight-shelf unit, she found that the concentration of debris was heavier and there were items, mostly books, that could not be salvaged. These things she tossed into the waste bins. Eventually, everything she and Zack used on a job, as well as all of their protective gear, would go into the bins and be taken to the medical waste facility.

Next of kin gave permission for Scene-2-Clean to dispose of any contaminated items, whether real or personal property. Anything that could not be perfectly cleaned had to go. That included furniture, floorboards, and drywall if necessary. Since starting her company, Sadie had developed a newfound respect for high-gloss paint, which didn't soak up bodily fluids.

Where contamination was heaviest, Sadie used emulsifiers to soften dried tissue and fluids. She reached a shelf that held several five-by-seven photographs in matching black frames. As she systematically wiped and sprayed the frames, something caught her eye. She stared at the photo in her hand. A happy couple dressed in their wedding finery, along with their grinning wedding party, smiled back at her. One of the tuxedo-clad men was definitely the same blond guy who had paid her a visit upstairs that morning.

Sadie let out a startled gasp, then stumbled and nearly dropped the picture.

She got to her feet, took a deep breath, and with the picture in hand, went up the stairs two at a time to the bedroom where Zack was working. He was on his hands and knees in a corner of the room, using a sharp blade to cut out and remove the stained carpet and underlay. He was totally unaware of the pretty brunette sitting on the bed, hugging her knees to her chest and rocking slowly back and forth. The savage slash across the woman's throat told Sadie immediately that this was Trudy Toth.

"Oh, I don't need this," Sadie muttered.

"What?" Zack asked over his shoulder.

"Nothing," Sadie said, stealing a sidelong glance at the apparition.

"Do *not* tell me there's a ghost in this room with me," Zack said with a long-suffering expression.

"Forget that. I need to ask you about this picture." She moved closer so she wouldn't have to shout through her respirator, and thrust the frame in his face.

"What about it?" He stood and took the frame. "You missed a spot along the edge," he pointed out.

"I'm not done cleaning it yet, but that's not what I'm talking about. Who do you see in the picture?"

"A bride, a groom, and, I assume, their best man and maid of honor. Is this a trick question?"

Sadie took the picture back, frowned down at it, then looked up again. Trudy looked much happier in the photo than she did right now with the grotesque slice in her neck.

"Never mind."

Sadie sighed and headed back downstairs. An unsettling thought occurred to her as she reentered the living room. She knew she wouldn't be able to return to work until she figured this out. She stepped into the kitchen safe zone, doffed her gear, and used her cell phone to dial Sylvia Toth.

"Hello?" Sylvia said.

"Hi, Sylvia, it's Sadie. Please excuse me for the strange question, but could you tell me who the best man was at your son's wedding?"

"His best man? Why on earth would you need to know about him?"

"It's kind of silly," she said, but her thumping heart said otherwise. "It's just that I saw their wedding picture, and the man standing beside Grant looks familiar to me. I think I've met him before." Certainly not a total lie.

"Oh. Well, that would be Kent Lasko."

"Kent Lasko," Sadie repeated. "And is he, well, is he still alive?"

"My goodness, of course he is! Why would you think he wasn't?"

"Just humor me for a minute, Sylvia. When was the last time you saw Kent?"

"Not for a while," she replied. "His mother is a good friend of mine. Probably the last time I saw him was at Ramona's sixtieth birthday party, three or four years ago. Ramona moved to Florida a few months after that."

Sadie rolled her eyes and made a huge effort to keep her voice calm.

"Okay, but if you don't mind me asking, how do you know Kent's still alive if you haven't heard from him or seen him in three or four years?" Sadie asked.

"For one thing, he sent a stunning arrangement of white orchids to the funeral," Sylvia replied with a little heat. "Plus Ramona and I still chat on the phone occasionally, and I'm sure she would've mentioned it if her son just happened to die."

"Of course. Thanks—and sorry for bothering you."

Sadie disconnected the call and shuddered at the realization that her visitor had not been a ghost. Her fingers trembled as she pocketed her phone. She knew that the living could be far more lethal than the dead.

3

"Sadie, you can't just call up the police and tell them that you normally see dead people at trauma scenes but since this guy was alive, he was breaking and entering," Zack said flatly. "Well, you could say that, but they'd probably put you in a home."

"I'm sure I can manage to put it a little more diplomatically than that," Sadie replied. Truthfully, though, she didn't know how she could word it without coming off as insane and risking her company's credibility.

"There's no sign of a break-in. He could've had a key, but it doesn't look like anything was taken or even disturbed. Hell, he could just be frigging morbidly curious, like half the freaks we meet."

Sadie nodded. "You're right."

"If he took something, that would be a problem. Even if he had a key, he doesn't have authorization to remove property from the house."

"I guess I've no proof he did anything besides walk through, either using his own key or because I left the door unlocked."

"But, hey, if it'll make you feel better, I'll call Petrovich and talk to him about it," Zack offered.

They were sitting out on the Toths' covered back deck. Their respirators were off, and Zack had just lit his second cigarette in a row. It had been raining for weeks; Seattle seemed to be going for a record. When the rain suddenly began to come down in torrents, the branches of a two-story-tall monkey puzzle tree in the yard started to bounce from the force. The damp gave Sadie chills—or it could've been apprehension. She rubbed her arms for warmth.

"If I were you and you were me, would you tell Petrovich?" Sadie asked.

"If I were you and spent my time talking to dead people, I'd probably just drink myself into a coma."

"Nice. Real nice," she muttered.

He chuckled and took a deep drag on his smoke, then tapped the ash over the rail onto the ground.

"Look, if you really want to go to the SPD, then I'll back you up, Sadie. You know I will."

"But?"

"But then you'd better be prepared for the shit to hit the fan. They're going to want to know why you didn't call right away. If it were me, I might be tempted to leave it alone."

Sadie examined a chipped fingernail and gnawed on the cuticle.

"What if he had another reason for being in the house? What if he did it, Zack?"

"Killed these people?"

She nodded.

"Petrovich called it as a murder-suicide. Detectives don't pull that decision out of thin air. He had evidence to back it up, and you can bet your ass he double- and triple-checked it."

Sadie was less convinced.

"I'll be right back," she told him. She slipped her respirator and gloves back on and reentered the house through the back door.

Upstairs she found Trudy Toth where she'd left her, still sitting on the bed, knees pulled up to her chest, rocking back and forth. She seemed totally zoned out and didn't even look up or turn toward Sadie when she entered the room.

"Did Grant do this?" Sadie asked. "Was your husband the one who killed you?"

Trudy kept on rocking, and the motion caused a flap of skin from the long gash in her throat to lift and fall rhythmically.

"How about Kent Lasko? Should I be worried that he was in the house?"

No answer.

"Well, I'll just take your silence as a no, okay?" Sadie snapped snarkily.

Trudy only rocked.

"You're a real peach," Sadie muttered and stormed back downstairs.

She opened the rear door and called out to Zack, "Okay, let's mop some blood."

"You're sure?" he asked, dropping his smoke and grinding it out with his shoe.

"Yeah, I'm sure. Let's get this job done so we can get out of here."

It was inching up to ten o'clock when Sadie pulled in to her garage. Every muscle in her body ached, even worse than the time she got suckered into trying a Pilates class. Cleaning those bookshelves had been murder.

The door from the garage opened into an extra-large laundry room. Sadie had had a shower installed in the room to make sure that when she came off a job, nothing from work would enter the rest of the house. The minute she was inside, she stripped and tossed everything she was wearing into the washer. Next she hopped into the shower and scrubbed until her skin was pink.

Dripping wet, she reached into a decorative trunk that she kept filled with towels. With a thick towel wrapped around her, she exited the laundry room and headed down the hall to her bedroom where she slipped into sweatpants and an oversized T.

A fluffy ball of white and black hopped in and stopped to watch her with vague interest.

"How's it hopping, Hairy?" Sadie asked her roly-poly bunny friend.

He twitched his black nose and hopped away. Hairy was a relatively new addition to her household. He had come from a house Sadie had cleaned a few months ago. The woman who'd died had left behind no family whatsoever, no one to care for the pets, so Sadie had taken Hairy, with the idea that it would be temporary. However, weeks turned into months and she never tried to find him another home. Hairy came kitty-litter-trained, and Sadie found him to be a soft addition that helped to tamp down the harsher side of her life.

She needed a drink, so she walked into the kitchen to see what was available. There was no beer, her first choice, nor was there any wine, her second. Double damn. Then she remembered there was vodka in the cupboard and tomato juice in the fridge, so she decided on a Bloody Mary.

She was just stirring the mixture and adding a drop of Tabasco when she heard someone in the living room. Sadie whirled around, knocking the glass bottle of tomato juice to the tile floor with a crash. Ugh, what a mess. She stepped over the puddle of broken glass and hustled into the living room, where she found Pam.

"Sheesh! Did you ever hear of knocking? You scared the crap out of me."

"Sorry," her friend answered. "You did say we'd get together tonight."

"I said *if* it wasn't too late."

"And you think it's too late at ten o'clock? What are we, twelve?"

Sadie laughed.

"Okay, fine. Come into the kitchen—I've a disaster to clean up."

Pam followed, chatting away. "I had the best day today," she said. She stopped short when they entered the kitchen and pointed to the slick red mess on the floor. "Is that . . . is it blood?"

Pam covered her face with her hands. Sadie walked over and whispered two words in her ear. "Tomato juice."

"Huh?"

"I dropped a bottle of tomato juice. God, you of all people—" She stopped short. "Never mind. Just go and wait in the living room until I get this cleaned up."

A few minutes later Sadie was sipping a strong vodka martini instead of another Bloody Mary.

Pam and Sadie had met several years earlier at a local elementary school where Sadie taught second grade and Pam was a special ed teacher. They'd bonded over their mutual dislike of the school's principal and all the bureaucratic bullshit involved in the school system. Pam had been recently divorced, and Sadie was going through a one-night-stand phase, so they'd quickly become friends. When Brian died, Pam was one of the few people who stuck around, particularly once Sadie decided on her new career.

"By the way, how was Dawn's party?" Pam asked.

Sadie frowned. "Noel asked Dawn to marry him and she said yes."

"Wow! They've only been together for a few months, right?" Pam raised her eyebrows. "I guess if it's love—"

"Let's talk about something else."

"You obviously don't like the idea."

"You know how I feel."

"Oh, come on. You're not still on about Noel looking like Brian, are you?" Pam rolled her eyes.

"I don't want to talk about it."

"Listen, Sadie, I wouldn't mess with you. Friends say the truth, right?"

Sadie only sipped her drink.

"So when I tell you that Noel absolutely does *not* look like Brian, what do you think?"

"That you're either completely blind or else you're a good liar. Or maybe you're trying to protect my feelings."

Pam looked contemplative and tapped her chin with the tip of her finger. "Maybe it's not about Dawn. It could be all about you. You're the one seeing Brian when you look at Noel. You've never properly dealt with your grief, and maybe this is the universe's way of telling you it's time you did."

Sadie glowered and her tone grew heated. "I'm warning you, Pam. Don't analyze me."

"I'm a special education teacher, not a psychiatrist," Pam said, holding her palms up in surrender. "But if I *was* a psychiatrist, I'd say that this is *definitely* all about you."

Before Sadie could come up with a scathing retort, her phone rang.

"Sorry for calling so late," Zack said.

"It's not late, Zack. It's not even eleven o'clock. What am I, twelve?" She winked at Pam.

"Okaaay. Well, I hate to do this to you when we're just starting that double scene, but I need to drive down to Portland. It's my mom. She fell, and she might have broken something."

"Oh no! Is she okay?" Stupid question. "I mean, is she at the hospital?"

"Yeah. I'm sure she'll be fine, but my sister's flipping out."

"Of course you should go."

"But the Toth house—"

"Will still be there when you get back. If it'll make you feel better, I'll save the toughest parts for you."

"Like what?" She could hear the smile in his tone.

"I dunno, maybe the skull fragments embedded in the living room wall."

"You're all heart."

She laughed.

"I'm driving down tonight," Zack said. "I should make it back by tomorrow night."

"Don't rush. Take all the time you need," Sadie said seriously. Although she hated working alone, she'd certainly done it many times before Zack joined Scene-2-Clean.

She put the receiver back on the coffee table and sighed.

"Don't suppose Zack was calling to say he was coming over to ravish you?" Pam smirked.

"His mother's just had some kind of a fall, so he's heading down to Portland."

"What a shame."

"Yeah. I don't think his mom's even that old. Midsixties."

"I meant about him not ravishing you."

Sadie laughed in spite of her attempt to stifle the giggle.

"He *does* have a pinchable ass, but we're friends and coworkers. That's all."

"You pinched his ass?" Pam asked incredulously.

"No, but I briefly considered it."

"You should've gone for it. One day you could invite him back here and give in to your urges. He'd probably love it. If not, you'd just end up slapped with a sexual harassment suit." She paused. "And if you're going down, go down big. Have rock-and-rolling mind-blowing sex. Don't just pinch his ass."

"Hmmm." Sadie chuckled. "I'm not stupid. I'm not going to mess with the first reliable employee I've ever had around for longer than a month." Her face grew serious, and she blew out a long breath. "I'm not looking forward to doing that job on my own tomorrow."

Pam winced. "If you need to talk work, please leave out the gory bits."

"I'm worried about ghost stuff, or the lack thereof, not gruesome stuff."

"Oh goody," Pam gushed, rubbing her hands together. "I love to hear your ghost stories."

That made her the only one. Pam, Zack, and Dawn were the only people who knew about Sadie's so-called talent—not counting the dead, of course. While Zack barely tolerated it and Dawn mostly ignored it, Pam was a tad overenthusiastic. As a matter of fact, she was convinced Sadie should tell the world so she could end up making the talk-show circuit.

Sadie told Pam about Kent Lasko's appearance at the Toth house earlier in the day and her subsequent realization that he wasn't a ghost.

"On one hand I think you should call the cops," Pam said. "But I guess it would trigger a ton of questions you're not prepared to answer. Unless you think now's finally the time to let the rest of the world know about your talents?"

"I'm still holding firm against the whole freak-side-show thing." She waved her hand in the air and shouted to the room, "Come one, come all! See the woman who mops up blood and talks to the dead!"

Pam giggled.

"I just wish I knew why the guy was in the house. Then I could put it behind me," Sadie said.

"So call him."

"Excuse me?"

"Give the guy a call. How many Kent Laskos can there be in Seattle?"

Sadie went and got her white pages, thumbed through the listings, and determined that there were in fact three listings for K. Lasko.

"That's not so bad," Pam said. "You're lucky the guy's name isn't John Smith. It's a little late now, but try those numbers in the morning and you'll have your answer soon enough."

"What do I say to him?"

"Just say, 'Hi, my name's Sadie and we met yesterday and I was just wondering what the hell you were doing mucking around inside a murder scene.' "

"Just like that?"

"Just like that."

Sadie thought about it for a moment, then slowly nodded her head.

"You're right."

First thing the next morning Sadie jotted the Lasko telephone numbers down on a slip of paper. She called each of the three listings from her cell phone on her way to the Toth house. The first number turned out to be Kelly Lasko, and the woman claimed to have no relation named Kent. The second listing was for a Kirk Lasko. Sadie had a nice chat with the man, but he was at least eighty, claimed to have no familial relations with the name Kent, and ended their call by making a lewd suggestion.

By the time she was dialing the third and last K. Lasko she was in the Toths' driveway. That number turned out to be not in service. As a final attempt, she dialed Information and asked if there were any new listings under the Lasko name, but nope. Nada. Zilch.

"Well, I tried," she said to herself.

It was time to get her mind into the mode of detachment necessary for work. She slipped through the back door of the Toth house and began to suit up. She was prepared to spend a full day there, because they hadn't made nearly as much progress yesterday as she'd hoped.

Sadie considered starting upstairs, but, truthfully, she knew that if Trudy was hanging out doing her bedroom zombie routine, it would disrupt the rest of her day. Instead, she set to work on the living room, where she'd left off. She managed to cover most of the circumference before she needed a break.

A square red candle on the fireplace mantel caught her eye, and she saw a sharp bone fragment protruding menacingly from it. She snagged the candle and two-pointed it into the rubber waste bin.

Her shoulders ached from crouching to clean the lower bookshelves for such a long time. Now that she was on her feet, she used the opportunity to bend and stretch a bit while she scanned the wall in front of her for more fragments.

She debated going to the van to retrieve the muffin she'd brought from home. She wasn't particularly hungry, but the acid in her stomach was building because she'd had only coffee before leaving home. She turned around and took a step—and went right through Trudy Toth.

"Eww, yuck!" Sadie shuddered and goose bumps popped out on her arms. "I *hate* when that happens!" She wagged a finger at Trudy. "Don't sneak up on me!"

Trudy's dark eyes were sad and filled with a pleading insistence that Sadie wanted no part of. Still, she felt her anger dissipate.

"It's okay to talk to me," she said gently. She realized that it was probably difficult for Trudy to hear her through the respirator, so she spoke up. "I can hear you, so go ahead and say whatever's on your mind. Just let it out. I promise that you'll feel much better if you do."

Trudy looked around the room; then her eyes fixed on the huge red stain on the sofa. Sadie realized that since Grant had shot himself after he killed Trudy, there was a good chance the woman hadn't even known until now that her husband was dead. Sadie watched as Trudy walked around and around the room, clearly mystified.

"This is great," Sadie groaned. "I've got a ghost in shock."

Working a double scene alone was difficult enough. She didn't need this kind of paranormal distraction.

Since Trudy did not look at all like she planned on talking, Sadie decided to go with the direct approach.

"Okay, listen up," she began. She cleared her throat and spoke loudly. "Trudy, I'm sorry to have to tell you this, but you're dead. Your spirit is stuck here because, well, I don't know exactly why. For some reason it just happens this way sometimes. I guess you didn't walk toward the light, or maybe you didn't even know there was a damned light. Anyway, Grant is gone too, but I don't see him. I guess suicides don't hesitate. They're prepared for the light." Sadie shook her head to stop her rambling. "Look, you just need to let go. Your time here is over and—"

Trudy wasn't even acknowledging that she heard Sadie speak. Instead, the woman walked to the sofa, which Grant had chosen as his final stop. She rubbed her finger into the stain.

"What the hell are you doing?" Sadie asked.

Trudy walked to the wall and began to print, using the blood on her finger. Astonished, Sadie watched as the spirit repeatedly dipped her finger into the grotesque inkwell to create letters. When she was done, the macabre message on the wall said *Not Grant*.

4

After scrawling the message, Trudy simply vanished into thin air.

Sadie followed the spirit's lead, except instead of following Trudy into another dimension, she chose to ignore the muffin waiting for her in the van and drive to the closest Starbucks for a large latte with an extra jolt.

While downing her latte, Sadie called her sister, Dawn. She needed someone to dump on about the situation.

"I'm not exactly up on ghost stuff, but if you look at the bright side, I guess it's good that this ghost is finally talking to you, right?" Dawn said around a mouthful of her lunch.

"Yeah, but technically she's not talking. She only wrote me a message." Sadie let out a breath. "Sorry for taking up your lunch hour with this."

"Hey, what are sisters for if not to talk to their sisters about conversations they have with ghosts?" She giggled. "So what's your next step with this woman? Do you believe her message that it wasn't Grant who killed her?"

Sadie contemplated the question while swallowing a mouthful of coffee. "I don't even know for certain that's what she meant."

"About this Kent thing—let's say he never showed

up inside the house and scared the bejesus out of you. How would you handle a ghost like Trudy?"

"I guess I'd just go about my work and ignore her until she was ready."

"What's the difference now?"

"You've got a real knack for pointing out the obvious. Thanks."

"Okay, while we're on the topic of the obvious, you're the only person on the planet who hasn't congratulated me on my engagement."

Sadie winced.

"I heard you're only supposed to congratulate the groom and offer best wishes to the bride."

"And you've done neither."

Sadie knew now was the time to make her point about Noel but she chickened out.

"Wow, I didn't realize the time. Can we talk about this later? We've both got to get back to work."

She hung up and finished her coffee on the drive back to the Toth house, all the time dreading having to deal with Trudy. But when she reentered the house, Trudy was still gone, doing whatever it was that spirits do when they're not looking for attention from the living.

Sadie focused on the task at hand and continued working. By close to eight o'clock, she was considering wrapping things up. Her back ached, and she seriously hoped that Zack would be back by the morning to help with the rest.

It was hard to believe she'd run this business completely on her own for the first couple of years. After that, there'd been a series of unreliable, queasy contestants for the job who'd lasted anywhere from one day to six months. Zack had made himself invaluable for the last year. Later this month, she thought, she would crunch the numbers and see if she could afford to give him a raise.

Sadie could hear the wind howling and the rain

coming down harder outside. She didn't mind the dark, drizzling winter months in Seattle—more often than not, that weather spoke to her mood. But not everyone handled the gloom the same. The Emerald City was breaking rain records this winter, and she knew that as the rains continued, some Seattleites were going to get depressed. Some would take their own lives or lash out violently toward others, and Scene-2-Clean would be called to sweep up what was left of the dead.

Sadie had scrubbed most of the spatter off the heavy granite coffee table but had been unable to lift it so she could clean where blood had oozed under its base. That would have to wait for Zack.

A side table sat to the right of the sofa, and Sadie decided that she'd call it a day after she removed the debris that marred its cherry wood. The gore had worked its way into the creases outlining a small drawer, so in order to get at it best, Sadie pulled the drawer out and dumped the contents onto a clear area of the floor. She sprayed cleansers on the table and then carefully worked a bristled brush into the cracks. Her gaze casually fell on the items she'd removed: a notepad, a couple of pens, and an address book.

The temptation was overwhelming. As soon as she was sure that the drawer and side table were spick-and-span, she snatched up the address book and flipped through the pages. The movement was awkward because she was still wearing gloves, but eventually she found the listing for Kent Lasko. The phone number penned neatly in the margin was the same disconnected one that Sadie had tried earlier and the address given was only a couple of blocks away.

Sadie looked up and gasped as Trudy suddenly reappeared, sitting cross-legged on the floor only a few inches away.

"Well, if it isn't the great scribe," Sadie said sarcastically. "I'm the one who has to clean up the mess, so

I'd appreciate it if you'd use a pen and paper next time."

Trudy didn't reply, but her fingers worked nervously in her lap.

There are no defensive wounds, Sadie noticed sadly. *Nothing that showed she tried to protect herself.*

Sadie could visualize the woman running in terror from her husband as he angrily wielded the knife, but she couldn't wrap her mind around someone just standing there and letting it happen. She pushed the disquieting thought aside.

"So you're just hanging with me, then?" Sadie asked. "Just going to watch me work? I don't usually like an audience."

To her surprise Trudy reached out, as if to cup Sadie's face or lift her chin. Sadie flinched and pulled away. When the dead touched her it was like fingernails on a blackboard.

Trudy shook her head, then made a strange gesture. She made a thumbs-up movement but lifted the gesturing hand with the other. She seemed to be struggling.

Maybe her hands had been cut, but Sadie couldn't see a wound. She felt sorry for her. "Don't worry. It isn't necessary to enter the next dimension intact."

Trudy covered her face with her hands and began to weep, her entire body shuddering with sobs. The sounds, the first Sadie had heard leave this woman's lips, were heart-wrenching. Trudy disappeared from view again, and it was a full minute before the sound of her cries subsided.

"There are days I just don't get paid enough to handle this crap," Sadie grumbled.

For once, Sadie didn't push herself to get the job done. A knot of tension had formed in her stomach, and she decided it was best to call it a day.

She left the majority of the supplies at the Toth house to use when she returned to finish the clean and jogged through the heavy rain to her van. She'd left her cell phone in the vehicle, and she quickly checked for messages while simultaneously turning the key in the ignition. She was hoping there'd been a call from Zack, but Dawn was the only one who'd left her a message. Sadie put the vehicle in reverse and dialed her sister's number.

"Just wanted to let you know that Maureen called," Dawn told her. "She found new tenants for the house on Hawkins Avenue. A nice couple. They'll be moving in next week. Unless, of course, you've changed your mind and want to sell the place?"

"There's no rush to sell," Sadie said. "Maureen does a great job as a property manager, and the place has gone up at least a hundred grand in the last few years. Nothing wrong with us banking more equity."

"Sure, but we both know that's not why you want to hang on to it," Dawn said dryly. "We've been renting out Brian's house for five years now. I've talked to Mom and Dad, and they're fine with selling it, but if you're still not ready, just say so."

"I'm saying so," Sadie snapped.

"Fine," Dawn said in her own clipped tone.

"Remember how proud Brian was of that house?" Sadie said. "All I could see was a dump, but he saw it had potential."

"Yeah, his idea of potential meant you and I spent a dozen weekends there patching and painting."

"But he was right. It looked great."

"Yeah."

After a minute, Dawn broke the quiet.

"By the way, Chloe is throwing us an engagement party on March first. She said you haven't replied to her messages asking whether that date works for you."

"You've only been engaged a couple of days. I don't understand why you need to have a party right away."

"Because it'll be fun."

"Well, some of us have to work and don't have time

for constant fun. Besides, I was hoping . . ." *That you'd come to your senses and cancel your engagement, so there'd be no party.* "Never mind."

"Hoping what?"

"That you'd take things slower."

There was a pause, and Sadie thought Dawn seemed to actually think about it, but then she realized the pause happened because the call had been dropped. When Dawn called back, she was fuming.

"Noel and I are getting married. You don't have to be jumping up and down with joy, but it would sure be nice if you could suck it up and at least *pretend* you're happy for me."

"I don't want to have this conversation over the phone," Sadie said. "Let's talk another time."

Dawn reluctantly agreed, and Sadie made a quick excuse to end the call.

Back at home, Sadie felt restless, so after showering, she got dressed again and headed out into the rain. She took her car this time—nobody liked to see the Scene-2-Clean van in a neighbor's driveway.

When she reached the Hawkins Avenue house, she used her spare key and let herself into the cozy split-level. Her footsteps echoed as she walked through the vacant home, flipping on only a couple of lights. She told herself that, as part owner of the property, she should do a walk-through while the place was still vacant.

After all, just because Maureen is taking care of the house, Sadie thought, *they shouldn't forget to perform their due diligence by giving an occasional visual inspection.*

Brian's old house had been vacant barely a month this time. Maureen had prepped the place for the new tenants with a fresh coat of paint. When Sadie closed her eyes and breathed deep, the smell of paint brought her back to the days when she'd helped Brian fix the place up.

She walked around the house and noticed the carpets were also newly shampooed. The house looked good, but Sadie knew Brian would've hated the priscilla curtains in the kitchen and the pale neutral shades. He'd loved strong, masculine colors with rich textures and deep tones.

Glancing into the backyard, Sadie smiled at the memory that Brian had wanted to build a rock-climbing wall on the side of the fence.

Sadie walked down the hallway, cut through the master bedroom, and hesitated only briefly before entering the small master bath. For a split second, she saw the room exactly as she'd found it on that morning five years ago. A rifle on the floor and Brian's lifeless body badly decomposed in the bathtub, his blood and brain spatter painting a macabre death scene on the walls.

Sadie climbed into the bathtub where Brian had lain. Her heart twisted in painful memory. He, like many suicides, had probably thought it would be an easier clean if he did it in the tub. Most people had no idea the kind of bloodbath a small room took when a bullet exploded someone's head.

With her legs pulled up close to her chest, Sadie waited. She knew in her heart that Brian's spirit wouldn't come. It never had before. Still, desperate yearning filled her with pathetic hope.

After a couple minutes she let her head drop to her knees and she moaned softly. She felt it was a cruel irony that she couldn't talk to those who chose suicide, as though God had cursed her with her gift as a joke.

She quietly sobbed against her knees, her body shaking with the force of her grief. After a while all her energy evaporated on a whoosh of exhaled breath and nothing was left in its place but pain.

When the phone rang, Sadie thought for an instant that she was still in Brian's bathtub instead of at home in her own bed. It took her a few seconds to reorient herself and fumble for the bedside extension.

"Hello?"

"Who's the jokester who wrote on the walls in blood?" Zack demanded. He sounded pissed. It wasn't a great way to wake up.

"You're back? And you're already at the house?" Sadie asked, swinging her legs out of bed and squinting at the clock. "Oh my God, it's nearly noon!"

She was up and stripping out of her sleepwear as she spoke.

"Yeah. I just got in and decided to come straight here. I thought maybe you'd gotten another call while I was in Portland."

"No, I overslept." She never overslept. Hell, she hardly ever slept through the night at all. "How's your mother?"

"Fine. It was a mild fracture. She'll be good as new in a few weeks."

"Good. Great." She took the cordless phone into the bathroom and turned on the shower. "I'll be there in half an hour."

"Do I want to know about this message on the wall?"

"Probably not."

With her hair still damp from the shower, Sadie slipped her hazmat suit over her clothes, zipping it up as she walked. Zack had left the back door unlocked, which annoyed the hell out of her.

"Anyone could walk right in here," she sniped, thinking of Kent Lasko.

"Sorry. Thought I'd locked it," Zack said, but he never looked up from where he was systematically cutting blood-soaked fabric from the sofa.

"You should be more careful."

He didn't reply but began cutting with harsher movements. She'd pissed him off.

"I'm going to finish upstairs." She paused. "I'm glad your mom's okay. It's good to have you back."

He glanced at the wall where Trudy's message was scrawled, and Sadie answered the question in his eyes.

"It was Trudy."

He sat back on his haunches and folded his arms across his chest. "You've never had one write you a note before, have you?"

She shook her head.

"I like it a lot better when they talk," he mumbled. "When only *you* can hear what they say. It's easier for me to pretend you're just crazy."

The look in his eyes told her he wasn't kidding.

"Face it—you'd be bored if I was normal."

He grumbled something about boredom not always being such a bad thing.

When Sadie got into the bedroom, it was as if Trudy was waiting for her. She greeted her with that strange thumbs-up gesture, and Sadie responded with a two-finger salute.

"You know, things will be much better for you once you let go," Sadie said gently. "You don't belong here anymore. It's time to move on."

Trudy's only response was to walk to the corner of the room where the carpet was crusty with hardened congealed blood. She began to rub her finger in it, and Sadie's anger spiked through her.

"No!" she hissed and moved to stop Trudy, but she needn't have bothered. In frustration, Trudy only pounded the floor with her fists, but her ghostly hands made no sound, and then she was gone.

Sadie was glad to see her go. It would be easier getting the job done without a crazy ghost hanging around, and the sooner she could finish this job, the better. This place was getting to her.

Sadie speedily worked through the bedroom, and Trudy didn't return to harass her. When she carried waste bins filled with carpeting downstairs, she saw that Zack had already removed all traces of Trudy's message. For a split second it bothered her that she hadn't thought of taking a picture, but she pushed that thought away.

The Toths had used a semigloss paint on the walls. If they'd used a flat paint, there would've been no scrubbing anything away and the drywall would've had to be cut out.

"We'll be able to start stage two tomorrow," Zack said as they doffed their gear in the kitchen.

"That'll be a relief," Sadie admitted. They both hated the awkward suits, goggles, and other gear necessary for working with blood.

In the second stage of the clean, they would need only to wear gloves to protect their skin from the harsh cleaning chemicals, and they could wear regular grubby clothes instead of the disposable Tyvek suits and face masks.

Sadie was bent over and tugging the booties off her shoes when she got the feeling she was being watched. She straightened and glanced at Zack.

"You were just totally checking out my ass!"

"Not my fault." He put his hands up. "If you're going to bend over like that, I'm going to look."

"Want to get a beer?" he asked a minute later, combing his fingers through his hair. "There's a place a few blocks away."

"Sure," Sadie replied as she stretched her aching back.

They took their own vehicles so they could go their separate ways afterward. Even though the rain was still sputtering outside, Sadie rolled down her window for the drive. As she followed Zack's car down the street, the damp, icy breeze blew in, smelling of wet earth and the fishy Pacific. By the time she'd driven the few blocks to the pub, the wind had blown death out of her thoughts.

They found a corner table in the trendy neighborhood watering hole and ordered a preppy microbrew. Most of the executive clientele had gone for the day, and the numerous televisions sounded loud in the emptiness. Sadie and Zack both turned when a newscaster began to talk about a woman's body discovered in her home earlier in the day.

"The mail carrier reported a foul smell coming from the home and contacted the police," the anchorman stated. "The medical examiner advised that the woman had been dead for a couple of weeks, but no foul play is suspected."

"A dripper," Zack commented and sipped his beer.

"Think we'll get the call?" Sadie wondered.

"Who else they gonna call but Slime Busters?" he joked.

The next news story showed Seattle PD handcuffing some thugs. Zack frowned at the screen.

"Do you miss being on the job?" Sadie asked.

"Nah," he replied, wiping his mouth with the back of his hand.

Sadie suspected he was lying, but the subject was moot. Zack couldn't go back to being a cop any more than she could return to teaching second grade. He'd taken a bullet for his partner, a noble thing to do. But then he'd gotten hooked on painkillers, roughed up a suspect, been caught on video by a citizen, and handed in his badge before they could ask for it. He'd spent a year washing Vicodin down with whiskey, getting into brawls, and doing other things he wasn't proud of before he snapped out of it and checked into rehab. One day he saw Sadie's van on the news. He called her and asked for a job, and Seattle PD's loss became her gain.

Zack ordered a heaping pile of nachos to go with their beers. After he'd eaten most of the chips, he got up to go.

"I'm beat," he said. "I'll see you in the morning."

"See ya in the morning," Sadie echoed.

She ordered a second beer but hardly drank any of it. She was looking around the pub and wondering if Grant and Trudy Toth had ever come here. That led her to wonder if Kent Lasko had joined them.

She knew she should leave, but she didn't feel like heading to her empty home. She approached the bartender and asked if she could take a look at his phone book. After he handed it to her, she quickly found the listing for Kent Lasko, the one with the disconnected phone. She figured if the number was disconnected it meant either that he'd moved since the number went in the white pages or that he'd changed his number and was still living there. She jotted down the street address and returned the phone book to the bartender.

Curiosity got the better of her and she decided to drive over. On the way, she told herself there was a good chance Kent had moved. Still, when she pulled up to the address and saw lights on inside the house, excitement raced through her. There was no way she would be able to sleep for wondering if he still lived in the house or if the new owner knew Kent Lasko's current address.

The rain was torrential now, and getting to the front door was like running through a waterfall. Just as she was about to knock, she heard footsteps and turned to face a man coming up behind her with keys in his hand.

Her face fell. This guy wasn't Kent Lasko. This guy was blond but thinner, taller, and a few years younger than the man she'd met. He was dressed in a designer running outfit and was obviously just returning from jogging.

"I'm looking for Kent Lasko. He used to live here."

"He still does," the young man replied. He stepped in front of her and opened the door.

"Hey, Kent, there's some lady here for you," he called. He turned to Sadie. "Come in."

"I'm fine," Sadie replied, choosing to remain on the front steps in the rain.

"Suit yourself."

The young man stepped inside, bent and untied his expensive jogging shoes, and tugged his dripping nylon hoodie over his head.

Kent Lasko walked around the corner from the hall. His mouth dropped in a fleeting look of surprise that was quickly replaced by a cool, practiced smile that made Sadie's skin crawl.

5

"Hello, I'm Kent. You probably know that since you obviously tracked me down." He stuck out his hand and offered a charming smile to go with it.

Sadie gave his fingers a quick squeeze.

"You were working at Trudy's house, right?" he asked. "It's a little hard to recognize you out of your blue astronaut suit."

Sadie nodded. "I'm Sadie Novak." She held her hand over her eyes to shield her face from the rain. "I tried calling you, but your phone number was disconnected."

"We had our number changed recently. Oh, and this guy who loves to run in the rain is my brother, Christian." Kent nodded to his brother. "Christian, Sadie here is working on cleaning Grant's house."

Christian's immediate reaction was to look appalled, but he recovered his manners, said hello, and offered his hand. When she shook it, Sadie noticed his eyes quickly appraised her damp shirt.

"Nice to meet you," he said. "The Toths were very nice people. It's a shame what happened."

"Yes, it is," she agreed.

"I'm going to go change," he said and excused himself, disappearing inside the house.

Then there was an awkward pause. She knew she should tell Kent Lasko why she'd tracked him down, but she hadn't really planned on actually finding him, so her confidence was a bit shaken.

"It's pouring. Come inside." He waved his hand and stepped aside to allow her entry. "My brother loves the rain, but personally, I think this weather is only great for crazy joggers and ducks."

"That's okay. Really," Sadie replied. *Because you're either a looter or a freak, and neither option appeals to me, even if you do have the bluest eyes I've ever seen.*

"How can I help you, then, Miss Novak?"

"You can tell me what you were doing inside the Toth house."

"I should've explained myself at the time, but truthfully, you didn't seem much interested. Maybe you were too involved in your work?"

"Yes." *Well, that and the fact that I thought you were a ghost.*

"It's no secret that I was friends with Trudy and Grant. More so with Trudy, I guess, and I was there to—"

"But you were Grant's best man, so why would you be closer to Trudy?"

"Wow, you really checked me out thoroughly." His eyebrows rose in amusement.

Sadie's cheeks heated even as a large drop of rain rolled off the tip of her nose.

"I saw you in their wedding picture."

"Right." He nodded and rubbed the back of his neck thoughtfully. "It's not really the kind of thing I want to talk about with a stranger, even if that stranger happens to be a particularly nice-looking woman who looks like she might drown on my doorstep."

Sadie's blush deepened, but she recovered quickly and squared her shoulders.

"You don't owe me an explanation, but I don't allow people in the house when I'm cleaning up a crime scene. And the police—well, I'm sure they wouldn't approve of the idea, either," she said coolly. "If you don't have a good reason for being inside the Toth house, then I'll need to notify the authorities."

"Wow, you're one tough cookie." He smiled appreciatively. "Okay, if you come in out of the pouring rain, I promise to tell you why I was inside their house."

Sadie didn't want to ignore all her mother's warnings about not going into a strange man's house, but she couldn't bear to be drenched further. She suggested they go for coffee to talk.

"Do you know Holly's?" he asked.

She said she did and they agreed to meet there. Sadie hustled back to her car. She reached the coffee shop first and ducked into the ladies' room and dried off with paper towels. Next she got her coffee and searched for a table that wasn't already occupied by a person with a laptop. She'd just sat down and had taken a few sips from her latte when Kent showed up. He got his own coffee and a slice of apple pie, then joined her at the small corner table.

"Great weather, huh?" he commented.

"Awful."

"Have some of my pie."

He offered Sadie her own fork, but she declined. She didn't want to make small talk.

"Tell me what you were doing at the Toth house."

"Right." He began fishing in the inside pocket of his jacket.

For all I know, this guy killed Trudy and Grant and then made it look like a murder-suicide, she thought. *He could be pulling out the knife he used to kill Trudy.* She tensed.

"The truth is that I was in Trudy's house to get this," Kent said, unwrapping a square of white tissue paper to reveal a stunning emerald pendant on a thick gold chain. It was amazing. Much nicer than a sharp knife used as a murder weapon.

"It's beautiful."

"The necklace belonged to my mother. Mom is a good friend of Sylvia Toth's."

"So Trudy somehow got it, and you thought you'd reclaim it for your mother before people started going through and dividing up the estate?"

Sadie was disappointed that he'd turned out to be a looter after all. Such a shame, because she was pretty sure from the way his denim shirt clung to his chest that the muscles beneath were rock solid. She cleared her throat when she realized that she was staring and forced herself to look down at her coffee instead of at his body. Damn, it had been a long time since she'd felt instant attraction to a man.

He was watching her, obviously weighing his next comment. Finally he continued. "I guess there's no harm in telling you the truth. You're not a friend of the family or anything, right?"

"Right. Just an employee hired by Sylvia Toth."

"Well . . . Trudy and I had an affair."

"Oh." Great. The guy's a looter *and* a home wrecker.

"It was a long time ago, but I gave her my mother's necklace when it looked like she was going to leave Grant. When she decided to stay and make the marriage work, well, I didn't have the nerve to ask for it back. After what happened, I couldn't stop thinking about it. I knew that when the time came to go through the stuff in the house, Sylvia would recognize the necklace and would ask questions about how and why Trudy had it."

"If it was a long time ago, how did you know she still had it? She could've pawned the necklace or even lost it or gotten rid of it."

Sadie focused on the pendant and found herself mesmerized by its antique beauty. The intricate gold was like lace around the emeralds, which glowed in the restaurant's lighting. She watched as Kent wrapped it again and then fisted it in his hand before he stuffed it back in his pocket.

"I *didn't* know for certain that she still had it, but she once told me she was keeping it locked inside her file cabinet so that Grant wouldn't find it. I knew she also kept a spare house key in the garden shed, so I went to the house and got the necklace."

"You shouldn't have been going through her things."

"Yes," he acknowledged. "Trust me, it wasn't easy going inside that house." He swallowed nervously. "But I really was only trying to protect Trudy's reputation. She wouldn't have wanted their families to think less of her, even in death."

Sadie frowned. Somehow she doubted that Trudy was haunting her own house because she was worried about her reputation.

"What happened to them was horrible. God, it broke my heart when I heard about it." His voice was thick with emotion, and he shook his head slowly from side to side. "I never would've thought Grant was capable of such a thing."

Sadie thought of Trudy's scrawled *Not Grant.* It could've simply been the ghost's utter denial of what had happened, or even wishful thinking. Somehow neither sounded right. She shuddered despite the hot coffee in her hands.

"So this is your full-time job? Cleaning crime scenes?" he asked, eyeing her curiously.

"Crime scenes and unattended deaths. We're officially known as bio-recovery technicians. Scene-2-Clean is my own company. I started it a few years ago."

"If you don't mind me asking, how on earth does a beautiful woman end up doing such an ugly job?"

His warm expression invited confidence.

"My line of work isn't exactly for everyone, but I like to think the job chose me."

He nodded as if that made perfect sense.

"What do you do?" she asked politely.

"I'm a real estate agent."

They talked about the burgeoning Seattle real estate market, the upcoming Seahawks game against the 49ers, and eventually the conversation wound back around to her occupation.

"I guess your line of work isn't exactly seasonal," he remarked.

"People die all year," Sadie said

Sadie liked Kent Lasko. She enjoyed the casual drawl of his voice, the striking blue of his eyes, and his toned body. The longer she talked with him, the more she found she didn't really care that he'd had an affair with Trudy Toth. After all, it was really none of her business.

"I should probably go," she said, getting to her feet.

He stood and helped her into her jacket in a gesture that smacked of a familiarity that wasn't totally unwelcome. She couldn't help but be disappointed that she had no reason to get his new phone number.

Kent had parked his car close to hers. Just as she was about to open her door, he called out, "Would you agree to dinner with me this week?"

Before jumping at the opportunity, Sadie quickly calculated whether or not this would be a conflict with her cleaning of the Toth house. Since Kent was neither the person who hired her nor the deceased she was mopping up, she saw no reason to say no. The niggling self-doubt was also put to rest by assuring herself that she would be with him in a public place.

"I'd like that."

They quickly set the date for two evenings later, exchanged phone numbers, and then she got behind the wheel. As she drove home, she found herself singing along to a love song on the radio, and the icy downpour didn't dampen her spirits at all.

*   *   *

True to her word, Sadie was up and at the Toth house early, but as early as she was, Zack had managed to beat her there. He was obviously trying to make up for missing a day, for which Sadie was grateful.

"We're ahead of the game this morning."

She looked around the master bedroom, moving easily without the restriction of the stage one gear. Signs of trauma had been eliminated, and now the room just looked like any other renovation.

Sadie tried not to give Zack any sign that Trudy was in the house with them. She respected the fact that doing crime-scene cleaning was hard enough without having some half-crazy boss chatting with the dead around you.

While they worked in the master bedroom, Sadie occasionally looked up to find Trudy standing in the bedroom doorway. Whenever she glanced her way, Trudy made nodding or waving gestures, as if she wanted Sadie to follow her in the direction of the upstairs den. Sadie was tempted, but Zack was working so efficiently that she didn't want to interrupt the flow by skipping off with Trudy. Instead, she discreetly stole an occasional glance at the woman while she continued her work.

"Okay, tell me what the hell's going on," Zack growled. He straightened and fisted his hands on his hips.

"What? Nothing," Sadie stammered.

"Bullshit. You've been looking over your shoulder all morning. It's driving me nuts."

So much for her attempt at being discreet. Sadie started to repeat that nothing was going on, but the look of annoyance on Zack's face changed her mind.

"Trudy wants me to follow her into the den."

He grimaced. "And she told you this?"

"Well, no. She's not the talkative type, but she's been waving me over."

He sighed, looked heavenward, and made shooing

motions. "Go ahead, then. You and your ghost go play. Get it over with so we can get back to work."

"Right." Sadie nodded sharply. She got to her feet and stepped quietly around the corner to follow Trudy down the hall.

"You're getting me in trouble," Sadie grumbled to the phantom's back. "Good employees are hard to find in this business, you know. Never mind hard— they're damn near impossible. Zack's been very tolerant of this kind of stuff, but who knows how long that can continue."

"I'm not going anywhere." Zack spoke up from behind her.

Sadie turned and bumped into him. She jumped backward, embarrassed and surprised that he'd overheard her.

"I was curious, so I decided to check out the den, too," he admitted sheepishly.

The office was meticulous, with the exception of a fine layer of dust that coated everything, since the room had gone unused for the last few weeks.

"That's one helluva fancy phone," Zack commented.

It had caught Sadie's eye as well. Funny that she hadn't noticed it when she'd been in the room to get the insurance papers.

"Looks like one of those videoconferencing things," she remarked. "Grant must've used it for his job. Certainly Trudy wouldn't have needed it. Sylvia told me she was a schoolteacher."

Trudy stood over by a four-drawer wooden filing cabinet in the corner, the same cabinet where Kent would've found the necklace. Trudy's hands made motions of attempting to open the top drawer, but her grip only passed through the handle. She tossed back her head and let out a loud moan of frustration.

Sadie walked over, opened the drawer, and looked in at nearly a dozen files.

"Okay, help me out here," she said.

"What do you want me to do?" Zack asked.

"I was talking to Trudy. Sorry."

He nodded. "I think I'll go back to the bedroom," he said in an I-can't-handle-this tone.

"Well?" Sadie asked, but Trudy just pointed at the buff letter-sized files.

Near as Sadie could tell, the folders held only household bills.

"Talk about organized," Sadie muttered as she pulled out a few folders and flipped through their contents. The first was labeled AUTO EXPENSES and contained everything from gas receipts to repair expenses. The next two files had expenses to do with renovating the house.

"Hey, I'm not an accountant," Sadie called out.

When she went to stuff the folders back in the drawer, she noticed a large gold envelope on the bottom of the drawer. Trudy was pointing excitedly.

"This?" Sadie asked.

Trudy nodded, and Sadie pulled the envelope out and opened it. It was filled with telephone bills.

"You want me to look at your phone bills?" she asked Trudy, watching the woman's face closely.

Trudy nodded emphatically.

"Thinking of changing your long-distance carrier?" Sadie joked, and Trudy rolled her eyes, an unexpectedly human gesture for a ghost, and then she faded away.

With the envelope tucked under her arm, Sadie walked down the hall and back into the bedroom.

"So?" Zack asked from the corner, where he was vacuuming up dead flies and maggots.

"She wants me to look at the phone records."

He nodded, pretending that this was the most natural thing in the world.

"Why don't you bring it with you while we get something to eat? I'm starved."

"You're always starved."

"You're never starved," he countered.

Zack was hell-bent on Tex-Mex, so they headed for Pesco's Taco Lounge. The place was a loud singles club at night but was great for lunch.

They decided on green-chile enchiladas, and Zack ate most of both their plates while Sadie scanned the phone records. She looked over the pages, but nothing jumped out and said Aha! At least not until she examined them a second time.

"Looks like they only moved back to Seattle in May. Before that, all the phone records are for a Portland address."

"Moved away for a few months but then returned to Seattle, maybe to be closer to Grant's mother?" Zack asked.

"I remember Sylvia mentioned a move to Portland that was just temporary. Grant was starting up a new sportswear store there and wanted to get it properly up and running before coming back."

Sadie frowned while her finger tapped a listing of long-distance calls made to a Seattle number.

"Would you consider six months to be a long time?" Sadie asked.

Zack's gaze followed a sexy brunette as she sauntered past.

"In what respect? It's a helluva long time to go without sex."

"I'm not talking about sex."

"It would be more fun to talk about sex." He wiggled his eyebrows comically. "But I guess six months isn't that long if you're talking about, say, how long someone's been married."

"If someone told you they'd had an affair—"

"So we are talking about sex."

"No sex," she nearly shouted and then blushed when others glanced their way. "If someone said they broke up with someone a long time ago, how long ago would you assume that was?"

"I don't know." He shrugged. "Maybe a year." He wiped at his mouth with his napkin.

"Yeah, that's what I thought."

"So, who's screwing around?"

"Trudy."

"Really? Who's she messing with, Casper the Friendly Ghost?"

"Ha ha." Sadie rolled her eyes. "She had an affair with Kent Lasko."

"She told you this?" His eyebrows rose in question.

"No, Kent did."

"Was that guy at the house again?" Zack leaned in on his elbows, his face suddenly dead serious.

"No. I went to his place last night."

"You went to *his* place?" He folded his arms across his chest. "This guy was skulking around a crime scene and you just decided to pay him a visit?"

Sadie shrugged. "I wanted to know what he was doing in the house. I found his address listed in Trudy's address book and decided to confront him about it."

When she saw the furious look on Zack's face, Sadie wasn't about to mention that she'd also agreed to a date with the guy.

"I'm not stupid. It's not like I went inside his house. We met at a public place for coffee."

The look on Zack's face said he was marginally appeased by that information.

"Anyway, Kent told me he was at the Toth house to retrieve a necklace. Supposedly it was a family heirloom, a gift he'd given to Trudy when he'd thought she would leave Grant. He didn't want Trudy's family to find the necklace and ask questions that might lead to them discovering his affair with Trudy. Guess he thought he was saving her reputation. But he said the affair was over a long time ago. According to this"— Sadie pointed to the papers—"six months ago Trudy was still phoning him from Portland almost daily. He had his number changed, but I recognize the number she was calling as Kent's old one."

Sadie drank from her water glass.

"Maybe he ended it but she wouldn't take no for an answer, so he had his number changed." Zack polished off the rest of the food on his plate and tossed his crumpled napkin on it.

"But then she moved back here with her husband and chose to buy a house two blocks away from her ex-lover? Why the hell would she do that if he'd changed his number and obviously wasn't interested?"

"People have done stranger things in the name of love."

"Yeah, but Kent said Trudy was the one who broke it off. He said she wanted to make her marriage work."

"She changed her mind. Guess she wanted to have her hubby and her side dish, too. It happens all the time."

"Right. There's no way a woman packs up and moves house to be closer to a guy she dumped unless they're still hot and heavy."

"Sounds right."

Her gaze met Zack's. "But that means Kent lied."

"Sounds like he's hiding something."

"Yeah," Sadie agreed. She suddenly felt sick to her stomach. She hoped that *something* wasn't murder.

6

They drove the unwieldy company van back to the Toth house after their lunch. They were halfway there when Dawn called Sadie's cell.

"Prepare to be mystified and amazed," Dawn said mysteriously. "I'm inviting you out for an evening of mystical entertainment."

"And that means . . . ?"

"Chloe gave me a gift certificate for a psychic reading for my birthday. When I called to make the appointment, they told me that they have a two-for-one deal this week. So you're coming with me."

"I'm probably busy," Sadie replied.

"You're just saying that."

"When?"

"Tonight at seven o'clock."

"I'm definitely busy."

"C'mon, it'll be fun. You'll see."

"I just can't. I won't be done working before seven o'clock."

"We'll be done by then," Zack piped up, and Sadie shot him a death glare. "Or not. Hell, we could be working on this one until next week." He grumbled something under his breath about never understanding women.

"We can meet up for drinks and appies first and just chat."

Sadie realized it would be the perfect opportunity for her to step up to the plate and tell Dawn how she felt about Noel. Truth was, she'd rather scrub decomp than have that conversation. But she knew she shouldn't put it off.

"Fine," Sadie said. "Where and when?"

She got the details and said good-bye.

"It's good that you're getting together with your sister. It'll do you both good," Zack said.

"Sure. Tonight I'm going to tell her why she can't marry Noel."

Zack didn't reply.

"I know what you're thinking," Sadie said.

"Oh, I bet you do." He chuckled.

"You think I should mind my own business and stay out of it."

"That about sums it up."

"She's my sister. I owe it to her to warn her that she's making a huge mistake."

"Uh-huh."

He pulled the van into the Toth driveway, and Sadie brought the phone records with her to put back into the file cabinet. There was no sign of Trudy anywhere. Sadie was both relieved and a little disappointed. It would've been nice to ask Trudy about her calls to Kent. Not that she expected an answer, since the essence of Trudy appeared still to be in some kind of shock and refusing to speak.

As Sadie plugged away at preparing the main floor for the restoration company, she thought about the phone calls and whether or not Kent had lied. She came to the conclusion that she was jumping to conclusions. After all, he didn't say *when* they broke up, only that they had. And he didn't really owe her an explanation. Besides the fact that she'd threatened to sic the cops on him if he didn't provide a reason for entering the Toth home.

Sadie briefly considered canceling their date, but

truthfully, the idea of having a conversation with someone new, alive, and breathing appealed to her immensely. At least she could keep the conversation lively with the pointed questions she intended to ask regarding his relationship with Trudy. She would satisfy her curiosity even if it meant no future dates with the hunky Kent Lasko.

By four o'clock the house was ready for the next and final phase, which involved meeting with the restoration company that would replace the carpeting removed from the master bedroom and also try to match and replace the section of blood-soaked hardwood that had been cut out of the living room floor.

Zack began packing up. Sadie knew there was no use procrastinating. It was time to go home, primp a little, and practice the lecture she'd prepared to give her sister at some point between drinks and appetizers.

As if reading her mind, Zack commented, "Take it easy on Dawn. Remember, your opinion is only your opinion."

Sadie rolled her eyes. "It's not like I'm going to freak out. I'll just lay out the facts and point out the obvious."

"That you think she's marrying Noel only because he looks like your dead brother?"

"Yes."

"Good luck with that."

Sadie's plan was to have a heart-to-heart chat with Dawn over food and drinks. She arrived at Fado's Irish Pub a few minutes early to prepare her thoughts. She'd already decided to take the direct approach. Even if Dawn was ticked off, Sadie knew she owed it to her sister to say what was on her mind.

But how do you tell your sister she's only getting married because her boyfriend looks like her dead brother? Sadie thought glumly.

The waitress brought the menu to the table, and a

sense of déjà vu swept Sadie into remembering an evening out with Brian a month before his death. Sadie and Dawn had joined him and his girlfriend at a pub much like this one. There'd been a bowl of nuts on the table, and Brian was acting his usual goofy self, so when Sadie had called him nuts, he'd picked a peanut from the bowl and flicked it so that it pinged off Sadie's forehead. A nut free-for-all had ensued.

Sadie closed her eyes, and she could hear Brian's rolling laughter and see his strong hands gesturing as he talked. She could see the way he would play air guitar just to embarrass his fiancée, Joy. And she could hear the sound of his deep baritone voice as he stated solemnly that no man would marry his sisters without being interrogated by him first.

The memory was a kick in the gut. She wondered if Dawn had given even a moment's thought to the fact that their brother wouldn't be at her wedding.

Sadie broke from her memories when she reached for her glass of Guinness and realized it was empty. She'd finished it and still there was no sign of Dawn. Scowling at her watch, she muttered, "Where the hell is she?"

A few minutes later, when she was angrily unfolding bills from her wallet to pay for her drink, Dawn rushed in.

"I'm sooo sorry I'm late," she breathed.

"Where have you been?" Sadie demanded sharply. "I've been sitting here for almost an hour!"

"I tried calling, but your phone must be turned off. I only got your voice mail," Dawn replied, sliding into the wooden chair across from Sadie.

"My phone's never off," Sadie said. She dug the phone out of her jacket pocket as proof, and then cursed. "I must've turned it off by accident." Then with a wave of her hand she added, "It doesn't matter. We agreed on six o'clock so we wouldn't be late for the crazy psychic and—"

"But look!" Dawn giggled hysterically and thrust her left hand in Sadie's face. "We were picking out my ring, and the jeweler could size it right there if we were willing to wait, and I just *had* to have it on my finger today."

"Nice. Very . . . sparkly," Sadie said, scowling at the cluster of small diamonds on her sister's finger. "Guess it's official."

"Yup, I'm getting married." Dawn thrust her hand out to admire her finger.

"While I was sitting here for an hour I was thinking about Brian. I wondered what he would've thought about Noel," Sadie blurted, her tone peppered with emotion.

Dawn looked stunned.

"Brian and Noel would've gotten along great."

"Riiight." Sadie snorted. "I don't think you've given any thought to Brian at all."

Dawn leaned forward on her elbows and scrutinized Sadie through slitted eyes.

"This pissed-off attitude isn't about me getting married, is it? It's about you missing Brian. About the fact that our big brother with the massive biceps isn't around to scare the crap out of Noel, the way he always liked to mess with his sisters' boyfriends." She sat back in her seat and sighed. "Our brother is dead and I miss him too, but that doesn't mean I'm never getting married or having children or living my life." She waggled a finger in Sadie's face and got to her feet. "And I'm not going to let you ruin my good mood today, so c'mon." She grabbed Sadie's arm and pulled her to her feet. "Pretend you're a happy, supportive sister and let's go next door to Maeva's Psychic Café before they give our appointment to someone else."

The psychic café had a storefront that sold everything from crystal balls to tarot cards and also had a counter where you could sit and nosh on nibblies while sipping herbal tea. The stools at the counter were full, but a young woman with multiple piercings in her nose, ears, and eyebrows told them that Madame Maeva would be with them shortly and encouraged them to browse.

"What a scam," Sadie muttered under her breath. "They want us to drop a wad of cash while we wait for an appointment that costs an arm and a leg."

"Technically the appointment cost us diddly-squat," Dawn pointed out. "It was a gift, remember? And nobody's forcing you to buy a thing. Oooh, look at these," she exclaimed holding up a pair of beaded earrings.

Sadie picked up a brochure from the counter.

"Oh, look, Madame Maeva Morrison will also do parties. How about instead of an engagement party we throw you a psychic party?"

Before Dawn could respond, the decorated clerk advised them, "Madame Maeva will see you now."

She motioned for them to follow her behind the counter.

They walked down a short hall with three brightly colored closed doors. The clerk opened the middle door, which was fire-engine red.

"Enjoy yourself," she said.

"Come inside and have a seat," a woman with a gravelly smoker's voice called out.

The room was dark except for the soft glow of half a dozen black and red pillar candles on a squat table. Around the table were huge matching black and red cushions meant as seating, and their host was sitting on one at the far end of the table. She had shoulder-length, curly black hair, a sharp pointed face that looked fortyish, and so many chains around her neck that Sadie wondered if the woman would be able to stand without help.

"Hello. I'm Maeva Morrison. Your friend Chloe

gave you a half-hour session as a gift, and you've brought your sister. How nice."

"Wow. She knows I'm your sister," Sadie said, elbowing Dawn. She sneered at the psychic. "Did you look into your crystal ball for that information?"

"Sadie," Dawn admonished. "Just sit down."

Dawn sank into a black cushion next to Madame Maeva and folded her legs into the lotus position. She nodded for Sadie to sit on the other side.

"That's all right." Madame chuckled. "I see believers and nonbelievers alike, and I can get a reading on just about anyone. As long as they pay my fee, disbelief doesn't affect me in the least."

"So you admit this is just a money grab?" Sadie asked in an acid tone. She eased around the corner of the table and took a seat across from Dawn, on Madame Maeva's left.

"You'd feel better if I did my work for free?" Maeva asked. "Do you think people would trust you more at your job if you did it for free?"

Because Dawn looked like she was ready to spit nails, Sadie retracted her comment.

"That was rude." Sadie cleared her throat. "And I apologize."

"No need for apologies, but we should get right down to work so we don't use up your entire session. Who wants to go first?"

"Oh, me!" Dawn squealed.

"All right then." Maeva smiled. "For an additional ten dollars I can tape your session for you."

"That would be great," Dawn gushed.

Maeva took the cellophane wrap off a new cassette tape and placed it in a recorder on the table. After pressing RECORD, she said, "In order to give you a proper reading, I need to hold both of your hands in mine. If you have a specific question or area of your life you'd like me to read, simply concentrate on that subject. I'll be glad to answer any questions later, but please try not to interrupt until I'm done."

Dawn eagerly placed her hands in Maeva's.

"You know, most people don't know this, but Sadie here has a similar talent—"

"Dawn," Sadie warned.

"Let's focus on you," Maeva said. "I need you to be perfectly quiet. Simply concentrate. I'll try and zero in on the questions that concern you, but I should warn you that the answers I see may relate to other matters entirely. I can't control the order in which things come."

The medium closed her eyes and began to hum a song softly under her breath. The tune sounded an awful lot like "We're Off to See the Wizard."

"You like *The Wizard of Oz*?" Sadie asked.

Maeva opened one eye and peeked at Sadie. "My humming assists me in summoning even the most reluctant spirits."

"And the song? Are we summoning Munchkins?"

"Personal choice. It's my favorite movie. Now, stop talking."

Sadie rolled her eyes and folded her arms tightly across her chest.

Maeva hummed for almost a full minute before she began to speak.

"This is an exciting time for you," Maeva murmured. "Congratulations on your engagement."

"Wow, you can tell that already?" Dawn gasped.

"Yes, because your engagement ring is pinching me." Maeva laughed and repositioned her hand in Dawn's. "Now back to work." Her humming grew louder. "You work in a doctor's office, right? A clinic. You've been hoping for a raise. Unfortunately, I see no promotion in your future, at least not there. You'll start another job soon, though, very close to where you're currently working. You'll love it there. Better

pay, more holidays, and"—she paused and winked—
"there are some great fringe benefits." More humming. "You've been worried about your mother. You think she doesn't get out much now that your dad's retired. I don't get a reading about your mom, but your dad should have a checkup. He hasn't been to a doctor in a while. It would be good for him to go."

There was more humming and more advice given over a period that lasted far longer than Sadie would've liked. At one point Maeva actually directed Dawn in the color to paint her kitchen, insisting that yellow would be much better than the off-white she'd selected.

Sadie's own thoughts drifted, and she thought about work and then Trudy. Then Maeva said something to Dawn that snapped Sadie's attention back.

"You should cancel the hold you put on that wedding dress. Unfortunately, you won't get your deposit back."

"But it looks perfect on me," Dawn protested.

Maeva shrugged and resumed her humming once more. "The style doesn't suit you. It's too poufy. You'd look better in something with straight lines. Besides, you won't need the dress, since you won't be marrying Billy."

Dawn gasped and yanked her hands from Maeva's grasp.

"That's all right. We're done," Maeva replied, calmly.

Dawn stared at the psychic with her mouth open and her eyes blinking back tears.

"You can't just end it like that," Sadie objected tersely. "You need to leave things on a more positive note."

"I'm not a motivational speaker," Maeva drawled. "I just call 'em as I see 'em."

Sadie gave Maeva a lethal gaze, then turned to Dawn. "Don't get yourself all worked up. It's all a load of hooey. She didn't even get your fiancé's name right."

"Billy's my pet name for Noel," Dawn whispered. "I call him Billy because he likes Billy Joel. He's always singing that song 'Just the Way You Are.' It's our song."

Sadie hated the smug look on Maeva's face and would've loved to slap it off her face. Instead she just laughed it off.

"Don't you see? Chloe probably told this woman all this information when she made the appointment," Sadie said. "Let's go back to Fado's and grab a bite to eat."

Sadie got to her feet.

"No." Dawn shook her head. "You should get your reading too. It's a two-for-one, remember?"

"And that sale is for this week only," Maeva added.

"Do it," Dawn said firmly. "Maybe she'll tell you that you're going to meet someone tall, dark, and handsome."

"Fine." Sadie plunked her butt back down on a large pillow.

"So if there is a dark stranger in my future, can you make him rich, too?" She asked, winking at Dawn. "Oh, and can we make this quick?"

"I don't offer drive-thru service," Maeva remarked coolly. "Concentrate on what you'd like to know." She positioned her cushion closer to Sadie's.

Sadie thrust her hands across the table and Maeva wrapped her cool fingers around them. The medium began her humming, and just when Sadie felt like she would be ruined from ever watching *The Wizard of Oz* again, the sound abruptly stopped.

Suddenly Maeva was on her feet and racing across the room. She grabbed a small garbage can and vomited violently and repeatedly while muttering angry curses between retches.

Sadie and Dawn faced each other with matched looks of disgust and revulsion and got to their feet.

Great. The woman has a stomach virus and she just touched me, Sadie thought. She couldn't wait to wash her hands.

They were headed for the door when Maeva swore loudly and muttered the name "Trudy" under her breath.

Sadie's mouth went dry and she felt the hair on the back of her neck prick up.

"Let's go," she whispered to Dawn.

"You should've warned me," Maeva said.

She turned to face them as she wiped her mouth with a crumpled tissue.

"Warned you about what?" Sadie asked warily.

Maeva narrowed her eyes and shook her finger at Sadie. "That you walk with the dead."

7

The bizarre visit to the Psychic Café pretty much killed Sadie's desire to confront Dawn about her relationship with Noel. Instead she decided to go straight home, where Pam was waiting to offer friendship, support, and a glass of California Pinot Gris.

"I don't get it," Pam said after listening to Sadie's complaints about the evening. "Which part bothers you most, that this psychic told your sister not to marry Noel before you could or that you're not the only person in the world with supernatural powers?"

"You're enjoying this a little too much," Sadie said dryly.

"Sorry," Pam replied through a smile that did not look the least bit apologetic.

"I'm not the bad one here. I only want Dawn to see the mistake she's making with Noel." Sadie put her feet up on the coffee table between them. "I don't want to see her get hurt. When Brian died she was a wreck."

"Not you, though. You were a rock. Hell, you held up your entire family. Although that wasn't necessarily a good thing. As I recall, you could have benefited quite a bit from a little psychological help. You still could."

Sadie scowled at her.

"I'm just saying the truth," Pam stated, her palms up in surrender.

"Remember the first time a spirit talked to me on a job? It was that old lady who got shot by a burglar."

Pam stifled a giggle. "You thought you'd flipped your lid. You were afraid to go back inside the house unless I went with you."

"Yeah, well, I went to see a therapist then, remember? He told me it was all a stress-induced hallucination because of Brian."

"And now you've had years of stressed-induced hallucinations. How does it feel?" Pam smiled.

"Now it feels great. I'm helping people. Sure they're already dead, but I'm still helping." She rubbed the back of her neck. "But in the beginning it wasn't great. It was awful, and I believed him that it was all caused by stress."

"But now you're fine. So what's your point?"

"Dawn's not fine. Maybe Noel is her stress-induced hallucination. If Dawn is looking to replace Brian with Noel and if I can get her to see that, then maybe I'll save her some heartache in the end. I want her to be happy, and I'm glad she's found someone, but a marriage based on her need to replace Brian can't be good."

"You've given all of this far too much thought." Pam leaned back in her chair. "And you do realize that no one else sees the resemblance to Brian except you?"

Sadie flicked that away with a wave of her hand, but Pam kept talking.

"Then I guess the good news is that, according to Madame Maeva, you won't have to worry, since Dawn and Noel won't be getting married after all."

"I'm not exactly ready to join the Madame Maeva fan club."

"You think she's a fraud?"

"I'm hanging on to some healthy skepticism."

"Um, isn't that a little like the pot calling the kettle black?"

"The first time I told you that I talk to dead people, you were freaked out, too," Sadie pointed out.

"Sure. It took some time to adjust to, that's all."

"It's a tough thing to swallow, and that's why I don't go around making it public knowledge," Sadie admitted. "Anyone who's as obvious about their so-called ability as Madame Maeva probably has none, beyond being a shyster. She's not like me. I provide a service. I help lost spirits find their way." She looked at Pam. "And, yes, it sounds crazy even when I say it. I'm not always successful, but I try—and I don't charge a fee for that service."

"So that's what pisses you off, that she's making money off her gift?"

"Yes. No." Sadie shook her head. "Hell, I don't know if she even *has* a gift. The woman actually hums 'We're Off to See the Wizard' while she does a reading!" She shouted. She took a calming sip of her wine. "Let's drop it."

But Pam wasn't quite ready to let it go.

"I guess Chloe could've given the psychic information about Dawn, but she doesn't know about your job and your weird abilities, right?"

"Dawn swears she's never told anyone. Not even Noel."

"And even if she had, how would Maeva know about Trudy?"

Sadie frowned into her glass, then finished off the rest of her wine.

"Maybe I was mistaken. Maybe she didn't say 'Trudy.' It could've just been a word that rhymed with 'Trudy.'"

"Like what?"

"I don't know. . . . 'Moody'?"

Pam laughed.

Sadie thought about the tape that Maeva had thrust

into Dawn's hands before they'd bolted from the premises. It would be easy enough to get the tape from Dawn . . . but suddenly Sadie was just tired and no longer cared.

"Can we change the subject?"

"Okay. How are things going at the new scene? Is Trudy still bothering you?" Pam asked.

"It would be easier if she would actually speak to me instead of waving her hands around and making strange gestures, like this—" Sadie imitated the thumbs-up motion Trudy had used a couple of times.

Pam curiously leaned forward.

"Was it more like this?" She made the gesture more precisely, with the palm of one hand assisting the thumbs-up hand.

"I guess so."

Pam's eyes grew wide.

"Oh my God, Sadie. Is this woman deaf?"

"Excuse me?"

"That looks like American Sign Language, and in ASL that gesture means 'help me'!"

The more Sadie thought about it, the more it made sense.

"She hasn't been ignoring me. She just hasn't heard me," she murmured.

She pulled her cell phone from her purse and scrolled through the listings until she saw Kent Lasko's number, then dialed.

"Yup?" was the greeting offered, and Sadie recognized the voice as that of Kent's brother, Christian.

"Can I speak to Kent?"

"Sure, hang on."

She heard him call Kent to the phone.

"Hi, Sadie."

"How did you know it was me?"

"My brother said a woman was on the line and she sounded hot."

"Oh." Sadie felt herself blush to the roots of her hair.

"You're not calling to cancel our dinner plans tomorrow, are you? Because I'm going to cook you a meal that'll knock your socks off."

Sadie cringed.

"Oh. I thought we were going out."

He was quiet for a few seconds.

"Would you prefer a restaurant over my gourmet cooking abilities?"

"No offense . . ."

He paused again.

"No problem. I know a great Italian place on Fifth."

"I know it."

"How's seven o'clock?"

"That's fine. By the way, can I ask you a question about Trudy?"

"Um, sure, I guess so."

"Was she deaf?"

"Yes, she was. She was born deaf, and she taught at the King County School for the Deaf. I just assumed everyone knew that."

"I saw a fancy phone in her den."

"Why were you in the den?"

"I needed to find the insurance papers," Sadie said quickly. "Anyway, I saw that fancy phone and it looked like something a deaf person would use, so I was curious." She was in a hurry now to end the call. "I'll see you tomorrow at seven."

"I'm looking forward to it," he said sexily.

Sadie turned to Pam. "She was deaf, even taught at the local school for the deaf. Do you think she was trying to speak to me using sign language?"

"It looks that way. Part of my training as a special education teacher had me studying basic signing to communicate with the autistic students who didn't have verbal skills."

"Come on," Sadie said, getting to her feet. "We're going out."

"I hope it's to see whoever can make you blush like that over the phone."

"Nope. We're going to visit Trudy."

"You can't make me," Pam stubbornly announced on the doorstep to the Toth residence. It was raining buckets, and Sadie was shivering under the small overhang at the back door while she struggled to find her key.

"Look," Sadie said, "the house is clean. There's no evidence of what happened here. You'll be fine."

Pam looked at her friend with a pained expression.

"I really don't know why I let you talk me into this."

Sadie unlocked the door and they stepped inside. Pam looked around, and Sadie pointed out that the only thing that was amiss on the main floor was that the living room was missing a sofa and a few floorboards.

"Is she—you know—is she here?" Pam whispered.

"You don't need to whisper," Sadie said with a smile. "Let's try upstairs."

When Pam seemed hesitant, Sadie added, "There's a very good chance she won't even show up."

"Okay." Pam sighed and followed Sadie up to the master bedroom.

Once inside the room, Sadie looked around with disappointment. No sign of Trudy.

"I'll check the den," she told Pam. "You wait here." And she ducked out of the room.

"Guess we're out of luck." She announced as she reentered a moment later.

"Good. Let's go," Pam said with relief.

"Not yet." Sadie grinned. Trudy had appeared, standing beside Pam.

"Oh God," Pam whimpered, looking to where Sadie was focused. "Is she here?"

Sadie nodded. "I wish you could see her. It would make this easier." Sadie turned slightly to face Trudy.

"You're deaf, right?" Sadie asked, carefully mouthing the words so Trudy could lip-read.

Trudy's response was immediate, an enthusiastic nod followed by a flurry of hand gestures.

"Whoa, hold on!" Sadie shouted. "I'll copy the signs to my friend so she can translate, but she only knows basic sign."

Trudy began to move her hands more slowly. With her index finger she drew a line down the palm of her other hand, and Sadie copied the motion.

"I think she wants to know what happened," Pam said.

"Well," Sadie began, "as I explained to you before, you're dead, Trudy. I wish there was a nicer way to say it, but there isn't."

Another hand signal followed, and again Sadie copied it for Pam.

"She wants to know how."

Sadie blew out a breath. "Well, if you're asking how I can see you if you're dead, then the answer is I don't know. Most people can't see you. Near as I can figure, you need to pass on some kind of message to me, and that's why you haven't moved on to the next dimension."

Trudy nodded slowly.

"Do you know how you died?" Sadie asked her.

Trudy's hands went to the brutal gash at her throat and made a slicing motion.

"Yes, you were cut there, but do you know who did it?"

She nodded yes with a sad look.

"It was Grant. He killed you and then himself," Sadie said.

Trudy frantically shook her head no and started screaming.

"Stop!" Sadie shouted and held up her hands in a calming motion. "Look, I know it's hard to believe, but it's important that you know the truth. If you stay in denial, you can't move forward. You'll just be stuck here."

Trudy was violently shaking her head *no*.

"Trudy, the police have evidence that Grant killed you with a knife, then shot himself downstairs."

Trudy threw back her head and screamed again, and the word "no" shrieked from her lips.

Sadie turned to Pam. "She's screaming no. I thought she couldn't speak."

Pam shrugged. "She's not mute. Many deaf people *can* speak, they just choose not to."

Once Trudy stopped screaming, Sadie asked her, "Are you trying to tell me it wasn't Grant who did this?"

"Not Grant." Trudy signed, sobbing.

"Then who? Who did this if it wasn't Grant?" Sadie demanded.

Trudy let out a long sigh and her shoulders relaxed. Then her essence began to shimmer.

"Oh no you don't!" Sadie shouted. "Don't you dare vanish before you tell me who did this!" But it was too late. One more simple gesture and Trudy was gone.

"Damn! She left," Sadie said. "She offered me a wonky peace symbol, and then she was gone."

"Maybe she'll be back?" Pam asked, but she was obviously relieved that her duties as translator were over.

"No. She's gone. For good. The shimmering," Sadie said, trying to explain, "it means they've gone over. I guess she delivered her message."

"That Grant didn't kill her?"

Sadie nodded and suddenly felt excruciatingly tired.

"Let's just go," she said.

"But you helped her go over. That's a good thing. Usually you're on a natural high when you help a spirit."

"It all feels wrong," Sadie said. "I didn't help her. Not really."

"Sure you did."

They didn't speak again until they were back in Sadie's car and pulling away from the curb.

"Do you believe what she said about her husband not being the killer?" Pam asked.

"I don't know." Sadie pursed her lips. "Sometimes the dead aren't much more reliable than the living. Maybe she just doesn't want to believe the truth."

Trudy's insistence kept playing in Sadie's head, and she found she wasn't quite ready to let sleeping dogs, or vanishing ghosts lie. After a restless night, she called Detective Petrovich and offered to buy him lunch.

"What's this all about?" he asked warily.

"You've been sending me business for a few years now, Detective. I probably owe you a lunch or two," Sadie said.

"I don't send you business," he replied evenly. "When asked about cleaning a victim's place, I simply tell the families that they should check the Yellow Pages. It's not my fault you're the only company listed to handle sweeping entrails. Scour Power only takes on drug lab shit."

"Okay, so it's not a thank-you lunch. Think of it as two professionals enjoying a bite to eat," Sadie said smoothly.

Pause.

"Look, I realize you've probably already heard, but I'm still a married man."

"Heard what?"

"I'm separated. The wife kicked me out, but still, I just can't . . . not that you're not a knockout, Sadie, but I'm not dating yet."

Sadie smiled into the phone and kept her voice even.

"Sorry to hear about your separation, Dean, but this isn't that kind of lunch." She paused, then added, "Not that any woman wouldn't be lucky to take you out."

She finally managed to convince Detective Petrovich to join her for lunch at Romio's.

Petrovich had his partner with him, a short, stubby man he introduced as Detective Sid Alden. Detective Alden was the polar opposite of Petrovich, who was tall, lanky, and good-looking in a hard-edged way.

"So you're the twisted gal they call Ms. Blood 'n' Guts, huh?" Alden asked.

"I do bio-recovery, yes." Sadie offered him a tight smile.

"I got the perfect joke for you, then," he began. "Why do all suicides have blue eyes?"

Sadie felt her stomach clench in preparation for his answer.

"They've got blue eyes 'cause one blew this way and the other blew that way." Alden bellowed and slapped his knee loudly. He failed to notice that nobody joined him. "I'll pick you up in half an hour, partner," he said to Petrovich with a wink. "Be good, kids."

When he was gone, Petrovich offered an apology on his partner's behalf.

"He doesn't know about, well, you know . . . your brother and all," Petrovich said by way of explanation. "He wouldn't have any idea how inappropriate that was."

"It's all right," Sadie said.

Petrovich had worked Brian's case, and because of that Sadie felt that an undercurrent of trust ran between them.

They made small talk until Petrovich was halfway done with adding calzone stains to the others on his tie. She ate a slice of her sausage, mushroom, and onion mini pizza before she broached the topic of the Toth house.

"It was an ugly scene, but, as you know, not our ugliest," Petrovich said, washing the calzone down with a Diet Coke. "Remember the time we had to call you in to mop up the guy who died in his hot tub?"

"How could I forget? After cooking in the tub for a week, the guy was black soup," Sadie said around a mouthful of her pizza. "Back to the Toth house—was there anything that made you think it wasn't a murder-suicide?"

"Nope. We did our due diligence. It was by the book. Why?"

"Sylvia Toth, the mother—she just seems to be having a hard time accepting it."

And so does her dead daughter-in-law.

"Parents of the perp always have a hard time." He wiped his upper lip with a napkin. "The knife used to kill the wife was cleaned, but it still had trace on it. The rifle he used was still in his hands. There was no forced entry."

"And there was gunshot residue?" Sadie asked.

Petrovich's jaw hardened. "Why do I get the feeling you're questioning my ability to do my job?"

"You're a great detective, Dean. The best. I'm just a little curious, that's all."

"Well, GSR can be unreliable after a body has sat there a few days like that, but, yeah, GSR on the hand and powder burns at the temple."

"Sounds right, then."

"Sure, it's right," Petrovich said, sitting up a little straighter. "All the evidence pointed to this being a crime of passion. Nothing premeditated here. The husband lost it."

He stuffed the rest of his calzone into his mouth, and Sadie could see he was working his mind as he chewed.

After swallowing, he continued. "The gun and ammo were both processed and found to have his prints, and the spatter pattern was accurate for his sitting on that couch and saying good-bye cruel world."

"You did your job and then some," Sadie said, offering the flattery she knew would get her more than if her questions sounded like criticism.

"Damn straight," he agreed. "The only thing that was a little unexpected was the fact that the husband's bloody yellow running shirt and pants were stuffed in the laundry hamper."

Sadie was about to sip her Coke but put it down. "You mean Grant killed Trudy and then changed his clothes?"

"And took a shower. There was blood in the drain."

"Huh." Sadie picked up the can again and drank her soda while she rolled that around in her head.

"I said it was unexpected, but it's nothing that sent up red flags or anything," Petrovich said. "The guy killed his wife in a rage. Then maybe he thought he could cover it up, so he showers, but then, in the end, he can't live with what he's done, so he goes back downstairs and puts a gun to his head."

Sadie nodded. "Sure."

"I even had a guy once who showered, put on clean clothes, went off to work, and stayed at his office all day after he'd slaughtered his entire family in the morning. Even took his boss out for a nice lunch. When he got home that night he took an overdose of sleeping pills."

"Wow." Sadie shook her head in astonishment.

"And in the Toth case, you put all that evidence together with the fact that Seattle PD had been there for a domestic squabble a week before, and you got yourself a pretty typical murder-suicide."

Sadie's eyebrows rose in question. "Grant smacked her around?"

"No evidence of that, but the neighbors called it in because they'd heard him screaming at her and throwing things for hours. When our boys showed up, they were patching things up and everything seemed hunky-dory. As a matter of fact, they were in the middle of makeup sex right there on the same sofa the guy killed himself on a week later."

Sadie was quiet.

He pointed to the remains of her pizza. "You gonna eat the rest of that?"

"Knock yourself out," Sadie replied.

They made casual conversation for the rest of their lunch until both of them had to return to work. Sadie took some bills from her wallet and thanked him for his time.

When she arrived at the Toth house, Zack was already there.

"I thought you'd be here first thing this morning," he said with a spark of annoyance.

Sadie bit her tongue and didn't remind him that she was the boss and he the employee.

"I took Petrovich to lunch."

Zack raised his eyebrows in question. "And?"

"And nothing. He did his job." She shared what the detective had told her about the evidence.

"He's crossing the line sharing that information with you," Zack said. "But maybe now you'll stop thinking something else happened."

"Trudy doesn't believe it."

He opened his mouth to say something but then just shook his head and changed the subject.

"You should've been here earlier. You missed the carpet guy that the restoration company sent."

"Damn!" Sadie picked up the business card that had been thrust through the front door mail slot. She had begun to dial the number on her cell when it rang in her hand.

"Scene-2-Clean," she answered.

"Hello, my name's Jackie. I saw your ad in the Yellow Pages."

"Are you in need of our services, Jackie?" Sadie asked softly.

"No. I'm in need of a job."

"We're not Molly Maid. You know that, right?"

"Sure."

"Did you check out our Web site listed in the ad?"

"Yes, I did."

"So you know we do mainly bio-recovery and deal with property that has been contaminated because of a traumatic or unattended death."

"Yes, and I'm already trained in crime-scene cleanup through the certification course in Dallas."

"You've done this work before?"

"I've been working in the biz for close to two years now in Texas, but I'm moving back to Seattle. I've already found an apartment, and now I'm looking for work. According to the Yellow Pages it's either you or Scour Power. I can handle the meth lab cleans too, but I'd rather not."

Hmm. Promising.

"We should talk in person," Sadie said, barely able to contain her excitement. They arranged to meet at a Starbucks within an hour.

"Sounds like she's got potential," Zack piped up.

"Yeah," Sadie said, nodding thoughtfully. "She's fully trained, working in the business in Texas, and looking to relocate."

"We could use another pair of hands. Maybe then we could expand to take some of the jobs outside of the city."

"Exactly. I was hoping to do that just before you started, but my last employee walked out on me at that hot-tub job. I could be wrong, but I've got the feeling she isn't coming back."

He laughed.

"I haven't renewed my ad in the *Times* for the last couple of weeks because it just wasn't generating any serious calls." She tucked her cell phone back in her purse and looked up. "But she found us. You know, even if she seems perfect, I'd like you to meet with her before she starts."

"That's not necessary."

"You'd have to work with her too, and besides, it won't hurt for her to see that Scene-2-Clean has a normal person balancing out my craziness. Not that I'd spring my odd talents on her. At least not right away."

"Oh, you mean you're not going to let her walk in on you talking to yourself a dozen times before you tell her what's going on?" he asked sarcastically.

"I think I'll cross that bridge if we get that far."

He rubbed the back of his hand across the stubble under his chin.

"Never thought I'd see the day when I'd be considered the normal one."

Sadie walked into Starbucks and ordered herself a double-shot low-fat latte, then took it to a small table near the front entrance to watch for Jackie. The face-to-face interview was a must in this line of work. She'd once had a young man sound perfect on the phone, but he'd dressed Goth and had his teeth sharpened to points. It wasn't that she had a moral problem with his lifestyle; she just knew she'd have to spend way too much time explaining him, so she had to pass.

Jackie arrived wearing the bright blue Gore-Tex jacket she had described, and her smile showed no hint of vampire dental work. In fact, she looked like a very normal midheight, late-twenties, pretty brunette. Which, of course, begged the question of why a normal woman wasn't, say, a Realtor, lawyer, or soccer mom instead of a blood 'n' guts worker.

They shook hands in greeting and Sadie glanced down at their grip. Jackie was missing two fingers, the ring and pinkie digits on her right hand.

"It happened a long time ago and it doesn't interfere with doing my job." Jackie offered the answer to the unasked question.

"Fair enough."

After Sadie bought Jackie a coffee, they got down to business.

"You've brought references?"

Jackie handed her a neatly stapled two-page résumé and Sadie took a moment to look it over. She managed to keep her expression bland, but she was pleased by what she read.

"You've been working cleanup in Dallas for two years?"

"Yes. My boss is great and I enjoy the work. I've learned lots."

"What's prompting your move to Seattle?"

Jackie hesitated. "I moved to Dallas to be with my boyfriend. That relationship ended and I had no other ties there. Seattle's my home. All of my family's here. As soon as I land a job, I'm moving the rest of my belongings back here."

A perfectly acceptable response. The only things stopping Sadie from hiring Jackie on the spot was the need to check her references and the hope that she wasn't going to demand an exorbitant paycheck.

"What brought you into the business?"

"I've worked as a paramedic, so the yuck factor didn't enter the equation for me. The money's better."

"Let's talk financial details, then," Sadie began. "What were they paying you in Texas?"

The figure Jackie provided was more than she'd hoped.

"You'd be on a three-month probation period, and

that amount's higher than I usually pay someone when they just start."

"Yeah, but if your turnover's as high here as it is in Dallas, then you rarely give a raise because most people quit long before their probation period ends. I'm coming to you fully trained. When you call to check my references, you'll hear nothing but good." She took a sip of her coffee. Her unwavering gaze met Sadie's. "I'll break a sweat and give you one hundred percent every single day."

Sadie nodded thoughtfully. "Tell me your worst."

"Multiple shotgun murder-suicide involving kids," Jackie said without hesitation. "Yours?"

"Unattended hot-tub death."

"Nasty soup."

"Provided your references check out and your criminal record check comes back clean, I'd say we've got ourselves a deal."

They shook hands across the table.

"Let me officially welcome you back to Seattle."

"It's a beautiful city."

"Hopefully you'll still be able to say that after you've soaked up its blood."

8

Sadie was in a great mood when she arrived home to prepare for her date with Kent, but her frame of mind changed to anxious when she looked in her closet. She knew that Pam would be able to help her out.

"I feel like a teenager all over again, and not in a good way. What should I wear tonight?"

"You're going to that Italian place downtown on Fifth, right?" Pam asked as she sat on Sadie's bed, leaning back against the headboard.

"Yes."

"Then you want something casually sexy but not too accessible."

"I have no idea what that means."

"Wear your snug black pants with heels and your lace tank top with the sheer black blouse over it. You'll look fantastic. Your main job tonight will be to stay dressed."

"Very funny, but I find it scary that you know my wardrobe so well." Sadie went into her closet.

"Just means it's time you did some serious clothes shopping."

"You're probably right."

"Oh and use your black Guess! clutch purse. It'll be perfect."

Sadie carried the clothes to a corner chair, then stripped and put on the outfit Pam had suggested.

"You're right—my black pants are snug. I think I'll wear the gray ones instead."

"The gray ones make you look frumpy. Wear the black."

Sadie tried on the gray pants anyway and saw that Pam was right, so she changed back. She angled her head and examined her reflection critically in a full-length mirror. "Good choice."

"Yeah, you look hot. Think you can manage your makeup and hair on your own?"

Once Sadie assured her friend she wasn't a total failure in that department, Pam left. Sadie carefully applied makeup and dabbed on a little perfume.

"Now what?" she murmured, glancing at the clock and seeing that she was ahead of schedule. "Nothing says desperate like showing up half an hour early."

Sadie walked to the living room and sat on her sofa, channel-surfing and trying to fend off Hairy, who sensed it was a good moment to cover her in rabbit fur. She watched part of a sitcom without really seeing it at all, and finally, when she knew she'd be arriving at just past seven o'clock, she locked up her house and walked to her car.

On the drive over she practiced casual conversation, small talk, and how to casually bring up Kent's so-called long-ended affair with Trudy.

When Christian instead of Kent met her at the restaurant, she knew she was in trouble. So much for thoughts of a romantic dinner date.

"My brother sends his apologies. He was showing some buyers houses and now he's stuck in a traffic snarl on the I-5."

"Oh." *Great. Just great.*

"I've been told to get you settled with a strong drink. Kent will be here any second. Here, let me take your coat."

For a second Sadie considered bolting out the door she'd just walked through, but instead she let him awkwardly fumble with her long trench coat and his own leather jacket. With some effort he got them onto the overstuffed rack near the door.

"Um, you know what—you don't need to do this. Really. I'll just go, and Kent and I can have dinner another time," Sadie said.

"No way. I was only a block from here, on my way to work, so it's no trouble at all. My pleasure. Plus Kent will kill me if I let you get away," Christian said, grinning warmly.

Sadie offered him her best okay-I'll-be-a-good-sport smile. With as much courage as she could muster under the circumstances, she followed the hostess to a cozy corner table.

"When Kent told me how you two met, I thought he was joking," Christian said. "Good thing you don't carry a gun on the job or you might have shot him."

He had Kent's hundred-watt smile, and when he turned it on Sadie relaxed just a bit. He was probably in his late twenties, and you could tell he had a way with women. It was a safe bet, that that smile had been used to weaken the knees of dozens of females already.

"I guess it was pretty strange, considering I thought he was a—" She stopped herself short of saying "ghost" and said, "Burglar."

"Oh, Kent's practically a saint. He's never so much as had a traffic ticket." Christian laughed throatily. "And I'm not just saying that because you're the best-looking date he's ever had."

Sadie laughed in return. "You've got his charm."

There was an awkward pause. They sipped their drinks and Sadie stole a glance at her watch. The seconds were ticking slowly just past seven fifteen.

Christian tunneled his fingers through his hair and his face grew serious. "You have a very, um, unusual job."

"Yes."

"Cleaning up Trudy and Grant's home . . . that must have been awful."

"You can look at it that way, but as I see it, I perform a service so that families of victims aren't traumatized twice."

He nodded and stared at her intently. Sadie felt like a bug under a microscope and changed the subject.

"What do you do, Christian?"

"Our uncle Ned runs a janitorial service. I work for him. It's mostly night work." He glanced at his watch. "And if Kent doesn't get here soon I'm going to be late."

"Did I hear my name?"

Sadie was relieved to see Kent approaching the table.

"I am so sorry for being late. I never should've agreed to take those clients out so late in the afternoon. You know what traffic's like. I don't know what I was thinking." He nodded to Christian, who was already on his feet. "I hope my brother was polite."

"A perfect gentleman," Sadie said.

"I'm off to work. Thanks for not taking off." Christian smiled at Sadie.

"Any plans after your shift?" Kent asked his brother, with a tightness in his voice beyond curiosity. "We still need to talk about a few things."

"I'll be around. See you later." Christian waved to Sadie on his way out the door.

Kent slipped into his brother's chair. He looked terribly yummy in a taupe knit sweater and dark slacks. He eyed Christian's drink, then picked it up and downed it.

"I inherited him after my parents kicked him out. He's got a job now, but I don't think I'm cut out for the big-brother routine."

"Christian seems nice, but I have to admit that if I lived with my sister, somebody would probably die."

"I try to see Christian's good points. Like he did

make me go jogging recently, trying to get me into shape."

"Jogging, huh? I used to love a good run. How did it feel?"

"Sore. Definitely. Very. Sore. And I spent far too much money on exercise wear. Christian took me to this megastore in the mall, and I dropped a wad of cash on clothes that I'll probably never wear again."

They laughed, and then the waiter appeared. They ordered and continued to chat amiably until the food arrived. After Sadie took a few bites of her chicken with lemon risotto, she confirmed that it was as good as it looked.

They were quiet while enjoying the food. Eventually Kent folded his napkin and put it beside his plate.

"Okay. Confession time," he said.

Her heartbeat sped up. Part of her wouldn't be satisfied until she knew more about his relationship with Trudy. The phone records still bugged her. Still, it had been a *long* time since she'd been on a date.

"What do you have to confess?"

"I said I'd cook for you, but you made a good decision about eating out. I'm not a great cook. I'd already spent hours sweating over a recipe I found on the Internet yesterday, so I was glad you vetoed that."

"Seriously?"

"My usual is either Kraft Dinner or hot dogs, though I have been known to creatively scramble an egg once or twice."

She let out a burst of laughter and didn't stop grinning like a fool until they got to dessert. Around a bite of cheesecake Kent mentioned that he'd gone to Portland for a sales seminar recently. Her smile faltered, and the wheels in her head began turning with thoughts of what she'd been dying to ask him all evening.

"Sylvia said Grant and Trudy lived in Portland for

only a few months before they moved back here," she said carefully, watching him to gauge his reaction.

"That's right." Grant nodded. He kept his eyes down and ate another bite of his own dessert before he continued. "I sold them the place here when they came back—but I guess Sylvia probably already told you that as well."

"No." That was interesting. It meant he would easily have had access to keys to the house. "I have to admit I'm surprised you'd sell them a place so close to your own home."

"Whenever he came over to my place, Grant would say how much he liked the area. It was his idea to check out older homes. He was good with his hands, and he knew he and Trudy could really fix a place up."

He reached across the table and linked his fingers with hers. Sadie cleared her throat nervously.

"But that must've made things really awkward for you—living so close, I mean." Her lips trembled slightly as she sipped some coffee. "Especially since you and Trudy had broken up so recently."

"It *wasn't* recent that things ended between us." He looked at her intently and tightened his grip on her fingers slightly until her gaze met his. "It was over a year ago that we broke things off. Before they left for Oregon. I kept in touch with Grant because we were still friends. Even though I felt guilty as hell—but I didn't want him to become suspicious. He called me when they were relocating back to Seattle and asked for my help finding a house. I know I betrayed him. But he was still my friend."

Sadie swallowed and could only nod in agreement as her gaze sank into his baby blues.

"You think I'm a jerk for screwing my friend's wife."

She didn't answer.

"You're right. It was a stupid mistake." His jaw tightened. "I wish I'd never done it."

Well, anybody could make a mistake, right? Sadie thought. *And the calls to Portland could've been Grant talking real estate with his friend.*

After dinner Kent retrieved her coat from the closet, clumsily hooking his own sweater on her zippered pocket as he helped with the coat. They comically untangled themselves and then he walked her to her car. She knew he was going to kiss her, and her heart was drumming wildly.

"Well, this is me," she said at her car.

He reached for her, then leaned in to kiss her tenderly and sweetly. When he slowly pulled back, Sadie had to stop herself from climbing all over him.

"That was nice," she said, swallowing a lump in her throat.

"Nice?" The corners of his mouth quirked in amusement. "Obviously I'll have to try harder."

He wrapped his arms around her, and this time the kiss was neither tender nor sweet. It was demanding, ravenous and passionate, and bordering on pornographic. As their tongues did the tango, his hands slipped inside her jacket to cup her breast and Sadie could barely refrain from bursting into the Hallelujah Chorus.

It was with great disappointment that she heard Pam's warning ringing in her ears and broke away.

"That was amazing," she breathed.

"Well, amazing is much better than nice." He smiled and bent to nibble her lower lip. "How about we try next for sensational?" He kissed her. "Then magnificent." Another kiss. "Stupendous."

She put her hands on his chest and gently pushed him away.

"It starting to rain. We should go."

"Right." He offered her sad-puppy eyes. "And you

won't come back to my place, even if I promise that I'll still respect you in the morning?"

She laughed.

He sighed dramatically but helped her into her car after just one more tonsil-inspecting kiss. She pulled out of the parking lot with a warm fuzzy feeling around her that totally belied the freezing drizzle that enveloped her car.

When Sadie woke the next day, the cruel light of day had her overthinking and -analyzing the night before. By the time she'd finished her first cup of coffee, the lingering tender feeling had been replaced with uncertainty.

She called Mrs. Toth to offer her an update on the progress she'd made at the house. Sylvia was pleased but simultaneously saddened by the idea that she would have to sort through her dead son's belongings.

"Do you have anyone who could help you with that?" Sadie asked.

Mrs. Toth thought about it for a moment.

"Maybe I should call my sister and ask her to come back to town for a few days."

"That would be a good idea," Sadie said soothingly. "It's an awfully big job for one person." Then she found herself guiltily wondering if Sylvia Toth would eventually call Kent to sell the house. "The cleanup is done and only the restorative work needs to be completed. I'll call you once the carpeting and flooring have been replaced, but in the meantime you can enter the home if you like."

When she disconnected from Sylvia, Sadie dialed the restoration company's carpet installer and rescheduled for that afternoon. However, it was something else that caused her to drive to the Toth house and walk inside Trudy's den late in the morning.

She sat down in the steno chair at the dead woman's

desk and went over the phone records again. Her forehead creased in concentration and she scowled as she confirmed what she'd noticed before. While Trudy and Grant were in Portland, someone had made frequent calls to Kent's home—and those calls were in the middle of the day, when Grant would've been at his new store. It wasn't behavior you'd expect from a woman who'd broken up with her lover and was determined to keep her marriage together.

Sadie sighed and drummed her fingers on the desk.

"I didn't expect to find you here this morning," Zack said from behind her.

Sadie jumped and her hand flew to her heart.

"Sheesh! Do you have to move so quietly?" she snapped.

"It's the ex-cop in me. I don't know any other way," he replied and moved to look over her shoulder. "The phone records again, huh?"

"Yes."

She told him about her date with Kent, leaving out the part about sexual tension and fiery kisses. Still, as soon as she mentioned the dinner with Kent she saw Zack's dark eyes go hard and angry. She told him about Kent's comments about keeping in touch with Grant, not Trudy, since the breakup.

"You don't believe him."

"These calls were made during the day. All of them. Grant would've been overseeing operations at the new store during that time. Maybe if one or two calls were made we could say that he'd chatted with his buddy on a day off, but there are dozens of calls here, all during store hours."

"You'd make a great cop," Zack said. "If you're interested in a career change, I could make a few calls."

She ignored his sarcasm.

"Look, I know none of this means he killed Trudy," Sadie said.

"I think it means that a man who's hot to get into your pants doesn't want to share details of an old affair with you."

"Be serious."

"I am. The evidence at the scene doesn't point to anyone else being inside that house. This case was closed as a murder-suicide. You talked to Petrovich and you agreed he did his job. From what I remember about when I used to work at that precinct, Petrovich may have been a sloppy dresser and a pig with food, but his work was pristine."

"Nothing's changed. Petrovich is still all those things."

"And Kent could be lying to you just because he feels guilty as sin."

"Because of the affair."

"Sure. He screws around with his best friend's wife, and then maybe he tries to end it, but she still wants him and eventually moves into his neighborhood. Besides, who cares if he's telling the truth about ending it a while ago? The damage was already done. The cold hard truth is that Grant found out about the affair. Maybe he found these phone bills."

"Trudy had them locked in her personal filing cabinet. She kept them hidden. Probably she was the one to take care of the household bills, since he was at the store such long hours. Besides, even if he saw the bills, she could easily have said she was talking about future houses with his good friend and Realtor, Kent."

"If it wasn't the phone bills, maybe she just came right out and told him about the affair. Confessed. He freaked out and killed her in a jealous rage before taking his own life."

"Sounds cliché," Sadie said, wincing. "But it also fits. I'm sure you're right."

"It doesn't matter if I'm right, or even if Petrovich is right, Sadie. The fact is, that's the scenario that fits the evidence. Evidence doesn't lie."

"Even when the victim herself says it's wrong?"

"Just try and leave the dead out of the equation," Zack said, raking his fingers through his dark hair.

"Lord knows, I've tried," Sadie said, throwing her hands up in the air dramatically. "The dead won't leave *me* alone."

"Okay, for argument's sake let's say that Trudy really has reason to believe it was someone else. Maybe that's because Kent surprised her. She was deaf, right? A deaf woman could easily be surprised by someone sneaking up on her wielding a knife. I bet Petrovich would tell you that Trudy had few defensive wounds—I'm betting the cut that killed her was made from behind."

Sadie pulled her mouth into a tight line as she recalled that Trudy's arms and hands were in fact unmarred. Damn! She hated that Zack's logic was winning out.

"No defensive wounds. You're right. But we've got a husband who's totally devoted to his wife. He loves her more than anything in the world and he just up and slits her throat?"

"Loved her so much he'd rather die than see her with another man," Zack said. "Women are more likely to be killed by their husbands than by a stranger. You know that."

"Yes," she said grimly.

"He snuck up on her, grabbed her from behind, and slit her throat," he said.

She shuddered.

"It would've been quick and she wouldn't have heard him coming."

"I guess . . ."

Sadie's voice trailed off and her fingers absently played with a stack of business cards on the desk. Then she really took notice of them. They weren't business cards, although they were the same size. They were actually cards showing the finger positions for the American Sign Language alphabet. Trudy probably used the cards in her work at the school for the deaf.

Sadie held a card up to her face and concentrated

as she put her fingers into the position of one of the letters. She held her hand up to Zack.

"What does this look like to you?"

He shrugged. "Like you're saying 'peace.' Why?"

"It's also the American Sign Language symbol for the letter K." She frowned. "K, as in Kent. It was the last sign that Trudy gave me before fading away permanently, after I asked her who did this to her. What if she was trying to tell me the name of her murderer?"

"Ah, hell, Sadie, didn't we just agree that the evidence points to the husband?" Zack's jaw tightened in irritation.

"I know, but—"

"Okay, then let's talk about Grant's death. Many people try to stage murders as if they're suicides, but that's not as easy as it sounds. When a scene is processed, they take GSR samples from the guy's hands and his clothing. They examine blood spatter patterns. Then there's examination and processing of both the gun and the ammo for fingerprints." As he talked, he ticked the points off on his fingers.

"Okay, okay, you're right." Sadie got to her feet and dusted off her hands. "I don't know why this job has such a hold on me."

She also didn't know why she was in such a hurry to believe that Kent Lasko, a man she would've slept with in a heartbeat, was capable of murder.

"By the way, Jackie's references checked out. I hired her, but I still want you to meet her." Sadie handed him a slip of paper with the woman's number. "She's expecting your call. Maybe you two can grab a bite to eat before she goes and packs up her belongings in Texas and joins our team."

"If you've already hired her, why do I need to meet her before she starts?"

"You've got better instincts than me. Let me know what you think."

The ring of the doorbell announced the arrival of the restoration company's carpet installer. Sadie greeted him and showed him the master bedroom. She was tired of thinking about Trudy and Grant and Kent, and was grateful for the amusing distraction of having the stout installer exposing his butt crack while measuring for wall-to-wall.

He showed Sadie samples, and together they decided on a neutral shade of Berber that was very close to what was already in most of the upstairs rooms. Even better, he told her the carpeting was in stock and since he'd had another job cancel he could have it installed the next day.

"That's great," Sadie said, walking him out. "The sooner this job gets done, the better."

She was suddenly anxious to rid herself of this house. Whether or not that included ridding herself of Kent as well was yet to be decided.

Just as she was pulling out of the Toths' driveway, Sadie got a call from a somber-sounding man who introduced himself as George Yenkow. She picked up on the grief in his voice at his "Hello."

"The medical examiner gave me your number. He said that you do this—this special cleanup that I need," he said softly. "My house . . . where my wife died . . ."

He seemed unable to finish.

"Yes, Mr. Yenkow, I specialize in the type of cleaning you need."

"I don't know how much your services cost. I'm not a rich man."

"Do you have home insurance?"

"Yes, but the policy is in my house and I can't—I mean, I will if I have to, but . . ."

"The insurance company will pay for my services, and if you'd like, I can search the home for the policy. There's no reason for you to go back inside the house unless you want to, Mr. Yenkow."

He thanked her profusely and gave his mother's address, where he was staying.

"That's not too far from where I am right now, Mr. Yenkow. If it's convenient, I could come over now to go over my contract with you and get the keys before going to your house, if it's nearby."

"The house is in Tacoma. I hope that won't be a problem."

Sadie cringed.

"Normally I work strictly in the Seattle area, Mr. Yenkow."

"Oh. Perhaps you can give me the name of someone who works in Tacoma, then?" he asked.

But there was no one else so Sadie agreed to the job and steered her car toward the address of Mr. Yenkow's mother.

An hour later she was leaving the Yenkow residence with a signed contract and house keys. She'd suffered through two cups of strong tea while Mr. Yenkow quietly unveiled the horrible truth of his wife's demise. He'd taken his mother on a trip to Los Angeles to visit her sister. They were gone for two weeks. Mr. Yenkow tried to call home a couple times but figured his wife must've landed the overtime hours she'd been hoping for at her night clerk job at the Holiday Inn. Turned out Mrs. Yenkow died of a stroke in their living room, probably the day after he left town.

Mr. Yenkow had had the bad luck to discover what had happened and would now have to live with the image of his wife's bloated, skin-sloughing body for the rest of his life. However, if Sadie could help him, he would not be traumatized twice by having to clean up the spill of decomp on his living room floor.

She needed to switch from her own car to the company van before driving the forty miles to Tacoma, so she headed home. It shouldn't be too much of a challenge—she would just make sure the van was

stocked and then head out. However, when she got to
her house, she saw a police car parked in her driveway
and an uneasy feeling skipped up her spine.

She could see an officer at her door, leaning on the
bell. She parked alongside the marked car.

"Can I help you?" she called out as she walked up
to her front door. "I live here."

The officer turned. "Sadie Novak?"

"Yes?"

"I'm Officer Mason. There's something I need to
discuss with you. Can we go inside?"

"Sure." A feeling of dread sat heavy in her stomach
as she fumbled with the dead bolt. "What's this about?
Has something happened to my family?"

"No, nothing like that."

They stepped inside, and she waited expectantly as
the officer dug a notebook from his pocket and flipped
it open.

"Miss Novak, it's my understanding that you've
been doing work for a Mrs. Sylvia Toth. Is that
correct?"

"Yes. Oh my God, has something happened to
Mrs. Toth?"

"That work was bio-recovery cleaning at her son
and daughter-in-law's house, correct?"

"Yes." She swallowed the lump in her throat. "I'm
basically done there now. Could you please tell me
what's going on?"

Before I blow a frigging gasket!

"Mrs. Toth claims she returned to her son's home
a short time ago to sort through belongings and discovered that a very expensive family heirloom was
missing."

Sadie felt sick to her stomach.

"A family heirloom?" she parroted. "An emerald
necklace, perhaps?"

"No, actually a platinum and diamond brooch. Apparently the jewelry in question was kept in a file cabi-

net in the home's den. Mrs. Toth says that the pin was always there and now it's missing. She also indicated that you were in that same filing cabinet to obtain the insurance papers necessary to file the claim."

"Wait a second." Sadie held up her hand. "Don't tell me Mrs. Toth is accusing me of stealing a diamond pin?"

"Do I have your permission to search your residence or would you rather I wait for a search warrant?"

Sadie's jaw dropped. When she recovered her power of speech, she replied, "Knock yourself out."

She folded her arms angrily and began to pace her living room.

"That woman has some nerve!" she muttered.

She wore a path across her living room for twenty minutes, thinking of all the names she was going to call Sylvia Toth when she phoned her and unleashed her fury.

She was in her kitchen getting a glass of water when Officer Mason walked in. He held up the long black trench coat she'd worn the night before on her date with Kent.

"Ma'am, is this your coat?"

"Yes."

Because it sure doesn't go with what you're wearing, she thought snidely.

"There appears to be something in the pocket lining," he said.

He turned the coat inside out and fished around the pocket until he was able to retrieve the item.

"Do you mind explaining what this was doing inside the lining of your pocket?"

He held up a stunning five-inch brooch encrusted with diamonds.

9

"Good news, Miss Novak," Officer Mason announced from across his cluttered desk at the police station. "Mrs. Toth says she won't press charges since she was able to recover the pin. You're free to go. Consider yourself lucky."

Sadie thought Officer Mason should consider himself lucky that she didn't boot him in the groin. Also, Mrs. Toth should consider herself fortunate that Sadie didn't rev up her car and mow the woman down in a parking lot.

"What about my statement?" Sadie asked through clenched teeth as she got to her feet. "I told you that Kent Lasko was obviously the one who stole the brooch and that he also took an emerald pendant. He made an elaborate show of getting his sweater snagged on my coat last night at dinner. I'm sure he somehow tucked that pin into the lining of my pocket in order to frame me. What are you doing about that?"

"Mrs. Toth doesn't know anything about a missing necklace and we haven't been able to reach Mr. Lasko," Officer Mason admitted. "I'll try him again later."

But the tired, dismissive look on his face said that he wouldn't bother.

"You should just be thankful that your client isn't

filing charges. I'm sure that wouldn't be good for your business."

Sadie's blood was boiling. She doubted the cop had even tried to reach Kent, but you could bet your ass *she* planned on getting hold of him. The possibilities for retaliation were endless. At the very least, she was seriously considering filling his car with all the maggots and decomp fluids recovered from her next job.

Officer Mason was bang on about one thing. Sadie knew a scandal like this could ruin Scene-2-Clean, so she was grateful Sylvia Toth had dropped the charges. Who the hell would use her services if they thought she would steal them blind? There was a good chance, however, that she could kiss all future referrals from detectives and the medical examiner's office good-bye if she didn't clear her name.

She took a taxi home from the police station. Clouds hung low, pressing against the city, and the weight of those clouds expressed Sadie's mood perfectly. She felt like putting her fist through a wall. Instead, as soon as she got home she tugged Hairy onto her lap and stroked him from ears to tail.

"I was framed," she told the rabbit.

Hairy didn't care about her plight. The black-and-white bunny only wriggled out of her grasp and hopped away. Sadie tried to put it behind her, but she was still seeing red. She snatched her cordless phone from the side table.

"That Kent son-of-a-bitch Lasko has some explaining to do," she said out loud.

She forcefully punched in his home telephone number, but she got no answer, not even a machine.

She thought of calling Zack, but she wasn't up to a lecture. No, she had to handle this herself. Getting abruptly to her feet, she snatched her jacket and keys. She was planning to take her car, but when she got into her garage she noticed the Scene-2-Clean van looked odd. Tilting her head, she looked closer.

"Oh God," she moaned, walking around the vehicle.

All four tires were flat. Not just flat but slashed, with deep gashes in the sidewalls. She straightened and looked around. The door leading from the backyard into the garage was partly open. She couldn't remember the last time she'd used that door. It may even have been unlocked. Stupid.

As she inched between the van and her car, she noticed a message scrawled in the dirt on the van.

Stay away from Taylor Street.

The Toth house.

Her hands shook with fear and anger as she squeezed between the van and her Honda. After opening the garage door, she put the car in reverse and sped down the driveway and out of her neighborhood. Minutes later she was parked in Kent's driveway, staring at his house.

Although it was early evening, there wasn't a single glimmer of light behind the tightly drawn curtains. Still, she couldn't leave without making sure.

Stomping to the front door, she rang on the bell. She could hear it sound inside the house. She considered that he could be out, maybe showing houses to clients or even just working at his office.

She called information for the number and was soon talking to the cheery receptionist at Kent's real estate firm. She informed Sadie that Mr. Lasko had gone out of town but another of their sales specialists would be pleased to assist her with her real estate needs.

"When do you expect Mr. Lasko back?"

"He didn't say."

Sadie hung up her phone, put it back in her purse, and stomped her feet like a two-year-old.

"Damn. Damn. Damn," she hissed as she walked back to her car. "What kind of man goes on a date with a woman and then slashes her tires before leaving town?"

The kind of man who also slips a stolen diamond brooch into his date's coat, her mind replied. *The kind of man who leaves threats in the dirt on a woman's vehicle to scare her.*

Sadie thought of Kent's steamy kisses and felt betrayed and defeated.

With her hand on the door handle of her car, she did an abrupt about-face and decided to take a quick detour around the back of the house.

The blinds covering the back windows were closed, but luckily they were the cheap metal kind and were slightly bent. After slipping between some small shrubs, Sadie was able to press her face against the dining room window and get a view inside. From her vantage point she could clearly see the kitchen eating area and the living room beyond. Nobody was lurking in the corners or cowering under the kitchen table. Apparently there was a good possibility that the dirtbag actually *was* out of town.

"What the hell are you doing?" The warbly old man's voice came from the next yard.

Sadie squeaked in surprise and jumped back from the window.

"I'm trying to find Kent Lasko," she replied, gathering her wits about her and walking toward the voice.

"Looks like you're a Peeping Tom," he shouted. "You can't be looking inside people's homes when they're not around. That's against the law!"

"It's important that I reach Mr. Lasko. Would you happen to know where I could find him?"

"No, but I'm head of the neighborhood watch, so if you don't move your arse out of his yard, I'm gonna call the cops on ya."

"I'm a friend of Kent's and I have an important message for him," Sadie explained, offering the neighbor a reassuring smile. "As head of the neighborhood watch, you're probably informed about the activities on the street," she continued in a relaxed and soothing tone. "Did you notice him leaving today?"

"Of course I noticed," he snapped. "The two of them were hauling suitcases to their car at four o'clock in the morning. I never sleep through the night anymore, so I catch stuff like that. We haven't had a break-in on this street since I was made captain of the block watch. Who the hell goes on a holiday at that time of the night?"

"A lying no-good asshole, that's who," Sadie murmured under her breath. She cleared her throat and said louder, "Did you happen to talk to Mr. Lasko or his brother and ask where they were going?"

"No, and now I'm missing *Law and Order*, so move it along before I call the authorities."

Sadie returned to her car, where she sat shivering in her rain-soaked clothes and fumbling for the ignition. She cranked the heat up as she drove away. With an exasperated breath, she realized there was nothing more she could do to find Kent Lasko. Still, she needed to make a living, so she would have to call a garage to take care of the tires on the company van.

Sadie searched her memory and came up with the name of the mechanic she'd used before. Unfortunately, he was also an acquaintance of Zack's. Regardless, she called Information for his number and dialed.

"All four tires?" Nick asked in disbelief after she'd explained the situation.

"Yeah, all four, and I need them installed immediately. Like tonight. I'll make it worth your while, Nick, but you can't tell Zack, because he'll go all cop on me."

"He *should* go all cop on you if you had four tires slashed," he grumbled. "But you're the customer. If I happen to run into my ol' buddy Zack, I won't mention it."

"It's no big deal," she assured him. "Really. Probably neighborhood kids. I left my garage door unlocked."

"Huh." His response sounded like he didn't really care.

By the time Sadie had driven back home, Nick's truck was already parked in her driveway. She let him into her garage and then left him alone to do his job.

She tried to busy herself with housework, but she was still jumpy about finding her tires slashed. Someone had come into her house. Even though it was only the garage, she felt invaded and vulnerable. She couldn't wait to blow off some steam. The best way she knew to do that was to work a scene.

As soon as Nick was done, Sadie paid him a hefty fee for the tires and his after-hours time and sent him on his way. She double-checked all her windows and doors and then left the house herself, eager now to tackle the job in Tacoma.

She called Zack and joked about finding out the real reason for the aroma in Tacoma.

"Oh, you mean all this time the smell wasn't from paper mills?" he joked back. "You need help?"

"Nah, I'm going to do the walk-through for paperwork and take the pictures."

"And there's something you aren't telling me."

Damn. Had he heard about the tires already? She'd kill Nick!

"Um, what do you mean?"

"C'mon, did you really think you could spend time at my old station and I wouldn't hear about it?"

"The brooch."

"Yeah, the expensive diamond brooch."

She took a deep breath and told him about everything except the tires. She probably would've even told him about the tires, but by that time he was blowing such a gasket about Kent Lasko planting a stolen pin in her pocket that she was getting a headache.

"And the worst part is you brought it on yourself

by agreeing to have dinner with a lunatic!" he screamed in her ear.

Sadie pulled the cell phone away from her head and shouted back. "We were in a public place the entire time and I only went so I could ask him about Trudy."

"You're not a cop, Sadie!" he yelled and added a few more curses.

"I gotta go," she said and hung up.

The drive over wasn't easy. She couldn't find a song on the radio good enough to distract her from thoughts about her trip to the police station earlier, the slashed tires, the threatening message in dirt, and her argument with Zack. Obviously, that was a lot of pressure to put on a song.

Instead, twice she punched in Mrs. Toth's phone number and twice she hung up before completing the call. She gave herself a mental pat on the back for not calling the woman and blowing off steam. The only thing that stopped her was realizing the truth. Mrs. Toth had acted logically. Let's face it: The woman let a total stranger into her son and daughter-in-law's house to clean, and the result was that valuable jewelry went missing. The conclusion Mrs. Toth drew wasn't a stretch, and Sadie highly doubted she would believe the truth if Sadie spelled it out for her.

Sadie turned her wipers on high to combat the constant drizzle. She took the Bridgeport Way exit into Tacoma. The street she was looking for was only a few blocks from Lakewood Towne Center, but she wasn't in a shopping kind of mood.

A turn down a side street took her to an area of older, unremarkable homes in a middle-class neighborhood with large lots and mature trees. She found the house, pulled into the long narrow drive, and pressed the remote provided to her by Mr. Yenkow. The door to the attached garage slid upward and she pulled her van inside and closed the garage door behind her. It was always nice to have a garage area as a safe zone where she could store her things and change. She also wouldn't have to cart her supplies through the rain to get them to the house.

The pungent smell of death hung in the air even in the garage. No matter how many unattended death scenes Sadie cleaned, the stench was never easy to handle.

Once she was suited up in full gear, she entered the house. First she would take pictures of the area to be cleaned, and then she'd search the home for the insurance papers needed to make the claim. Mr. Yenkow had said his wife took care of the bills and he had no idea where she kept such records, so Sadie expected it might take a while to find the documents. The day was young, though, and she was confident that there'd be time to get down to the nitty-gritty.

Telltale flies greeted her when she entered the house. Since the body had been removed a week ago, many of the flies and maggots would have died off by now, but there were still enough of them to cause her to wave them away. At the end of the job, she would sweep up all the dead ones throughout the house and flush them down the toilet—although the idea of filling Kent Lasko's car with them was appealing.

The scene was contained in the living room, where Mr. Yenkow said he had discovered his wife. Since the woman had passed a couple of weeks before he'd found her, there was no doubt it was an image he wouldn't quickly forget. At least Sadie's work would prevent this family from undergoing further trauma. When she was done, the place would be like new. Still, it was doubtful that Mr. Yenkow would choose ever to move back in. People seldom did.

Sadie had no problem locating exactly where the body had been. Small bits of tissue that had sloughed off it clung stubbornly to the carpet. Dried skin and yellowish fluid covered an expanse in the center of the living room and the surviving flies and maggots were having a drunken party in the residue.

Mrs. Yenkow had been a petite Japanese woman in her early sixties. She had a penchant for seductive lingerie, specifically fuchsia teddies. Sadie knew this because Mrs. Yenkow, or the essence thereof, stood before her now, worriedly wringing her hands.

"Hello," Sadie said and the woman jumped.

"You—you can see me?" she stammered, her eyes growing large in her round face.

"Yes, although I'd rather not," Sadie said, referring to the ghost's scantily clad body. Most of the time it was a relief to see the body of a natural death as it had passed, rather than its decomposing corpse. Today she wasn't so sure.

Sadie looked up at the ceiling instead of directly at the woman.

"I thought I was losing my mind," Mrs. Yenkow continued, giggling nervously. "I hid when George came home, of course, because I didn't want him to see me like this, but for some reason I haven't been able to change my clothes. . . ." Her voice trailed off.

"George? Oh, right. Mr. Yenkow. I met him earlier today."

"It would break his heart to see me wearing this. He might figure out about me and Ted."

"Ted?"

"He's our neighbor."

"Ahh." Sadie nodded in understanding. "That's why the lingerie?"

"Yes. Please pardon my appearance."

First Trudy and now Mrs. Yenkow. Was nobody on this planet faithful anymore?

"I don't understand it," Mrs. Yenkow murmured. "People have been coming and going, but nobody seems to be able to see me. At least, not until you showed up." She shook her head slowly from side to side. "By the way, who are you?"

"George hired me to clean your house."

"Really? That's quite the getup you have on." She smirked and waved her manicured hand at Sadie's blue Tyvek jumpsuit. "I usually just wear a sweat suit when I clean. You must use some pretty powerful cleansers."

"You might say that."

"Oh, I get it!" Mrs. Yenkow clapped her hands together excitedly. "This is my anniversary gift, right? George did that before—you know, hired Molly Maid to come in and tidy up for my birthday. So sweet of him, really." She was wringing her hands again and began pacing.

"Mrs. Yenkow, I think we both know that's not why he hired me," Sadie said softly.

"Of course it is," she protested. "The place is an absolute mess and I've been working such long hours at the hotel it's been hard to find the time to get everything done. When I retire next year it'll be different, though. Why, just look at the dust that's collected on the furniture—and what's that sticky, disgusting goop all over the floor?"

"That would be you, Mrs. Yenkow," Sadie said evenly.

"What?!"

The woman had finally stopped pacing, but now she looked as though she'd been slapped.

"You had a stroke and died alone here in your house while George was out of town. It was probably shortly after Ted left you that first evening, because nobody noticed you'd passed until George returned. For some reason, your spirit has held on to this place."

"No," Mrs. Yenkow whispered. Then she shook her head violently and her voice rose to a shout. "You're insane! You're a crazy person! How can I be dead? That's just not possible."

"I'm afraid it is."

"If I'm dead, then how come we're standing here talking?" she demanded triumphantly, placing her hands on her hips and thrusting out her chest, making her look even more ridiculous in her tight lace teddy.

"When I clean death scenes, the spirit of the deceased can sometimes communicate with me. I don't know why it happens, but it usually means they're in denial about their passing, or sometimes they have a message that they want me to relay to those they've left behind."

"Noooo!" she screamed, and the shrill sound was a siren in Sadie's head that caused the fillings in her teeth to vibrate. Then, just as suddenly as she had appeared, Mrs. Yenkow was gone.

"She'll be back," Sadie grimly said to herself.

There'd been no shimmer or gradual fading to indicate that the spirit had made the transition to go beyond this world.

With her ears still ringing, Sadie began her search for the insurance documents. She looked in all the usual places, like drawers and cabinets, and finally located them in a shoe box on the top shelf of the bedroom closet. She took the paperwork out to the van.

Then she made a few more trips back and forth to bring in supplies and waste bins. She needed emulsifiers to soften the dried tissue, cleansers, and scrub brushes.

Sadie worked hard and sweat soon ran down her back and pooled under her breasts. She'd wanted to clean this job alone, to work through her day's frustrations, but after she and Zack had talked on the phone he had insisted on showing up.

"I'm sorry. I shouldn't have gone off on you," he said.

"I'm okay."

"Okay, huh? Is that why you've been scrubbing the same square inch for ten minutes?"

"I hate that Sylvia Toth accused me of stealing." Sadie was surprised at how calm her voice was, since her heart was thumping so hard.

"Nobody who knows you would call you a thief," Zack said.

"The cops found it in my coat, Zack. If word gets out, Scene-2-Clean could be ruined."

Zack's face grew serious. His dark eyes were hard and slitted, and Sadie could see the cop he used to be written all over his face.

"Let's start again—and this time tell me everything."

She told him about the tires then, using the same detached, calm voice that was contrary to the way her blood was boiling beneath the surface of her skin.

"I'm going to kill him," Zack snarled when she'd concluded her tale. "I'm going to rip his arms right out of their sockets and stuff them up his—"

"First you'd have to find him," Sadie interrupted. "And I want first crack at killing him."

They worked together then, ripping out the carpet and scrubbing the floor beneath.

"I can do what's left on my own," Sadie announced.

"Okay. I'll carry the bins out to the van and then be on my way," Zack said.

Once he'd left, Sadie was revisited by Mrs. Yenkow.

"I bought a card for George for our anniversary. I didn't get to give it to him," she said.

Sadness colored the woman's tone, and Sadie felt a surge of emotion. She knew it all boiled down to moments like these.

"I can help you, Mrs. Yenkow," Sadie said, suddenly eager to do just that. "You're still here because you wanted George to have that card. Do you remember where you left it?"

Sadie found the card in the dresser, where Mrs. Yenkow had said it would be, and at her insistence Sadie read it to the woman out loud.

"You'll always be my knight in shining armor," she read. The words were printed in glittery silver letters over a comical Adonis riding an equally funny stallion. Inside Mrs. Yenkow had signed it, "Forever, your Pooky-Bear."

"I really loved him." Mrs. Yenkow sniffed.

"And yet you were sleeping with the neighbor," Sadie couldn't resist adding. She immediately regretted her tone when she saw the injured look on the woman's face. "Sorry. That's really none of my business."

"Our sex life may have been lacking, but that doesn't mean we didn't love each other deeply," Mrs. Yenkow said haughtily.

Although it was difficult to take a sixty-year-old woman in a fuchsia teddy seriously, Sadie got her point.

"Right. Again, I'm sorry."

"We were married for over forty years. That's not an easy thing to accomplish. Sure we had some rough times, but I assure you that most of it was perfectly fine."

God save me from forty years of "fine," Sadie thought.

"I'll make sure that George gets the card, Mrs. Yenkow. Is there anything else? I'm here to help you."

"It must be hard for you to be a sort of middleman," Mrs. Yenkow said.

"I sure fought it in the beginning," Sadie admitted. "I thought I'd been cursed." She chuckled. "But you know what? It's given me a purpose on this planet that I never had before."

"Don't tell me you actually enjoy this?" Mrs. Yenkow asked incredulously.

"When I can help, yeah, I love it." Sadie grinned. "Is there a message you want me to give to George with the card?"

"Can you just make sure that he knows that I loved him very much?"

"I'll tell him," Sadie said, her tone softening.

"Good." Mrs. Yenkow sighed. "I feel kind of funny."

Sadie watched as Mrs. Yenkow's edges faded and a soft flicker began at her fingertips and toes and worked its way inward.

"You're ready," Sadie said breathlessly. Sometimes the wonder of it all still amazed her. "Good-bye, Mrs. Yenkow."

The woman faded, her essence shimmering until, finally, she was gone.

Sadie broke into a laugh and fisted the air.

"Yes!" she cried. "I've still got it!"

She stripped off her gear in the garage and dumped it into one of the remaining bins before climbing into her van. She turned up the radio on the drive home and loudly sang along. She realized that this was what had been missing lately. The adrenaline rush of pure joy she got from helping someone go over.

At home, she did a triple rinse and repeat to wash away the stench of decay. Then she brushed her teeth and gargled to remove the taste of it from her mouth. It never totally worked. At least not as well as a few shots of sambuca.

With the tall dark bottle and a shot glass in hand, Sadie made her way to the couch and used the remote to flip on the TV. She was channel-surfing and on her second shot of the licorice-flavored liqueur when Dawn called, wanting to chat.

"You'll never believe the strange day I've had," she said.

"Did it involve the police or conversing with a ghost wearing nothing but a lace teddy?"

Pause.

"Never mind," Sadie said. "I've had a weird day myself but you go first."

"Well, our office received some letters that were to go to a company on the floor above us, so on my break I walked them up. I like to take the stairs as often as possible because it's good cardio."

"Hmmm." Sadie downed her second shot and poured herself a third.

"Anyway, to make a long story short, I got a new job."

"What?"

"Dr. John Irwin, who runs the office upstairs, offered me a job. Turns out his office manager quit on him this morning because of a family emergency, and he was pulling his hair out when I showed up."

"So you're going to walk out on your current job, just like that?"

"Of course not. I'd never get a good reference that way, right?"

"I'm not a good one to ask. When employees quit Scene-2-Clean it's usually sudden and they run away screaming or crying."

"Riiiight. Well, in the *real* world we give two weeks notice," Dawn said. "Anyway, he's hiring a temp from an agency until I can finish off my two weeks, and I'm going to go up at the end of each day to train for an hour or two. And get this—he's going to pay me almost double what I'm making now! That's not even the best part. He seems like a really nice guy. Not like the ass I'm working for now. Dr. Irwin is kind and considerate. I'm going to love working for him. Don't you see? It's just like Madame Maeva predicted."

"Hmm," Sadie said, flipping channels once again, trying to find a show that wasn't about cops or crime scenes.

"You know, if Madame Maeva can help me find a new job, I bet she could find you a man."

Before Sadie could respond to that comment, Dawn put her on hold to take an incoming call from Noel and then left her in limbo so long that Sadie realized she'd been forgotten and hung up.

Half an hour later it occurred to her that she had the television tuned to a bad cooking show and still had no idea what they were making. Thanks to Dawn, her brain had been tuned instead to Madame Maeva of the Psychic Café. The more she thought about the woman and her so-called knack, the more an interesting idea percolated in her mind.

With another shot of sambuca for courage, Sadie found Madam Maeva's Psychic Café listing in the phone book and dialed quickly before she could change her mind. Since it was just after eleven, she was mentally preparing the message she'd leave on the company's machine.

"Hello?"

Unfortunately, Madame Maeva herself answered the phone. Sadie was tempted just to hang up but Sambuca was a powerful persuader.

"Hello?" Madame Maeva said again.

"This is Sadie Novak."

"Yes, I know."

"It doesn't take a psychic to figure that out. Lots of people recognize my voice," Sadie said, immediately going on the defensive.

"Actually, I have caller ID."

"Oh."

"But you weren't calling to test my abilities over the phone."

"No, I'm calling to set up an appointment. You never finished my reading."

"I can't give you a reading—at least not without vomiting all over you."

"But it was a two-for-one deal," Sadie protested. "It's false advertising to offer two for one and then back out on the second one."

"Tell your sister that she can bring someone else. Anyone else."

"I'll be honest—I'm trying to locate someone and I don't know where else to turn."

"I don't do missing persons."

"I wouldn't ask unless it was important." Sadie stopped short of begging. Maeva was quiet, but Sadie could sense her wavering. "Look, this guy is at the very least a thief who tried to frame me. At worst he may have murdered two people."

"Fine." She sighed and relented. "Come in tomorrow morning when I open at nine, but if I throw up, you pay double my regular rate."

"Deal," Sadie said and added silently, *with the devil herself.*

10

The jangle of the door chimes sounded shrill in the quiet of the Psychic Café. The store had just flipped its little sign from SORRY, WE'RE CLOSED to COME ON IN, WE'RE OPEN. The same clerk read a book behind the counter and nodded a hello to Sadie.

"I can bring you right in," she said, getting to her feet and adjusting her peasant skirt.

The woman led the way down the short hall, past the bright red door Sadie and Dawn had gone through before. At the end of the hall, she opened a canary yellow door for Sadie.

Madame Maeva sat behind a desk in a room lined with filing cabinets and bookshelves filled with hardcovers that ranged from business to how-to topics. The entire room screamed office efficiency, not clairvoyant voodoo. It was a far cry from the dark room where they'd sat on the floor.

"No comfy pillows?" Sadie asked, taking a seat in one of the stiff-backed chairs on the other side of the desk.

"I thought it would be best if we kept a desk between us," Maeva explained. "I was a little surprised to hear from you so soon. Usually the true skeptics take longer to come around, if they ever do."

"You were right about Dawn's job. She found a better position in the same building." She held up her hand. "Don't get me wrong—that doesn't mean I've turned into an instant believer. It's just that I'm a little desperate here." She pulled her chair closer to the desk. "So, how do we get started? Do we hold hands again, or what?"

"No offense, but I'd rather not touch you," Maeva said, shrinking back and wrinkling her nose with distaste.

"None taken, but for the record, I don't dance with the dead."

"I never said you *dance* with the dead. I said you *walk* with the dead."

"Whatever." Sadie waved it away. "I do bio-recovery cleaning. I cleanse the vicinities of traumatic or unattended deaths."

She took a business card from her wallet and pushed it across the desk to Maeva, who examined the front and back.

"Who's Zack Bowman?" she asked, regarding the name and phone number printed on the back.

"An employee. And friend. He takes the business calls if I'm not available, so I printed his number on my cards."

"Does he also walk with the dead?"

"Look, since the deceased is long gone before I arrive on the scene, I can assure you there is no dancing or walking involved."

"Cut the crap," Maeva barked. She folded her arms across her chest and regarded Sadie coolly. "You know *exactly* what I mean. What are you? A guide? A doorkeeper?"

"I don't even know what that means."

"I am a medium, a clairvoyant as well. I can get a reading off most people and have often been successful in making contact with those on the other side."

"Your mother must be very proud." Sadie chuckled sarcastically.

"Why do you pretend to be a disbeliever? You can't possibly still be in denial of your own abilities?" She impatiently drummed bloodred fingernails on her desk. "Oh, I get it. You think you're the only special person on the planet." She drew quotes around the word "special" and laughed throatily.

"I don't know what you're talking about."

"Like hell you don't," Maeva snarled. "The minute I touched you, I knew your power was as strong as my own or greater. Lay it on the line, sister. What are your talents? Do you hear them? See them? Offer them sexual favors? What exactly do you give to the souls of the dead that makes them seek you out?"

Sadie didn't want to have this conversation. She'd fought for five years to keep her abilities secret from as many people as possible. She didn't want to open up a Sadie's Psychic Café and offer specials of the week for helping the dearly departed. The entire thought appalled and repulsed her.

"I should go," she announced, getting to her feet.

"So you're afraid—is that it?" Maeva asked, leaning back in her chair. "You think as long as you keep your little talent a secret, you're not like me. You're not a freak."

Taking a deep breath, Sadie sat back down and reconsidered. Like it or not, she was running out of options for how to handle the Toth situation.

"Sometimes when I'm cleaning a scene, the spirits approach me. They talk to me. Some are quite chatty, but others not so much. It's not something I control. I don't call on them—they just show up."

"Interesting. Why do you think they come to you?"

Sadie shrugged. "Probably because nobody else can see them."

"That's not it. They must want something from you. Can you clearly see their physical presence, or do you just get a feeling that they're in the room?"

"I can see them as clearly as I see you. Their bodies usually appear to me as they were when they died. Sometimes that part can be a little gross."

"And they just talk."

"They talk and I listen."

Sadie couldn't help but fidget in her seat. This kind of discussion unnerved her. She didn't want to find out that her own abilities were being advertised on Maeva's bulletin board or Yellow Pages ad.

"Nobody can know," Sadie said, her voice pleading.

"Someone must already," Maeva said. "I can't imagine you've kept it totally hidden. Your sister hinted of something when she was here, but of course you cut her off."

"Doesn't matter."

Three people knew of her ability—Pam, Dawn, and, of course, Zack. Even *they* could barely conceal their desire to call her a weirdo. She was sure of it. Yet here she was, spilling her strangest secret to a woman who defined weird by vocation.

"I can keep a secret," Maeva assured her. "But tell me, what do the dead talk about?"

"Sometimes they have a message. Other times they're in denial about their own fate. I try to help them realize that they have to let go of their presence here and move on. Most of the time it helps, and they sort of glimmer, fade, and *poof!* they're gone."

"Poof?"

"Poof."

Maeva threw back her head and laughed for a full minute. Sadie was fuming.

"What the hell's your problem?"

"Nothing," Maeva chuckled. "It's just good to come across someone as strange as myself."

"I wouldn't go that far."

"I bet you inherited your talent," Maeva said.

"You'd lose that bet." Sadie sniffed at the thought

of her mother or father having any kind of super natural abilities.

"Hmm. Lots of times these kinds of things are inherited like brown eyes and blond hair. You must've been scared to death as a child when you first had some mutilated corpse show up to talk about the weather."

"Nothing like that happened when I was a kid. This is all kind of a recent addition to my repertoire. It showed up after somebody in my family died."

"I see." Her eyebrows rose. "You're not the first to become aware of a talent after a traumatic event. Go on."

"Well, the first few times it happened, of course, I thought I was losing my mind." She closed her eyes and blurted out, "So I went into therapy for a while."

"Did it help?"

"Yeah, it helped convince me I was crazy and that if I continued to tell people that I saw dead people I'd be locked up."

"So you ignored it."

"I tried to, but it wouldn't go away." Sadie shook her head at the memory. "Eventually I found it was easier to help the dead than to run screaming in the other direction. It took a while to realize they wouldn't hurt me and it scared the hell out of me. Still does sometimes," she admitted. "But I guess I've gradually gotten more used to it, and I enjoy being able to help them."

Maeva nodded knowingly. "You said the spirits fade most of the time, but what happens when they don't choose to go *poof*?"

"I can't force them to leave. I can only suggest it's in their best interest. If they choose to remain here, I think they stay in a kind of limbo. Maybe they wander the earth haunting whoever or wherever." Sadie chuckled and waved her hand. "Could we please talk about the real reason why I'm here?"

"No." Maeva held up her hands in a halting motion. "You've already told me you're looking for a guy who is a criminal of some kind. Like I told you and your sister, I prefer that the person I'm reading *think* and *focus* on their question, not tell me out loud. If I know everything in advance, then I get readings that involve your emotions, but nothing that's necessarily true to the situation you're concerned about."

"Fine. I promise to think and focus."

"Do you want the session taped?"

"Sure."

Maeva took a new cassette out of its wrapper, slid it into the recorder, and pressed the RECORD button.

Sadie reached her hands across the desk, but Maeva shook her head.

"There's no way on God's green earth I'm touching you. We're going to have to try things a little different. The message may not be as clear, but it's the best I can do."

She got up and closed the blinds on a small window, then turned off the overhead fluorescent lights, plunging them into semidarkness. Maeva took her seat and cleared a stack of papers from the center of her desk. She instructed Sadie to lean forward with her elbows on the desk and to put her hands up.

"Turn your palms toward me and I'll do the same."

There they sat, with their elbows on the desk and their palms facing each other in a ridiculous kind of suspended high five.

"My hands are going to be only about an inch away from yours, but I don't want you to grab my fingers or touch me. Understand?" Maeva asked gruffly.

"Yes."

Maeva shuffled her elbows across the desk until her palms were closer to Sadie's, and then she began humming. Sure enough, it was that tune from *The Wizard of Oz*.

"Don't you know any other songs?" Sadie quipped. "That one's getting old."

"Shut up," Maeva sniped. She squeezed her eyes shut and resumed humming.

After three or four minutes Sadie began to feel something. Her hands were becoming warm and tingly. At first she thought it was from being in such an awkward position, so she shifted a little in her seat. Then her hands also began to vibrate. There was a strange tickling, as though her palms were against Maeva's humming lips. Sadie blinked in surprise, because now that her eyes had adjusted to the dim lighting, she could actually see her fingers trembling, and hard as she tried, she couldn't seem to stop them.

"There are cleaning supplies," Maeva murmured. "Buckets, mops, brushes, cleansers, and some kind of rolling cart." She pursed her lips into a thoughtful frown and then resumed humming. "It's raining hard and the roof is leaking. Not a lot, but there's a bucket catching the drips. You hate skiing."

Sadie harrumphed.

Maeva opened one eye and looked at Sadie. "Well, don't think about skiing if you don't want me to talk about it," she chastised.

Maeva hummed again, louder this time, and the vibration in Sadie's hands grew more intense. It became a struggle to prevent her hands from touching Maeva's because they seemed to be drawn together by some invisible magnet. Sadie noticed that Maeva's fingers were trembling as well. The psychic looked as though she was in pain, and she had a fine mist of perspiration on her upper lip.

"I don't know why he did it," Maeva suddenly gasped. She moaned softly, then blew the next words out as if it was a huge effort. "I'm sorry, but I just don't know."

She yanked her hands away abruptly, and it was as

though invisible strings broke from Sadie's fingertips. Her hands dropped to the desk.

"That's all I've got," Maeva announced.

She stood, opened the blinds, and turned on the light.

"Well, that wasn't very helpful," Sadie remarked sulkily.

She folded her arms and tucked her fingers under her arms. She was extremely grateful that the tremor in her hands had stopped, but they still tingled.

"I can only tell you what I see," Maeva said. Snagging a tissue from a box on the corner of her desk, she dabbed the sweat from her face.

"But you didn't see anything," Sadie protested. "All those supplies are the things I use to clean trauma scenes, and a rolling cart could be the dolly that I use for the heavy bins. I wasn't even thinking about my work. I was only focusing on a guy who might be a murderer. I came here to get answers about him."

Maeva merely shrugged. Then she dug in her desk drawer for a pack of cigarettes, tapped one out for herself, and offered one to Sadie, who declined. Maeva lit her smoke and looked thoughtful.

"I don't know what to say. You of all people should know this kind of thing isn't scientific. All I can tell you is I gave you the information that I received, and the response felt right when I gave it."

"You said you don't know why he did it, but I wasn't even focusing on *why* Kent did it. I'm not even sure I care. I just really need to find him and clear my name about the diamond brooch and put him in jail for murder!"

"Who's Kent?" Maeva asked, taking a hard pull on her cigarette and blowing the smoke out in a long stream.

"The man I came to ask about! The one I focused on!" Sadie shouted. With exasperation she got to her feet. "This was a complete waste of time."

"Wait a second," Maeva said. "I don't know about

this Kent guy. When I said I don't know why he did it, I was picking up on someone else. Another person and question you were focused on."

"Who? What question?"

"You were wondering why Brian did it—why your brother killed himself."

Maeva pressed EJECT on the recorder and handed the tape to Sadie.

Sadie stood there looking like a deer caught in the headlights. She swallowed thickly and said, "I've got to go."

Sadie's fingers still tingled when she started her car. She drove around aimlessly as she mulled over what Maeva had said. Her directionless driving landed her parked once again on the street in front of Kent Lasko's house. There was still no sign of life.

She dug out the cassette tape of Madame Maeva's psychic reading from her pocket and slipped it into her car system. Maeva's smoker's voice filled the car with her annoying humming. The entire session was less than five minutes, and Sadie punched the OFF button when it ended. Her stomach roiled with apprehension and the hairs on her arms stood up when Maeva mentioned Brian's name.

She used her cell to dial Dawn's number and didn't bother with a friendly greeting.

"Did you tell Maeva about Brian?"

"What?"

"You heard me. Did you tell that crazy psychic about our brother killing himself?"

"Of course not! Why would I say anything to Madame Maeva about Brian?"

"Then it must've been Chloe."

"She wouldn't do that."

"Check. Call her right now and see if she said something about Brian when she got you that gift certificate for the Psychic Café."

"What's going on, Sadie?"

"Just call her and then call me back on my cell."

Sadie pulled away from Kent's street and drove to a small convenience store. She went inside and bought a Diet Coke and a chocolate bar.

Dawn called back while she was munching the candy. "Chloe never said anything to Maeva about Brian. She arranged the appointment with the girl up front and gave only our first names for the appointment. That's it."

"Do you believe her?" Sadie asked.

"Of course I believe her! Now what the hell is this all about?"

"Later. I've got to go."

She took a bite of the sweet chocolate, and as she chewed she listened to the tape one more time. She stopped it when Maeva said, *You were wondering why Brian did it—why your brother killed himself.*

Had she really been thinking about Brian? As she washed a mouthful of chocolate down with soda, she had to admit that a part of her was *always* thinking about Brian and asking that question. Five years had passed and she was no closer to an answer.

By the time she had finished her Diet Coke, she was willing to admit that Maeva had something. What she had, Sadie wasn't sure. Sadie was annoyed that she'd expected Maeva to offer up help. She doubted the psychic could use psychic powers to locate Kent Lasko. Turned out it had been asking too much.

Sadie put her car in gear and drove back over to Lasko's house. She'd been sitting in her car scowling at the house for about ten minutes when she noticed the elderly next-door neighbor, Captain of the Neighborhood Watch, giving her the hairy eyeball from his living room window. Figuring that he might follow through on his earlier threat to call the cops on her, Sadie started her car. She was just about to drive away when an older-model Sunbird whipped into the Lasko driveway and Christian Lasko hopped out.

Quick as a bunny, Sadie cranked the wheel of her car and parked directly behind the Sunbird. She jumped out of her car and jogged up to greet Christian, who dropped his keys in surprise when he spied her approaching.

"I thought you were out of town," Sadie called out as she quick-stepped up behind him.

"Out of town? Why did you think that?" He offered a tense smile over his shoulder while he snatched up his keys and jammed one into the lock.

Sadie just laughed loudly and maniacally. This caused Christian to look extremely anxious.

"Kent's not home," he said over his shoulder.

He stepped inside and tried to shut the door, but she put her hand up to stop it.

"I'll leave him a message that you dropped by. He'll call you when he gets back," Christian said.

"When he gets back from hiding?"

"No, when he gets back from Tahoe." He looked at her strangely. "His buddy has a place there. He called last night and asked Kent to come up, so Kent booked himself the first flight out. He'd live on skis if he could. I drove him to the airport when I got back from my night shift."

"You know what I think?" Sadie asked, not giving a damn if he wanted to hear her opinion or not. "I think Kent took off to avoid dealing with me and the police. He left town because he knew I'd be hunting him down and wanting to kill him for what he did."

Christian's eyes got big, and then they got angry. "Get out of here."

He tried to close the door, but Sadie held it firm.

"I want that emerald pendant," she said. "The one Kent took from Trudy's house. I'm going to give it to Mrs. Toth. He had no right to take it, and I'm not taking any chances that he might try and plant it on me to make the police think that I was the one who stole it! Hand it over."

"You're crazy," Christian said. He opened the door wide, throwing Sadie off balance, then thrust the palm of his hand out, pushed her back a step, and forcefully slammed the door shut with a loud bang. She heard the dead bolt slide into place as he shouted, "Leave, or I'll call the cops!"

That hadn't gone nearly as well as she had planned. As she walked back toward her car, she noticed the elderly neighbor giving her a surly look between his drapes. Sadie was tempted to show him her middle finger. Instead, she went grocery shopping for more junk food and then straight home.

She didn't sleep well that night—and it wasn't just because she'd consumed a lot of Cheetos. Ever since Brian had decided to eat his gun, she'd had a recurrent dream that she was running to his house to try and stop his impending suicide, but she was always too late. She woke from the dream panting and exhausted, as if she'd run a marathon. She hadn't had the dream in months, but Maeva's comments and the horrible events of the last few days had stirred her thoughts to go to that dark place.

When the morning dawned and Seattle's mountain view was once again blocked by gray and gloom, it matched Sadie's mood perfectly. She dragged her ass to her van with a travel mug of scalding coffee and wound her car down the I-5 to the Yenkows' house. Zack was already there, busy setting up the ionizer to deodorize the place.

"If I'd realized you were going to be such a go-getter today, we could've driven in together," she said.

"I tried to call, but I only got your voice mail," he explained. "I figured you were already here."

"Damn. It's my new cell phone. I seem to accidentally shut it off when I don't even realize it." She looked around the room. "After you're finished with the ionizer, you can take the rest of the day for yourself. There's not much left to do, and I can finish up."

"That's your way of saying you don't want me around," Zack replied. When she started to protest, he held up a hand. "That's okay. You've been going through a lot. I don't blame you for wanting some time alone. As a matter of fact, maybe you should take the day off. You look like shit."

"Thanks," she said sarcastically.

Sadie sat down on a nearby sofa and scrubbed her hands through her hair thoughtfully.

"He did it, Zack. Kent killed them and made it look like a murder-suicide. I've been racking my brain and trying out different scenarios, but I just can't figure out how he did it."

Zack pinched the bridge of his nose and squeezed his eyes shut. The lines around his eyes deepened, and he looked older than his forty years.

"Sadie, I'll say it again: If all the evidence points to a murder-suicide, then that's exactly what it was. Stop looking for more. This guy Kent probably has his own agenda that's all about making sure you don't broadcast his affair."

Sadie got to her feet and began walking around the living room, looking at it with fresh eyes to make sure she hadn't missed anything.

"Okay, if he didn't kill Trudy or Grant, why would he steal that diamond brooch and put it in my coat?"

"People are generally crazy," he said, joining her in squinting at the floor from different angles. "Stop looking for an explanation. The guy might have taken the pin as some kind of souvenir of their affair, or maybe he thought he could pawn it for cash. Hell, he could be a kleptomaniac who panicked when he realized that what he had was worth real money." He shrugged. "This is not your problem. Stay out of it."

Tears sprang to her eyes and she rubbed them away.

Zack came closer and wrapped his arms around her. For a second, she allowed herself to feel warm and secure in his embrace. Then she pulled roughly away.

"Thanks for listening to me go on about this," she said quickly when she saw his hurt look. "You're a good friend."

"Right," he said abruptly.

They dusted off the near emotional upset and went to work to set up the rest of the deodorizing equipment. Then they removed the bins, which would go into locked storage until waste pickup.

This time Sadie felt the drive back to Seattle was almost cathartic. The traffic on the I-5 was uncharacteristically easygoing—nobody cut her off or hugged her bumper. By the time she got home, she felt relatively relaxed. She powered up her computer and tackled the paperwork that had been begging for attention for weeks.

She called a couple of insurance companies that needed reminders to send her a check for jobs done in previous months and paid a few of her own bills. Once the pile of paper had been reduced by half, she rewarded herself by playing a few mindless rounds of FreeCell.

When the phone rang, she was grateful for the distraction as she reached for the receiver.

"We need to talk."

"Who is this?" Sadie asked.

"Maeva Morrison."

She could hear the woman dragging on her cigarette and blowing out smoke.

"I can't think of anything we need to talk about," Sadie replied with complete honesty.

"Well, too bad. You left something behind last time you were here."

"What?"

"Your ghosts."

"Okaaaay," Sadie said and laughed in spite of herself. "Maeva, how do I put this in a polite way—have you been smoking crack?"

"I just had a séance. It's a monthly event I put on for a local well-to-do family. They get together with me to try and make contact with their dead father."

"Don't you feel the least bit guilty for taking advantage of their grief by taking their money?" Sadie inquired.

"Get a grip. They're just hoping Good Old Dad will reveal the whereabouts of the valuables he stashed before he died."

"Okay, but I really don't see what any of this has to do with me."

"Usually the father's spirit shows up and offers hints and riddles. He's quite a jokester and in no hurry to lead his lazy family to his fortune, but he gives them just enough to offer them hope and keep them coming back for more."

"How fun for both you and him," Sadie drawled sarcastically. "And?"

"And this time the father did *not* show up at all, but one of your ghosts did. I'm pretty sure it was the one from that murder-suicide scene you were thinking about."

"Trudy?" Sadie asked, sitting up a bit straighter.

"It wasn't a woman," Maeva said, dragging again on her smoke. "It was a man. He called himself Grant."

"What?!" Sadie shrieked.

She was on her feet now and nearly dropped the phone. In her attempt to catch it she knocked the remaining papers to the floor, where they scattered. She shook her head hard and reclaimed her sense of skepticism.

"Okay, this sounds too convenient. Like maybe you did some research and somehow found out about my dead brother and then found out about the murder-suicide scene I just finished. All just to make money off me."

"That's bullshit," Maeva spat angrily. "Why is it that you expect me to believe in *you* and *your* abilities, but you feel you don't have to reciprocate? Do you honestly believe you're the only person on earth cursed with supernatural abilities?"

Well, yeah, up until this point I'd been happily living my life in denial, thank you very much.

Sadie managed to rethink her position and relented ever so slightly.

"Fine. Let's say for argument's sake you're telling the truth. What the hell do you want me to do about Grant's visit to you? He never even tried to contact me. I don't have any control over these spirits or, apparently, who they contact." And because the last bit sounded a tad like jealousy, she added, "And I really don't care who Grant contacts."

"Here's my theory on that. He killed himself and I think suicide victims probably go straight over to that next dimension. You seem to get spirits talking to you before they move on, but I'm betting you don't get many suicides that are chatty, right? Not even your own brother."

Sadie didn't speak.

"We could work together," Maeva suggested. "I have a plan that might work, but we'd have to do it as a team."

"Yeah, nut and nuttier."

"Are you in or out?"

Sadie bit the corner of her lip.

"I'm in, on one condition. After this is all said and done, you have to try and contact Brian for me."

11

Sadie figured that mopping up body parts and easing spirits into the next dimension was her calling. The reality of death, its effects and remnants, were so much a part of her everyday life that she was rarely rattled. However, as she slunk in the shadows at the back of the Toth house in the dead of night, she suddenly knew fear and all its cousins.

"Hurry up," Maeva hissed.

"I *am* hurrying," Sadie whispered back.

They'd parked more than a block away because Sadie didn't want neighbors to see her parking at the house. They reached the backyard and jogged diagonally across, their shapes mostly hidden in the shadows of the tall cedars. The rain was coming down in torrents, and Sadie's feet made sucking noises in the spongy moss-mixed grass.

"Ewww!" Maeva cried suddenly.

"What?" Sadie froze in place and furtively glanced around.

"I think I stepped on a slug."

Sadie grumbled something about making Maeva *eat* a slug, then continued her quick-walk to the back door. She fumbled around in the dark to find the dead-bolt slot, and when she finally got the door open, she ushered Maeva inside, then quickly closed and

locked the door behind them. Maeva reached to flick
on the lights.

"No," Sadie hissed. "I told you, no lights. Sylvia
Toth already thinks I'm a thief. She may have told
the neighbors to call the cops if they see me around
the house."

"And yet you still have her key," Maeva pointed
out.

"Actually, the police took my key at the station.
This is a copy. I always make a duplicate because
sometimes Zack and I work separately, or the restoration company needs to get into the property when I'm
not available. It makes things easier."

"Uh-huh," Maeva said. "Admit it—you were coming back here with or without me."

"No way. I am so done with this place," Sadie
whispered.

"Unless Mrs. Toth has the place bugged, you can
probably speak up." Maeva chuckled, her own voice
just above a whisper.

"I don't feel very good sneaking in here," Sadie
admitted, her tone growing only slightly louder.

"We'll be quick. Show me where Grant died and
we'll get started."

Sadie brought Maeva through the solid wood door
that separated the kitchen from the living room.
Thankfully, the heavy drapes were shut tight. Nobody
looking toward the house would be able to see two
women lurking inside.

Sadie watched Maeva pull a pack of matches and a
thick black pillar candle from her oversized purse. She
lit the candle, then placed it in the center of the large
granite coffee table.

"I'll attempt to summon him to this spot. Most spirits are more receptive at their point of departure,"
Maeva said. "Your being here also should help."

"I don't see how," Sadie said. "I told you that

Grant never appeared to me. Trudy was the only one I saw."

"And I told you that I think that's because you don't connect with them once they've moved on. You won't need to communicate with him. That's my job. The place of a person's death is charged with their energy, yet you only see their physical presence *before* they move on to the next plane. I, on the other hand, can make contact with them only afterward. Between the two of us, we cover all bases." She smiled.

"Right. Cue the *Twilight Zone* music."

"Maybe Grant's spirit guide helped him over before he was ready. That happens, you know, and that's why spirits like to contact me."

"This conversation is giving me a headache."

Sadie had happily made her way through life without ever knowing about things like spirit guides, and she wasn't sure she wanted to gain this knowledge now. It seemed as though it was tempting fate.

The candle flickered and long shadows fell along the walls, adding an eerie feel to the old house.

"Have you always been able to contact the dead?" Sadie asked just to break the silence.

"Yes. I thought everyone else could, too. My parents dragged me off to a psychiatrist at five years of age when I insisted ghosts were real. The doctor tried to *cure* me."

"What happened?"

"I got tired of going to sessions, so I learned to lie. Eventually everyone was convinced I just had weird dreams. Then I discovered a distant relative who also had weird dreams." She laughed.

"I used to wish I was only dreaming," Sadie said. "And when I started doing trauma cleaning I thought it would be short-term. A way to heal after Brian. I figured I'd do it for a few months, then go back to teaching elementary school. I knew I was helping other families in this job, but I didn't enjoy it enough to want to turn myself into a social pariah. When the dead began showing themselves to me and I made my peace with that, well, it gave me a reason to keep doing what I do. A purpose beyond the fact that I now make twice what I used to teaching school."

Maeva nodded. "With me, I don't actually get to *see* their presence. They can be dead a very long time and sometimes I can still make contact. A family once asked me to contact their grandfather, and I had no luck, but their great-great grandmother had a lot to say. Mostly, I feel obligated to be their messenger."

They shared a quiet moment of realization that they were on the same side before the heebie-jeebies reminded Sadie they needed to move on.

"Okay, so now what do we do? You've lit a candle—and it smells great, by the way," Sadie said.

"It's vanilla."

"Any significance to that?"

"It reminds me of home baking, without the calories."

"What else do we do?"

"We wait."

"That's it? We just camp out and hope Grant likes the smell of vanilla, too?"

"Pretty much."

"How do we know if he does show?"

"It's hard to say. Some spirits announce themselves in an obvious way, and others are a quiet whisper that I need to concentrate on. In case he's the quiet type, I should try and make contact."

Maeva sat down cross-legged on the floor next to the coffee table and began humming to herself. Reluctantly, Sadie joined her in the sitting, but not the humming.

Twenty or thirty minutes went by, and whatever it was that Maeva expected to happen didn't.

"I'm not getting anything. Zip. Nada," Maeva admitted. She got to her feet, stretched, and dusted off the back of her pants.

"I guess we tried," Sadie said, glad to be able to stand up, since her ass had begun to fall asleep on the hardwood floor.

"You know, I really thought that being here, where he died, would encourage Grant to show himself. If he had issues to resolve, I thought this would be the place to do it." She shook her head from side to side. "I hate to say it, but maybe you were right. Maybe it wasn't even Grant Toth who showed up at my séance last night. I was sure it was, but I've been wrong before."

"You said that you felt a connection to Trudy when he visited."

She shrugged. "Maybe that was a leftover vibe from *your* visit. Although the spirit did call himself Grant— but who knows?" She waved a hand to encompass the Toth house.

"Did you get a vibe from him . . . like a feeling that he'd killed himself?"

"Yeah, but unfortunately, there's probably been more than one man named Grant who ate lead. Probably even more than one in greater Seattle. Too many souls choose to jump ship before it docks."

"And I've got the calluses on my hands to prove it," Sadie murmured.

Sadie felt herself warming up to Maeva. There was something to be said for being able to have a conversation about the dead with someone who knew the ropes, so to speak. Sadie felt almost envious. Maeva had taken on the same execrable calling, but she embraced it publicly instead of cowering behind a cloak of secrecy or, in Sadie's case, a hazmat suit.

They headed out the back door, the same way they had come in, and walked silently through the heavy rain down the back alley. They turned up the next street and stopped where Maeva had parked her Mazda behind Sadie's car.

Maeva pressed the pad on her key chain to unlock her car, then abruptly stopped.

"Oh no," she said, slapping her forehead with the heel of her hand.

"What?" Sadie asked, but it dawned on her at the same time. "The candle! You left it on the coffee table, didn't you?"

"Sorry. It's totally my fault. Give me the keys and I'll go back for it." She held out her hand.

"No, I should be the one to go. The Toth house is kind of my responsibility."

"I'll come with you."

"There's no sense in both of us going."

"Do we really need to get the candle? I buy them in bulk."

"If Mrs. Toth notices it, I could be up a creek," Sadie said, already turning away and running in the direction they'd come.

Sadie ducked back into the dark alley. The hood of her jacket blew off her head as the winds picked up, and her hair became immediately drenched from the downpour. She broke into a run. It was nearly one o'clock in the morning now, and exhaustion would slow her if she let it. She just wanted to get the damn candle and get her ass back home to bed.

The rain tapered to a stop just as she crept across the sodden backyard again. She let herself in the house through the back door and wiped her feet on the mat before she cut silently through the kitchen and entered the living room.

Her breathing was hard and labored.

Man, I'm out of shape. Can't run two blocks without panting like I've run a marathon.

But it wasn't that thought that caused her to abruptly halt where she stood. Every breath that left her lips appeared in a puff of white. The room was cold. Freezing.

The rain that dripped off Sadie's soaked body, puddled, then instantly froze into a sheet of black ice at her feet. She shivered as a drop of rain at her temple crystallized and iced over on her face.

"Holy shit."

Every fiber of her being told her to bolt, but she swallowed her fear and forced her feet forward to the center of the room, where the candle sat waiting expectantly in the middle of the granite coffee table. Every breath that left her mouth hung in the air like frozen mist. She tasted fear in the back of her throat and her heart jackhammered painfully.

When she reached the coffee table, she extended a trembling hand for the candle. Before her fingers even made contact, it leapt off the table, hung momentarily suspended in midair, then flew across the room and crashed against the bookshelves.

"Oh maaaan," Sadie whined, jumping back. "Grant, is that you?" Her voice came out as a squeak. "Look, I'm new to this, okay? Well, not new to talking to the dead, but new to talking to the real dead—um, never mind. It's kind of hard to explain." She took a deep breath and blew it out slowly, fighting for control. "I'm just going to treat you as if I can see you," she said, speaking more to herself than to the cold room. "I'm guessing you have unfinished business to discuss, but, quite frankly, I'm not sure I can help you. Maybe I should go back and get Maeva. She's better at this kind of stuff, I'm sure."

Sadie turned to walk back the way she'd come, but the heavy oak kitchen door slammed shut with such force that the entire room shook.

A whimper escaped her throat.

"You're freaking me out," she said, realizing that was the understatement of the year.

"Okay, so you don't want me to get Maeva. That's cool. You know I helped Trudy, right? She was at peace when I saw her last."

The candle lifted from the floor where it had landed.

Once again it hung weightless in the air, but then it moved, as if carried, over to the wall. Like a black crayon, it drew on the wall, and soon a large heart shape appeared with the name *Trudy* in it.

"You loved your wife very much, didn't you?" Sadie asked, and she gasped as invisible arms seemed to wrap around her and warm her in a hug. "I'll take that as a yes."

When the embrace ended she was plunged back into the glacial cold.

"From everything I've heard, Trudy was a very nice woman." *Besides the fact that she screwed around on you with your best friend.*

Sadie cleared her throat.

"Let's cut to the chase, then," she said, deciding to take the plunge. "I need to know for sure. Did you kill her? Did you kill Trudy?"

A single book rose from the bookcase across the room. It hung for a second, as if held by an invisible string, then suddenly it was ferociously propelled toward Sadie. It narrowly missed her head, crashing into the wall behind her.

She yelped.

"I guess that's a no." She swallowed the lump in her throat.

With a thunderous clamor, a multitude of books flew from the bookcase. They began to spin in a huge cyclone in the center of the room, creating a frosty tornado. The curtains lifted away from the picture window, twisting and beating against the glass from the force.

Sadie ducked just before the books hammered the walls in all directions. One glanced off her shin, but she was lucky. Some of the hardcovers hit the wall with such force that they remained embedded in the drywall.

Her feet felt leaden as she slowly began to back out of the room. The granite coffee table, which probably weighed close to two hundred pounds, rose off the floor and spun like a feather before being dropped back onto the floor over and over again, until Sadie thought the sheer weight of it would surley break through the hardwood and crash into the subbasement below.

Finally, Sadie's feet found traction and she spun on her heel and fled the house. She didn't pause to lock up and she didn't stop running until she'd made it the full block over to where Maeva remained waiting for her.

"What happened?" Maeva asked. "Are you all right?"

Sadie held up a finger to beg a moment to catch her breath and gulped air into her lungs.

Maeva took a step closer and picked something out of Sadie's hair. Her eyes grew huge.

"My God, you're covered in ice!"

12

Sadie wasn't at all surprised when Officer Mason knocked on her door late the next morning.

"Mrs. Toth called to report that someone appears to have vandalized her son's home."

"You've got to be kidding?" Sadie gasped. She didn't know if the officer bought her look of surprise, so she followed it up with, "Why on earth would someone do that?"

"Takes all kinds," the officer said, narrowing his eyes. "I just came from there and the place was trashed. Well, not the entire place. Just the living room. Stuff was thrown around and broken, and books were actually jammed into the drywall. There didn't appear to be forced entry, and since you had a key—"

She held up her hand to stop him. "Right. I *had* a set of keys but then turned them over, remember?"

"You could've easily made a spare set."

"Yes, and as a matter of fact I *did* make an extra copy of the key. It's routine for us to have at least two sets. The spare set went to the restoration company. They were to continue with the next stage of the work. They'll be handling the painting and carpet replacement upstairs, as well as fixing the hardwood in the living room. The restoration companies I use are reputable, but maybe they forgot to lock up and some teens decided to party." She was talking fast and forced herself to take a deep breath.

"I'll need the name and number of that company."

"Of course."

Sadie went to her den and retrieved a business card. She would have to call the restoration company in advance and warn them that the police would be calling regarding vandalism at the house. She would make sure they were aware that she didn't think they were at fault; the police were just doing their job. She walked back to the foyer and felt marginally guilty when she handed the card to the officer.

He looked at it and then tucked it into his pocket. Then he pulled his face down into a frown and addressed Sadie. "The Toth neighbors heard quite a ruckus there around one o'clock this morning. Where were you at that time, Miss Novak?"

"I was at home. Asleep."

"Any witnesses available to verify that?"

"My rabbit, Hairy, but besides him a friend of mine came over. We stayed up late, and since she'd had a couple of drinks I insisted she stay the night. You just missed her."

"Then I'll need her name and number as well," Officer Mason said evenly. He didn't look all that pleased that she had a possible alibi.

Sadie managed to look annoyed instead of nervous as she scratched out Maeva's private residence number and sent Officer Mason on his way.

At least it wasn't a total lie. The two women *had* come back to Sadie's and had drinks last night. Maeva had wanted every last detail about what had happened inside the house, and Sadie had required many shots of sambuca before she'd been willing to talk about it.

Maeva hadn't stayed the night so much as she'd just left when they were finishing discussing the matter, which had been this morning. Before she left, though,

Sadie had the foresight to construct the alibi that she was certain would be required after Grant's destructive temper tantrum.

With Officer Mason's car backing out of her driveway, Sadie called Maeva to give her a heads-up.

"We did nothing wrong," Maeva assured Sadie. "So stop sounding so guilty."

"Sure." Easier said than done. "I think it's best if we don't talk again for a while. Until this whole Toth thing goes away."

"You're being paranoid."

"There's stuff you don't know," Sadie said, thinking of the slashed tires. "So far I've got people from practically every dimension out to get me, so, yeah, I'm a little freaked out."

After she hung up, Sadie showered, then washed down some aspirin with extra-strong coffee. Once she felt almost human, she headed to her office and powered up her computer. She figured that she would bury herself in alternate depths of paperwork and computer games.

She finished her filing and began playing FreeCell on her computer. Although her hand was clicking on the cards, her mind was ticking off everything she knew about Trudy, Grant, and Kent. She got the feeling that she was missing something obvious. Something just out of reach. She snagged the phone on her desk and dialed Detective Petrovich's cell line.

"Can I buy you coffee?" Sadie asked after he grunted a greeting.

"People might start to talk if we keep getting together," he pointed out.

"Since when do you care what anyone thinks?"

"I'm off at six. I can meet you at the Blue Dog at eight."

Sadie's hand was numb from FreeCell by six, so she stopped by the market to pick up some fruit and some kitty litter for Hairy before meeting Petrovich.

She found the coffee shop (converted from an old house), and when the detective showed up she was already on her second latte, which didn't help her nerves. Petrovich was dressed for casual comfort in Levi's and a leather jacket over a gray sweatshirt, but he still didn't fit in with the university crowd that filled the place. He also had dark bags under his eyes that begged an explanation, but Sadie didn't pry.

She greeted him and bought him a coffee, plain and black—nothing fancy-shmancy—and a tuna melt to go with it.

"Thanks for agreeing to meet me," she said as they sat down at a cramped table against a bright orange wall.

He shrugged. "My other choice was to spend the night unpacking."

"You moved?" Moving was enough to put bags under anyone's eyes.

"Yup. Had to." After a pause he added. "My ex is going for a bigger chunk of my cash. I needed a smaller place, so I got one about a block from here."

"Oh." Sadie reached out and covered his hand with hers. "Dean, I'm sorry. This must be a rough time for you."

"I'm good." He tugged his fingers away and added, "What do I need with a bedroom all to myself? A bachelor place is fine. More than fine." And the anger in his eyes challenged her to say it wasn't.

"Sure," Sadie said.

He clapped his hands together and changed the subject. "So, what's up? Is this about you tossing the Toth house?" He smiled at her from over his coffee cup.

"That's not funny."

"Depends on what side you're looking from." His grin widened. "From what I gather, all the guys at the station are getting quite a kick out of it. They're thinking the blood 'n' guts girl finally went off the deep end."

She winced.

"They think I've flipped out."

"Some. Others think you're just on a crime spree from seeing too much."

Ouch.

Her gaze grabbed his and held.

"I didn't steal that brooch, and I didn't toss the Toths' house."

"I'm not saying you did, although that's exactly what Sylvia Toth is saying."

Oh God.

"You know, it would be good if you just lay low and stay away from that woman."

"I intend to," Sadie assured him.

Sadie waited for Petrovich to take a sip of his coffee, then drank a little of her own. After a deep breath she forged ahead.

"I asked you to meet with me 'cause I'm hoping you'll back me up. Maybe you can put the rumor mill to rest by tossing out some facts on the situation, or at least a good character reference. Scene-2-Clean will be hit hard if word spreads I'm a vandal and a thief."

He nodded seriously. "Don't know how much help I'll be, but sure, if I hear anyone bad-mouthing you, I'll set them straight."

"That's all I ask." She offered him a bright smile.

"Of course, if we had someone else to put out there as a suspect, it sure would help."

"I'm working on that."

He shook his head. "I don't like the sound of that. Leave the investigations to us."

"I'm just trying to save my ass, Dean. You know damn well the force doesn't have the manpower to put it all out for a jewelry theft, house break-ins, or tire slashing."

"Tire slashing?" He leaned in.

"My company van had its tires slashed, and the culprit left me a message in dirt on the van telling me to back off from the Toth house."

"When did this happen?"

"A couple days ago."

"Damn it, Sadie, you should've called me!" He thumped the table hard, and her coffee sloshed out of the cup.

Petrovich dug out a notepad, and she filled him in on what few details there were.

"Best advice I can give you is to stay away from there," he said, waving his pen in her face. "Things will settle. Time will pass. Everyone will forget about the Toth situation when the next thing comes down the pike."

"Some might forget, but others won't. It only takes one to keep the rumors going. I rely on business sent my way by SPD and the ME's office. If they suspect that there's even a slim chance I'm guilty, nobody will send business my way. I can't blame them. I'll keep away from the Toth place, but I need you to look harder into Kent Lasko."

Sadie intended to avoid Mrs. Toth at all costs, so she was stunned when she returned home, pulled into her driveway, and saw Mrs. Toth zip her small Chevy up behind her. Now what?

Nervously, Sadie climbed out of her car and watched as Sylvia Toth approached with a look of blatant, unadulterated hatred.

Uh-oh, this can't be good.

"How dare you!" Sylvia shouted furiously as she approached. "What the hell's your problem, anyway?"

Sadie took a step back.

"What kind of a sicko takes advantage of someone's grief by trashing their dead son's home?"

"I'm sorry to hear your son's place was damaged, but I can assure you that I *wasn't* the one who did it." Sadie stood her ground and met the woman's gaze. "Now why don't you go on home before either one of us says or does something we'll regret."

Sadie turned and walked to her front door, hoping Mrs. Toth would just get back in her car and drive off. She didn't. She followed Sadie and continued to shout.

"I should've known there was something wrong with you," Sylvia raged, pointing her finger accusingly at Sadie. "Anyone who's in your line of work, who gets their kicks working with blood and gore, must have something wrong upstairs."

She tapped the side of her head and then made the cuckoo sign. Sadie's blood began to percolate, and she bit down on the inside of her cheek to stop herself from screaming back. The only thing that kept her from telling the old biddy off was the reminder that the poor woman had just lost her family.

"I understand your anger, but like I said, I did *not* trash your son's living room," Sadie said between clenched teeth.

"How did you know it was just the living room, huh?" Mrs. Toth demanded triumphantly.

"The police told me," Sadie said. She glanced across the street, where a curious neighbor was unloading groceries from the trunk of her car. Most of the soccer moms and the nine-to-five dads had avoided her like the plague since they'd discovered her profession. A shouting match on her front lawn was not exactly going to win her any neighborhood popularity contests.

"Why don't you come inside? I'll make tea and we can talk about this like mature, rational people," Sadie suggested magnanimously.

"That would assume that we're both sane, but apparently only one of us is," Mrs. Toth screamed shrilly. "I wouldn't be caught dead spending time with you."

"That's exactly how most people *do* end up spending time with me," Sadie muttered to herself.

Mrs. Toth spun on her heel. Sadie should've got while the getting was good, but she couldn't help but blurt, "I don't think Grant killed Trudy."

Mrs. Toth froze comically with her right foot lifted in midstep. She turned around ever so slowly, and Sadie hated the look on the woman's face—anger first, but then desperation mingled with hope. Sadie knew that she would've worn that exact same expression had someone told her that they didn't believe Brian had taken his own life.

"What did you say?" Mrs. Toth whispered.

"I don't have any evidence, you understand, just a gut feeling and . . ." She gave her head a shake. "Forget it. I shouldn't even discuss this with you."

Mrs. Toth straightened and took a step toward her.

"A cup of tea might be a good idea."

Once inside Sadie's kitchen, Mrs. Toth sat with her hands tightly folded on top of the table while Sadie took as long as possible to make one small pot of tea. When she'd fussed enough with cream, sugar, and flowery napkins, like this was some kind of a garden party, she took a seat across from Mrs. Toth.

"I have no hidden agenda here," Sadie began. "This tragedy has already torn you apart, and I don't want to hurt you any more than you've already been hurt."

Mrs. Toth simply stared into her cup of tea. A slim tear traced its way down her cheek.

"I've never believed Grant was capable of murdering Trudy. It just doesn't make sense. He was just so damned devoted to her. Trudy and his stores—those were the two things he loved the most." She sighed and took a sip of tea, then put the mug down and looked up at Sadie. "I don't mean that he didn't care for me. He did. It's just that his love for Trudy was everything. He worshiped her. As much as he loved that damn sportswear store, he would've given it all up if Trudy had said boo. She was everything to him."

"Tell me about the stores," Sadie said, trying to make small talk.

"Grant prided himself on that damned store and everything in it. He wouldn't even consider stocking any of the top-selling brands if the company had so much as a hint of unethical business practices. He said that he felt globally responsible for the products he sold." She smiled in memory, but then her smile faltered. "Does that sound like the kind of man who turns around and butchers his wife?"

"No. No, it doesn't." Sadie shook her head sadly. She knew she shouldn't share what was in the forefront of her mind, but she couldn't see a way around it. "I have to tell you something now, Mrs. Toth, and you're going to think I'm crazy. Please, just hear me out."

Mrs. Toth gave her a look that said she already thought that someone who mopped up body parts for a living wasn't all there.

"Sometimes when I clean someone's home, I feel a special connection to the person who has passed. I know it sounds nuts, and it sounds the same way to me when I say it out loud, but there are times when the person who died communicates with me."

"I don't understand. You mean you feel ghosts when you're cleaning a house?"

Sadie wondered what she'd gotten herself into, but she pushed on. She had nothing to lose, since Sylvia Toth already thought she was talking to a lunatic.

"I can actually see the spirit of the person who's passed. Sometimes, for a short period of time, I can even communicate with them."

The woman didn't run screaming from the house, but she didn't embrace the idea, either.

"You're telling me that you *saw* my son's ghost and he said he didn't kill his wife?"

Sadie shook her head. "No. Grant didn't say anything like that, at least not directly. I saw Trudy, and she *did* tell me that."

One look at Mrs. Toth and Sadie knew she was losing her audience. Disbelief radiated from her every pore, but still Sadie went on.

"Trudy didn't speak to me, but she kept showing me hand gestures. That's why I asked around and found out that she was deaf."

"You think she was trying to tell you something?"

"Yes. Unfortunately, I can't control how long spirits are in a state of limbo. She left before I could get the full message."

"But she did say, I mean, sign, something to you?" Mrs. Toth asked, still looking at Sadie like she was a crazy person, but Sadie could tell that part of her really wanted to believe.

"I think that what Trudy was trying desperately to tell me before she slipped over was that Grant wasn't the person who killed her."

"Then did she tell you who *did* do it?"

"Not exactly, but when I asked her who it was, she showed me this hand gesture." Sadie held up her fingers in imitation of what Trudy had shown her.

"The peace sign?"

"It's also the letter K, in American Sign Language. I think Trudy was trying to spell out the name of the person who killed her, but she passed over before she could finish."

"Someone whose name starts with the letter K?"

"Yes."

Neither of them spoke for a full minute. Sadie was wondering if Mrs. Toth was afraid to bolt for the door.

Mrs. Toth shrugged her shoulders. "None of this makes sense to me."

"And I don't expect it to," Sadie rushed on. "But there's more. Kent Lasko was inside your son's house the very first time I went there to clean. Later, he told me he was there to claim an emerald necklace that he'd given to Trudy. He needed to take it from the house because"—Sadie paused, not wanting to tarnish this woman's image of her daughter-in-law—"he said the necklace belonged to his mother."

"Kent's mother, Ramona, is a good friend of mine. I know she does have an emerald necklace that she plans to pass on to a daughter-in-law one day. Why on earth would Trudy have Ramona's necklace?"

Sadie shrugged.

"Trudy didn't even like to own fancy jewelry," Mrs. Toth continued. "That diamond brooch was a gift to me from my husband, God rest his soul, but Trudy wouldn't even wear it. She was terrified of losing it. That's why she kept it hidden away in a file cabinet. She said that she'd keep it in there and only take it out on special occasions. When she did wear it, she touched it continuously to make sure it didn't fall off. I was hoping one day I'd have a granddaughter who would wear it." She paused and glared at Sadie. "That's why I noticed right away it was missing. I can't believe you took it. I trusted you."

Sadie shook her head vehemently. "I know the police found that brooch in my coat pocket, but I swear on my brother's grave that I wasn't the one who stole it. I had a date with Kent Lasko, Mrs. Toth. I was a fool to go out with him. He obviously asked me out to dinner only to plant that brooch on me."

"That doesn't make sense. Why would he take the brooch and give it back to you?"

"Maybe he just meant to get the emerald necklace and the brooch was wrapped with it. It was probably a mistake. Maybe he knew that I would turn it over to the authorities, or maybe he wanted to distract me from my suspicions that he had something to do with what happened to Grant and Trudy."

At her look of disbelief Sadie weakly offered, "I

know it sounds crazy. I wish I had all the answers, but, truthfully, I don't."

Sadie had gone this far and she knew there was no saving face with this woman anyhow, so she went for broke and spilled the rest.

"I was in your son's house last night. I went there in the middle of the night to try and contact his spirit."

"So it was you who destroyed the house!" she gasped.

"No! Remember when I said I saw only Trudy's spirit and not Grant's? Well, I was trying to contact him, and I believe that what happened in the house was his way of sending me a message. I know I'm asking you to swallow a lot here, but last night Grant's spirit showed up. He touched me when I asked if he loved his wife, and his touch was warm and tender, as if he was agreeing with that statement. Then he used a black candle to draw a heart with *Trudy* written inside of it."

"I saw that heart."

"Well, when I asked Grant if he'd also killed Trudy, his spirit went nuts. He flew into a rage and flung things around the room. He even lifted that heavy coffee table like it was a toy, and he threw books everywhere. I can't help but take that reaction as an adamant no."

Mrs. Toth's eyes glistened with tears.

"I wish I could believe in this—this craziness. I want to believe Grant wasn't a murderer, but you're also asking me to think that Kent murdered them instead, and that's almost as unlikely. I can't see Kent ever hurting Grant or Trudy. He was the best man at their wedding. He and Grant were buddies since college."

"Sylvia, would you rather believe that Grant killed his wife and then himself?"

She wiped away a tear. "My sister told me if there was any evidence that pointed to someone else, the police would've found it."

Sadie had no answer for that.

Mrs. Toth got to her feet. "I need to think about this for a while."

Sadie walked her to the door. She doubted she would ever see the woman again, and it was probably just as well.

"Thanks for hearing me out," Sadie said. "I don't want to intrude on your pain. You won't hear from me again, and I won't be going near Grant's house. You have my word." Sadie bent to her purse, withdrew the final key for the Toth house, and handed it to Sylvia.

"Can I just ask you a question?"

Sadie nodded.

"Did you see your brother's spirit and talk to him when he died?"

Sadie swallowed. "No. I wish I had."

Mrs. Toth nodded and opened the door. The minute she stepped outside, a sharp crack rang out and a bullet dug a deep gash in the door frame an inch from where they were standing.

Mrs. Toth screamed but stood frozen to the spot. Sadie watched as a dark green, older-model Toyota gunned the accelerator past the house, only to slam on the brakes, skid to a stop, then rocket suddenly in reverse. A hand holding a gun extended from the driver's window.

"He's coming back!" Sadie screamed.

She yanked Sylvia Toth by the arm, but not before a second shot split the air.

Mrs. Toth crumpled to the ground like a rag doll, and Sadie pulled her inside the house and slammed the door shut. She dragged the hysterical woman to the hall, and only there did she look seriously at the wound. Her shoulder was soaked in blood, which was quickly pooling on the floor.

"Don't leave me," she cried, her good arm locking on Sadie and her eyes pleading.

"I'll grab the phone to call for help and I'll stay with you until they get here," Sadie assured her.

Mrs. Toth's eyes were wide with fear as she released Sadie's arm.

Sadie crawled on her belly toward the other end of the room to get to the phone. She reached the cordless receiver just as a third shot exploded her picture window and she was showered with glass.

13

After the ambulance attendants sped Mrs. Toth away, Detective Petrovich walked Sadie through an icy drizzle and into the back of his unmarked car. The drive to the station was quiet. It wasn't until she'd given her statement three times and written it out fully that she heard any news of Mrs. Toth's condition.

"She's in surgery. The bullet caught her in the shoulder, but although she lost a lot of blood, she'll be fine," Petrovich said.

"Thank God," Sadie murmured.

"I need you to go through these books and see if you can identify the make and model of the car." He tossed two binders in her direction. They landed with a bang on the metal table, causing Sadie to jump.

"I told you it was an older-model green Toyota and the driver's-side door had some rust."

"See if you can narrow down the year," he said with a bite.

"You think I had something to do with this, don't you?" Sadie whispered, her fingers trembling as they turned to the first page in the binder. "You think I tried to kill Mrs. Toth."

"Of course not," he said, scratching the top of his head. "Besides, we tested your hands for gunshot residue, and it's obvious from the trajectory of the bullet that the shooter was in the street. Just like you said."

She nodded.

"But why the hell did this happen at your place? Sylvia Toth said that she told nobody she planned on going to see you."

"Maybe someone followed her."

"Or they were told to be there."

"You don't think I asked someone to come by and shoot her?" Sadie asked in disbelief. She narrowed her eyes angrily at him. "Dean, if you're suggesting for one minute I did this—"

He cut her off.

"The neighbors saw you two fighting in your driveway just minutes before."

"She was pissed at me about that diamond pin and her son's house being busted up. Still, she came inside and we had tea together and tried to work things out."

"You hate tea."

"Which proves how desperate I was to end things on good terms! I was trying to take the bad attention *away* from Scene-2-Clean. I don't want to attract more!" Her eyes grew dark and somber. "Did you even bother to try and track down Kent Lasko, like I told Officer Mason to do? I bet Lasko never went to Tahoe. That's just a lie he told to cover his ass while he slashed my tires."

"As a matter of fact, we found Kent Lasko," Detective Petrovich said evenly.

Sadie looked up hopefully.

"You found him? That's great! Was he holed up at a friend's house somewhere? Did you test *his* hands for gunshot residue? That guy's as guilty as sin. I'll bet he'll even confess if you lean on him. Hell, I certainly won't complain if you want to bring him in and rough him up—"

"We didn't talk to him because he was up the mountain at the time." Detective Petrovich shouted above her ramblings. "His friend was in the condo, and he verified that Kent is with him and they're skiing! I'm sure once we dig, there'll be a dozen people who'll vouch for seeing him there. We both know that there's no way he could get from Tahoe in time to shoot Sylvia Toth."

"Damn! Double damn!" Sadie muttered. "You're sure?"

"We'll check, like I said, but we have no reason to believe his friend would lie. The guy seemed genuinely surprised to hear why we were calling, and he was ready to vouch for his friend in a heartbeat. Kent Lasko has never had so much as a parking ticket."

Petrovich drummed his fingers on the table and watched her intently.

"You know, there's another possibility you should think about." He paused and Sadie looked at him expectantly. "It's possible the shooter wasn't gunning for Mrs. Toth. You already had your tires slashed and were given a warning."

Sadie's eyes grew big for a moment before her body just sank into itself. She felt deflated and suddenly very tired. Her instinct was to shake her head in adamant denial, but she needed to face the truth.

"Somebody thinks I should mind my own business in the Toth case," Sadie said. "And I guess there's a chance that somebody isn't Kent Lasko."

"The graveyards are full of people who were murdered for sticking their noses where they shouldn't have, Sadie. Please tell me you're walking away from this thing and you'll leave me to find the shooter."

"I'm done." She blinked back tears. "And on that positive note, I think I'll go," she said and got to her feet. "I got a window to fix. You know how to reach me, if you find out anything."

"And you know that you're expected to stay in town until this matter is cleared up."

With a harrumph and as much dignity as she could muster, Sadie stormed out and took off for home.

When she got there the glass company was replacing the window. Still, the broken bits of glass and the blood had to be cleaned. Sadie eyes blurred with tears as she swept up the remnants of her window and wiped up Sylvia Toth's blood. Then she buried herself in the rest of her housework and paperwork for the remainder of the day and well into the evening, not wanting to pause for even a moment to think.

It was dark when she finally sat down. Icy rain pinged off her windows, and she started up the gas fireplace in the living room. Every time the wind gusted or the house creaked, her stomach clenched in fear.

Hairy was no help whatsoever in offering comfort to his stressed owner. Instead, the bunny hunkered down with a faded stuffed toy bunny (Mini-Hairy) in his basket and couldn't be bribed or coaxed into her lap—not even with the promise of the yogurt rabbit treats that were his favorites.

"You should know that I'm seriously considering trading you in for a Doberman pinscher," Sadie grumbled, but Hairy only twitched his nose without fear.

Sadie was tempted to go out somewhere, anywhere, just so she wouldn't have to stay in her home feeling like a sitting duck. But she was afraid to open her damn front door. Her butt felt frozen to her couch. She was so spooked that even Pam's intrusive nature would've been welcome, but her friend wasn't around to offer her usual platitudes. This was the first time Sadie had felt inclined to agree with her mother— maybe she needed to find a man.

Even TV couldn't distract her. Her gaze kept drifting occasionally over to the door frame, where a substantial hole announced where they'd dug out the bullet. Every time she glanced in that direction she felt sick.

Finally she couldn't stand it any longer and she called Zack.

"I hate to bother you," she began, "but I didn't

get a chance to check on the ionizer at the Yenkow house today."

"Been there, done that."

"Oh." Of course he had. "Thanks."

"No problem."

When she was quiet he sounded worried.

"Sadie?" he asked. "Are you there?"

"Yeah." The wind howled, her old house creaked, and the bullet hole seemed to mock her like a bad horror flick. "Don't suppose, if you're not busy, you'd be willing to come over?"

"Now? Tonight?" he asked, surprised.

"Yes."

"I'll be there in ten minutes."

It was closer to twenty before he showed up. When there was a pounding at the door, Sadie cursed and hated that she felt skittish about answering. She would've checked the peephole, but she didn't have one. She desperately wanted to turn the fear in her belly into anger, which was too bad for Zack.

"So what's up? What the hell happened?" he asked before he even slipped his arms out of his jacket.

"For once, Zack, could you not be such a man?" she snapped.

His eyebrows rose in amusement.

"You'd rather I be a woman? Because I don't think I'm that much in touch with my inner drag queen."

"How about you come in and make small talk and polite conversation?" Sadie realized she was shouting, so she took a calming breath, then added in a small voice, "Can I get you a beer?"

He nodded. "Sure."

She brought them each a can and they took a seat, she on the sofa and he on a chair. His look was deceptively casual. Only the tightening of his jaw and the deepening lines around his eyes hinted that he was either worried or pissed.

They chatted amiably about the weather that was

howling outside her door and about various jobs in the past. Finally there was a pause, and Zack slammed his empty beer can down on the coffee table and faced Sadie.

"Dammit, Sadie. When are you going to tell me why there's a bullet hole in your doorjamb?"

"I was getting to that," Sadie sighed. She downed the rest of her beer, then spilled out everything, from her meeting with Maeva last night to her statement at the station a few hours earlier.

When she'd finished, Zack's legs were eating up her floor like a caged animal. He muttered a lot to himself, and his hands were balled into fists. So far he wasn't exactly being the picture of comfort that Sadie had hoped.

"I've let this slide long enough," he stated flatly when he finally stopped pacing. "Hand me your phone. I'm calling in some favors."

She shook her head vehemently.

"No. Absolutely not." She was on her feet just inches away from him. "I can't let you get involved in this, Zack. This is my problem."

"Now I need you to stop acting like a woman," he snarled. "You can't dump this crap on me and expect that I won't do a damn thing to try and fix it."

"I only told you because we work together and this involves a client." At his skeptical look she continued, "And because you're a friend."

"A friend. Right," he said, tight-lipped. "That's just great."

He dragged his fingers and mussed his hair further, then moved closer and put his hands on her shoulders. The warmth of his touch gave Sadie a feeling of uneasiness.

"I remember when you first told me about your . . ."—he searched for the words and dropped his hands to his sides—"your conversations with people who aren't there."

"You caught me chatting with that young mom in Renton." She chuckled at the memory. "You thought I was crazy. You probably still do."

"To tell you the truth, I don't know what to think about all that." He was pacing again, his hands flying in the air with emotion. "The only thing I *do* know for sure, Sadie Novak, is that you aren't a liar. Not by a long shot. I've seen you go above and beyond the call of duty to help hurting families. When we were cleaning that old house in Bellevue, you knew the family was hard up for cash and you slipped a couple hundred bucks of your own into a drawer where you knew they'd find it."

"You weren't supposed to see that."

"You also took a chance on an ex-cop when nobody else would. So if you say that you get feelings and see things that I don't, then I'm willing to step up and say that's just fucking A-okay with me." He shook his head slowly from side to side. "But this isn't about you telling dead people to walk toward the light because they got lost along the way, and this isn't about some deaf woman who got her throat slit. This is about *you* being a target."

"I never said that."

"You didn't have to. You'll have to fire me to stop me from making an effort to look into this, and even then I couldn't make any guarantees."

She nodded slowly.

"Okay."

She knew then that if she was honest she would admit that this was exactly why she'd asked him to come over in the first place. Deep down she knew Zack wouldn't be able to just stand aside if someone took a shot at her. She got him the phone and listened while he made small talk with some guys in the police department whom he used to work with. He mingled greetings with inquiries as smooth and casual as could be.

While she listened, she forced Hairy onto her lap and stroked the length of his silky fur, bribing him with a fistful of yogurt yummies to hold him still.

"I'll take another beer now," Zack said when he was done.

Placing the phone on the coffee table, he settled back into the chair, deep in thought.

She nudged Hairy to the floor and got them each another can.

"So?" she asked as she popped the tab.

"Not a whole lot," he said. "Nothing sets off any alarms in this case. Grant went jogging, probably to cool off after arguing with his wife. When he came home he was still pissed, so he went upstairs and slit his wife's throat. Afterward he panicked at first, stuffed his bloody clothes in the hamper, and had a shower. He either realized he'd never get away with it or else he was filled with remorse, because he went down to the living room and ate his gun."

"Just like that? A guy goes for a jog and then nearly decapitates his wife but takes off his bloody clothes and has a shower before blowing his brains out? Does that sound right to you?"

"Sure." He took a long pull on his beer. "Many times if a guy kills his wife in a spur-of-the-moment crime of passion, afterward he'll take a while to compose himself. Sometimes he'll even start to clean up the scene."

"You saw Trudy's scene. Nobody tried to clean that up before we got there."

"Right, but let's say he's freaked out after killing her. He takes a shower to figure out what to do and the clothes go in the hamper out of habit. Then he realizes there's just no way to cover it up, so he doesn't try to clean up. He's overcome with guilt and can't take it. He goes downstairs and puts the gun to his head."

"And the weapons were found in the house?"

Zack nodded. "They found the knife back in a butcher block on the kitchen counter. He'd washed it, but not good enough."

"And prints?"

"If there were any, he washed them off the knife, but, yup, prints on the gun were his."

She shook her head slowly from side to side. "I don't know . . . it still feels wrong to me. If this *was* a murder-suicide and I'm to buy what you're saying, why would Trudy insist it wasn't Grant and why would Grant put in so much effort to deny it?"

Zack shifted uncomfortably in his seat. "I can't speak on behalf of ghosts. It flies in the face of all the training I've ever had. If I had to give you an answer based on what you've told me, I'd say Trudy was either in denial or feeling guilty because of the affair. Most likely, Grant found out she was screwing his best friend. As for that whole spooky scene with the cold room and the books being thrown, well, maybe Grant's message is that you should butt out and get lost. Not every person likes someone poking around in their private business. Could be that ghosts feel the same way about that kind of stuff."

A weary smile broke her lips.

"Are you actually talking about ghosts with me and sounding rational?"

"Yeah. Guess it's official." He chuckled. "You've caught me in your vortex of weirdness."

It was nearly eleven, so when her cell phone rang, Sadie frowned and was going to let the call go to voice mail, but Zack picked the phone up from the table and handed it to her.

The call was short but not sweet. She made notes as she talked.

"We've got a job to take on at a convenience store in Chinatown," she said to Zack when she was finished. "A sawed-off-shotgun job. It's bound to be real messy."

He nodded. "I heard about that one." And his mouth quirked at the corners like he was containing laughter.

"What?"

"Nothing. It was sad, really. And brutal." But he kept on smiling. "The owner was chased around his store and finally shot by some crackhead."

"You look like you're all broken up about it," Sadie said dryly.

"Who called it in?" Zack asked, clearing his throat and wiping away his grin.

"The son. It's a family business and they need the place cleaned as soon as possible. The store's their only income. We'll need to get in there tomorrow and see if we can finish up in a day."

"That's quick." He quirked an eyebrow. "Are the vultures circling?"

It sure wasn't unusual for family members to be more concerned about what the deceased left behind than about the person who had passed. That was an even uglier side to her business than the gore they cleaned.

"Mom-and-pop business, and it just sounds like they're hard up for the cash the store brings in. They've already called the claim in to their insurance company, and the son is going to fax the paperwork over tonight."

"Mighty efficient of him." Zack finished off the rest of his beer. "I haven't worked a store location with you before. Should be interesting."

"Watch, they'll want us to try and salvage all the shelved goods."

"That'll be fun."

Sadie noticed the smirk playing on his lips again.

"There's something you're not telling me."

"Oh, you'll find out soon enough." Zack got to his feet, yawned, and stretched. "Fetch me a blanket and a pillow. I'm crashing on your couch tonight."

When she frowned, he pointed a finger in the direction of the busted door frame.

"Someone shot up your house today in broad daylight. Do you really want to be home alone tonight with only your rabbit for protection?"

When Sadie woke up to the smell of freshly brewed coffee, she briefly thought that it would be nice to have a man around again, or a roommate. It was amazing how easily she could be lulled into a false sense of comfort just by the promise of instant caffeine.

"We need to get moving," Zack barked at her when she walked into the kitchen. All her romantic notions were pretty much washed away immediately.

"It's just after seven." Sadie yawned as she poured coffee into her *I ♥ Seattle* mug. "We're not meeting Bart Woo until nine. Why the rush?"

"Just don't want to waste the entire day, that's all," he grumbled into his mug.

She silently made two pieces of toast, put them on a plate, and slid it in front of him. Maybe he was grouchy because he needed food. It couldn't be a hangover—they'd stopped at two beers. Sadie grabbed her coffee, sat down at the table, and watched as Zack rubbed the back of his neck.

"Now I get it." She cringed. "Guess I should've warned you that my sofa is a real bitch to sleep on."

"It feels like I slept with a noose around my neck," he snarled.

"It's not easy being a macho he-man protecting the women of the world, huh?"

"If we do this again, I'm sharing your bed."

She glanced up and saw the look on his face that he wasn't kidding. She reddened and busied herself with fetching him two aspirin before heading for the shower. After she dressed, she grabbed another cup of coffee and they loaded the van with supplies and hit the road.

When she stopped the company truck in front of their destination, she looked over at Zack.

"Oh God," she said, then turned and raised her eyebrows at him. "You could've warned me."

"What, and miss the look on your face when we got here? Not a chance."

Zack smiled, and Sadie only closed her eyes and shook her head as they climbed out of the vehicle and walked toward the store. The neon bright red awning overhead read HOT TAMALES EROTICA.

"The family lives in an apartment above the store," Sadie said. "We'll get the key from them and I'll get the contract signed before we go inside."

They took a few steps and were immediately greeted by a young Chinese man, who rushed over. He was frantically waving his arms, making shooing gestures, and shouting, "No, you can't park there! You must move your vehicle to the back. Park in the alley, not in front of the store!"

"Mr. Woo?" Sadie asked.

"Yes. Yes," he confirmed. "Move your truck and I meet you at the back entrance before you scare away all our customers!"

Sadie eyed the four-foot inflated pink dildo in the display window and mumbled to Zack, "I don't think there's a whole lot that would scare off his clientele."

She maneuvered the van slowly down the narrow lane, which was riddled with potholes. In order to allow other vehicles access down the lane, she had to park extremely close to a Dumpster. It was so tight that she couldn't open the driver's door, so she exited via the passenger side.

Bart Woo looked a lot more relaxed, even a little too relaxed. He waved them inside with a huge smile that certainly didn't scream grieving son.

"You'll get the place done today, right?" he asked. "So we can reopen tomorrow?"

"I can't make any guarantees, Mr. Woo. We haven't even seen the place yet."

She handed him her contract to look over, and he signed it after giving it only a passing glance.

"You realize that if something is uncleanable, whether it's real or personal property, we have to toss it. I'll provide the insurance company with an itemized list, so you should be reimbursed, but much of your product may need to be destroyed."

"Yes, I understand," he said hurriedly. "But you'll try and keep what you can clean, yes?"

"Yes."

"Fine. Start now, okay? The sooner you start, the sooner you finish and I reopen my store and restock my shelves with stuff from the storeroom."

Bart Woo handed Sadie a key to the premises, then scooted back upstairs to his apartment. Zack was almost finished suiting up.

"This is a shotgun job," she reminded him. "It'll be slow going because there'll be lots of debris. Remember to watch for sharps."

Bone fragments could be razor sharp and would easily slice through their gloves if they weren't careful. The cut itself was the least of their worries. It was all the potential diseases swimming in the blood that upped the level of risk.

Once they were fully suited, they stepped out of the stockroom and into the outer store. It wasn't the destruction that caused Sadie to stop short and had her eyes bulging.

There was something about standing in a store with floor-to-ceiling sex aids that made her feel distinctly uncomfortable.

Hot Tamales Erotica looked like a war zone—a combat area littered with packaging shrapnel and coated with slimy joy gel that was mixed with blood spatter.

14

Bone fragments were embedded in walls, shelves, and product. Bart Woo was either paranoid that they would steal from him or terrified that they were being overly slow in their cleaning efforts, because he repeatedly popped in unannounced.

"I'm sorry, sir, but I don't know how you put up with him," Sadie grumbled to Mr. Woo Sr., who walked up and down the aisles in dazed confusion. The entire right side of the man's rib cage was blown away.

It didn't matter that the older Mr. Woo probably couldn't hear her from behind her disposable respirator. He also didn't appear to speak English.

"No spatter here, but the packaging has been destroyed," Zack called out. "Should I toss it?"

Sadie glanced over her shoulder in his direction.

"Yeah, toss it," she replied, clearing her throat uncomfortably.

"You sure?"

Zack closed the gap between them, took the object in question, and nudged Sadie under the chin with it.

"A woman living alone could find something like this useful."

Sadie looked down at the huge black dildo and blushed bloodred.

"Get lost," she muttered with a nervous giggle and turned away.

"Of course, if that's not your thing, there's always these."

She turned again and he snapped a pair of fur-lined pink handcuffs onto her gloved hand.

"Zack, stop it!"

He tugged her close.

"If Bart Woo would leave us alone in here for a while, I could probably help get rid of that stressed look on your face."

Her eyes were huge and she swallowed thickly.

"We should probably just get back to work."

He released her and they busied themselves at opposite ends of the store. By three o'clock, they'd been hard at it for nearly six hours straight. They were both low on energy and decided that they were long overdue for lunch and an infusion of caffeine.

Bart met them in the storage room while they were doffing their Tyvek suits and stuffing them into the bins.

"Where are you going?" he asked. "You're not even done. You still have work to do!"

"Mr. Woo, we've worked for hours without stopping. We're just taking a break. We'll have lunch and come right back."

"You have lunch here. I'll order you a nice stir-fry from next store. You'll love it."

Sadie planted her hands on her hips and just barely managed to keep her anger in check.

"We're on target to get the cleaning done today, Mr. Woo, even if we take a one-hour break. Still, there are portions of the drywall that had to be removed. All that will have to be replaced, and I still need to contact the restoration companies."

"I'll hang posters over the holes in the wall for now," he said with a shrug. "I just need to be able to sell my products and make money."

Zack stepped up to stand shoulder to shoulder with Sadie.

"I'm sure your father wouldn't mind if you took a

day or two off to mourn his passing and deal with your grief," he drawled evenly.

"My father worked his fingers to the bone selling cheap imported paper fans at this location for over twenty years," Bart Woo snapped. "I took over the store last year when he was about to lose everything to the bank. Of course, being old-fashioned, he didn't like the changes I made or the products we'd be selling," he admitted. "However, when he saw that we made more money in a single year than he'd made in the last ten, he didn't mind." Bart Woo smiled. "As a matter of fact, he took great pride in learning about our products so he could make knowledgeable recommendations to our customers. My father never missed a day of work his entire life. He would want me to keep that tradition going."

"Point taken." Sadie nodded. "But we're still going out for lunch. See you in an hour."

They stepped outside into a light drizzle that misted over them as they strolled down the lane and entered South King Street across from Hing Hay Park. Looking left and right at the multitude of choices, Sadie debated her options.

"How about dim sum? There's a place up the block—"

"I know a great deli around the corner," Zack said. He stepped up onto the curb to his right and began to walk.

"We're in Chinatown," Sadie reminded him, quickening her pace to keep up. "I figured while in Rome . . ."

"Even the Romans would've gone for a sub from this place."

Sadie found it hard to argue with that kind of logic. As it turned out, Zack was right. Although the Formica-table decor of the tiny diner left something to be desired, there was no refuting the fact that the thick sandwiches looked mouthwatering.

With most of her sandwich still left, Sadie pushed her plate away, dug out her phone, and dialed Detective Petrovich to ask about Sylvia Toth. He told her he'd heard that the woman was recovering well from her surgery but was still heavily sedated.

"She's out of surgery," Sadie told Zack after she hung up. "I'd like to go visit her."

"Not a good idea." He pointed to the remaining piece of Sadie's sandwich, and she nodded her okay for him to eat it.

"Why not? I'll bring flowers and stop by for a second to see how she is."

"You already know how she is. Petrovich just told you. Don't visit. Get a florist to deliver the flowers instead."

Sadie rested her head in her hands.

"I feel so guilty."

"Why? You didn't shoot her."

Sadie started to pursue her point but then realized that there would be no reasoning with a man who had a blob of mustard in the corner of his mouth and a cop demeanor.

"My first patrol was in this neighborhood," Zack said in an unusual show of nostalgia for his ex-life, or else an attempt to change the subject. "Man, did we have trouble with the Asian gangs. Biggest problem was that much of the older Chinese community is so tight-lipped they never wanted to press charges."

Sadie was barely listening. Instead, she scrolled through the listings on her cell phone and punched SEND.

"Who are you calling now?" Zack asked.

"Kent Lasko."

Zack opened his mouth to speak, but disbelief apparently had fused his voice box, because no sound came out. He snapped his jaw shut and quietly dabbed at the mustard on his mouth. His eyebrows drew together as he shot daggers at her.

"He's not home," Sadie replied. Not to be deterred, she dialed the real estate office next. She was told the same thing as before, that Mr. Lasko was out of town but another agent would be pleased to help her with her real estate needs. Nobody at the office seemed to know when he was expected to return and no one had another number to reach him.

With a sour look on her face, she stuffed the phone back into her purse.

"Didn't Petrovich tell you he's got a rock-solid Tahoe alibi?"

"Not for when that diamond brooch showed up in my pocket," Sadie snapped. "And we both know he didn't need to be here to have someone take a shot at my house."

"Let the cops handle things," Zack said, downing the rest of his Coke. "Focus on something else." He leaned in and whispered, "How about you think about that raspberry gel that grows hot when you breathe on it?"

"Be serious."

"I'm dead serious," Zack replied. "Fine. If you won't do that, you could call restoration companies to find out who might be willing to put off a job in progress for the chance to work on renovating a sex shop."

Sadie grinned. "You've got something there. That kind of spin might actually get someone on the job quicker."

She called the regular companies they used, but unfortunately, not as many restoration professionals were voyeurs as one might first expect. One company offered to fit Hot Tamales in next week, but nobody was willing to drop a current job just for an opportunity to work around dildos and furry pink handcuffs.

"Bart is going to be pissed," Sadie remarked.

"Yeah, but he looks like the kind of man who was born angry."

As if to prove Zack right, when they returned to

the sex shop Bart was glaring down at them from the
window of the upper suite, which looked out on the
alley. When they went inside to work, Mr. Woo Sr.
was walking the aisles, mumbling to himself in Chinese. Sadie wished she had her iPod so that she could
drown out his voice.

They'd removed most of the visible blood and tissue, as well as all products and hardware that were
beyond cleaning. Now they painstakingly worked to
find and eliminate all the bone fragments. The shrapnel caused by the shotgun blast covered a shockingly
wide area, and some bits were embedded so far into
the drywall that the wall itself had to be cut away. A
shame, since the paint used in the shop was a high-
gloss type, which would usually tolerate a disinfectant
spray and a scrub clean for blood quite well.

Mr. Woo must've been standing behind a large glass
display case when he was shot, because it had been
decimated during the incident. The spray of glass
mixed with blood and tissue was bad, but equally dis-
turbing was coming upon the odd fluorescent rubber-
ized material. Apparently, vibrators didn't tolerate
gunfire much better than humans did.

They filled close to a dozen large rubber bins with
destroyed product and shelving. Zack's eyes were
laughing behind his face mask whenever he noticed
Sadie collecting a few more vibrators in animal shapes
to clean or remove. He was enjoying this a little too
much.

It was a relief to enter the second stage of cleaning
once the blood, tissue, and sharps were removed. Now
they could simply wear gloves to protect their hands
from the cleaning products and not worry about cuts
and diseases.

True to their word, they managed to finish the job
at Hot Tamales Erotica that night, even though it was
the middle of the night.

"I've got one more thing I have to do," Sadie remarked as she yawned and stretched in the storage room. "You wouldn't happen to have your handheld tape recorder on you?"

"I think it's in the truck. You want to borrow it?" Zack asked.

"Just for a minute."

She put the recorder in her purse and walked across the street to a twenty-four-hour food mart. A bored-looking Chinese teenager slouched behind the counter, flipping through a porn magazine.

Sadie purchased a couple chocolate bars and went to the counter to pay for them.

"You wouldn't happen to speak Mandarin, would you?" she asked the clerk.

"Me and most of the neighborhood."

"Would you mind doing me a favor?" She dug a pen and paper from her purse and wrote out a couple lines, then took out the handheld tape recorder. "I'm taking a course at the university, and I need to be able to say this paragraph in Mandarin. Could you translate it into my tape recorder for me?"

He read the piece of paper, then looked up at her like she was insane.

"I'm not going to say that."

She pulled a five dollar bill from her wallet and slid it across the counter.

"For ten I'll teach you the top Mandarin curse words."

"What I wrote down on that paper will be fine."

A minute later she walked back across the street. She let herself into the storage area, tossed Zack a Hershey bar, and told him she'd be right back.

Inside the store she walked up to Mr. Woo Sr. and motioned for him to stop pacing the aisles. Once he realized she could see him, he approached her, frantically speaking Chinese.

Sadie rewound the tape recorder, turned up the volume, and pressed PLAY. The clerk's voice sounded, reading the Mandarin version of the lecture Sadie usually gave to the spirits to help them realize that they were dead and they no longer held claim to this life.

Sadie watched as the old man began to nod. With a saddened expression he put his hands together prayerfully and offered her a bow before his essence slowly shimmered and faded away.

"Everything okay?" Zack asked Sadie as she stepped back into the storage room.

"Great," she replied, a big smile on her face. Her head buzzed with the charge of energy she got after helping a spirit. "Let's go tell our client the job's done."

"It's two o'clock in the morning. We could just leave him a note."

"Nah, I want to deliver the good news in person."

Zack smiled. Sadie wasn't the only one who enjoyed banging on Bart Woo's door and waking him to give him the news.

"Even though the cleaning part is done, nobody is available to do the drywall repairs and painting for a week," Sadie said.

"No matter. When a man comes in looking for a blow-up girlfriend he doesn't notice if there are a few holes in the walls," he replied sleepily.

"Riiiight," Sadie said.

She whistled happily as they finished loading up the van. Zack offered to drive, and she tossed him the keys, then surprised herself by dozing off for a few minutes. When she awoke, she thought they were at her house, but instead they were pulling into Kent Lasko's driveway and Zack had turned the truck's lights off.

"What are you doing?" she asked, bolting upright.

"Thought we'd pay Kent's brother a little visit and find out what he knows."

"Christian works nights as a janitor," she said. "He won't be home."

The words were hardly out of her mouth when she noticed the flicker of the television behind the drapes covering the picture window.

"Good news," Zack replied. "He's off tonight." He opened his door, then focused a serious gaze on Sadie. "Don't suppose I could convince you to wait here."

"Fat chance," she replied and was out of the vehicle and bounding up the sidewalk ahead of him.

He caught up and grabbed her arm.

"Let me do the talking," he said in a whisper as they reached the front door.

Sadie nodded her agreement. She realized Zack was the only one present with previous experience in interrogation techniques.

Sadie rang the bell, and immediately the sounds from the television were silenced.

When the curtains parted slightly, Sadie knew they were out of luck.

"He knows who it is," she said. "He's not going to answer the door."

Zack listened with his ear pressed to the door.

"C'mon," he said.

He yanked her by the hand and they quick-stepped around to the back of the house. He stopped behind the back deck, where they were partially hidden from view by a tall cedar. He pressed his finger to Sadie's lips in a shushing motion.

"Stay hidden," he whispered harshly in her ear. "Promise me."

Before Sadie could say anything, Christian Lasko appeared, slipping out of his back kitchen door and quietly locking up. He turned and tiptoed down the back porch.

"Going somewhere?" Zack asked, stepping out from the shadows.

Christian jumped.

"Who are you? Get—get out of my backyard before I call the cops," he stammered.

"I *am* the cops," Zack said evenly, and everything in his posture and tone acknowledged it as fact. "Where are you sneaking off to, Christian?"

The young man straightened his spine defensively. "I was just putting out the trash."

"Except you forgot to bring it out."

"Okay." He threw up his hands. "You caught me. I'm going for a run first and then put out the trash. Big deal."

"It's only a big deal if you're a liar."

"Look, I've already told the other cops everything and there's nothing else to tell. My brother's skiing in Tahoe, so he couldn't've tried to kill that old lady."

"What about Trudy and Grant?"

"What about them? Grant and Kent go way back. They were pals. Grant would never do anything to hurt him or Trudy." He shook his head. "It's too bad Grant went all nutso, but it has nothing to do with us. This is harassment. You guys need to leave us alone."

"If your brother wouldn't do anything to hurt them, why did he steal a diamond brooch from their house and plant it on the cleanup girl?"

"Is that what she said? My brother would never steal a thing. He's Mr. Clean," Christian scoffed. "You've got the wrong guy. You should be looking at that crazy broad who did the cleaning, not at Kent."

"Watch who you're calling a crazy broad!" Sadie spat, stepping out from behind the tree.

"I'm so done with this, man," Christian said, balling his hands into fists and taking off as fast as his expensive Nikes would carry him.

Zack glared at Sadie and tossed her the keys to the company truck, then angrily stalked back to the front drive, where he climbed into the passenger side.

"I guess you're ticked that I didn't keep quiet," Sadie said after a few silent minutes of driving.

"You guess right."

"I'm sorry. I should've let you handle it."

"You promised."

"Well, technically I didn't promise. I didn't get a chance to promise."

He looked at her with an icy scowl.

"But it was like a promise," Sadie added quickly.

They drove on in silence. Before long they pulled up to her drive and she parked the van in the garage. Before she could close the garage door, Zack was headed for his car, parked on the street where he'd left it the night before. Obviously he wasn't interested in spending another night on her killer couch.

Sadie followed him to explain.

"Sorry, but I just don't like being called a broad or crazy," she called to his back.

He turned and planted his hands on his hips.

"Is it better to be called a thief?" he demanded. "Because you and I both know your reputation and your referrals from detectives and the ME's office are going down the toilet unless you can clean this up."

She jammed her hands into her pockets and nodded. "You're right, but what can I do?"

He blew out a long breath and shook his head slowly.

"I haven't a clue."

Sadie slept restlessly that night. Even after she'd checked and double-checked her doors and windows, she just didn't feel safe. She felt like she had two choices—an alarm system or an attack dog. Since there was little likelihood that Hairy and a dog would get along, she thumbed through the Yellow Pages first thing in the morning.

Pam showed up early, wanting to assist Sadie in her search for an alarm company.

"Don't use the one with the biggest ad and don't use the one with the smallest," Pam advised as Sadie scanned the advertisements.

"And make sure that you get one that does monitoring and not just one that has a loud, annoying siren," she added seriously.

"For a woman who's never had an alarm system, you sure have a lot of opinions on the matter," Sadie commented dryly.

"You sure are cranky."

"I'm not cranky. I'm just tired."

"And sex-deprived."

Sadie glowered at her friend while she gulped her third mug of coffee.

"Don't get your back up, I'm only pointing out the obvious," Pam said. "And I've been thinking that you should consider sleeping with Zack."

Sadie put her mug down.

"I thought we agreed that would be the worst possible thing I could do and that getting involved with him would lead to certain disaster for me and my company."

"Yes, but now it doesn't matter because you've got multiple disasters happening all around you. Besides, if he quit you have another employee starting in a few days."

"You think I should have sex with my employee only because I've got another employee all lined up?"

"And also because he's got one helluva ass."

Any other day, Sadie would've laughed, but she was quickly losing her sense of humor. She ignored Pam and dialed the third alarm company advertised on the page. She asked questions and took notes about prices and services, and then she called two more. She found one that was recommended by the Better Business Bureau and could even send a techie over that very day for the installation.

"He'll be here in a couple hours," Sadie told Pam. "You're welcome to stay and see if he also has a great ass."

"No thanks," Pam said. "I think I'll go by Logan's office and check to see what he's up to."

"You should stay away from Logan. Let him move on."

"Move on? Why the hell should I let him move on?" Pam bit back.

"You guys haven't been dating for a long time. Give it up," Sadie grumbled.

It was just as well that Pam didn't stick around to admire the technician's ass, since it turned out he was a she. Within an hour every window and door in Sadie's home was fitted with little sensors that would announce a break-in. She was shown how to program in her own code, and then the service woman handed her a thick manual to study at her leisure.

Regardless of the fact that it cost more than she expected, Sadie felt a whole lot better just having the system in place.

She needed to send invoices to three insurance companies and to pay her medical waste bill. She also needed to put lime on the moss patches on her lawn and do some laundry. Instead of doing any of these tasks, she drove into a Seattle area with numerous hospitals, known as Pill Hill, and rode a hospital elevator to the third floor of one of them.

As she walked down the hall, an old man passed her, wearing a hospital gown that was open in the back, exposing his wrinkled butt to the world. Unfortunately, since the man was obviously deceased, she was the only person who got to cringe at the sight.

She dodged the spirit and walked into Sylvia Toth's room, where she found the woman sitting up and playing cards with another lady. The woman had bottle-blond hair with a couple inches of pure white at the roots and was at least ten years older than Sylvia. Both women looked up at Sadie with surprise when she walked through the door.

"I wanted to see how you're doing," Sadie said, "but you've got company, so I'll just go."

Mrs. Toth blinked at Sadie, but she didn't seem to

know what to say. Finally proper upbringing won out, and she was forced to make an introduction.

"This is my sister, Janet," Sylvia explained. "She's from Portland and will stay with me until I've recovered."

"Hello, I'm Sadie."

"Nice to meet you," Janet said, breaking into the hacking cough of a longtime smoker. She got to her feet and they shook hands. Then she took the flowers from Sadie's arms. "Aren't these lovely."

"How are you feeling?" Sadie asked, tentatively approaching the bedside.

"Kind of tired, actually," Sylvia answered, turning her head away.

"I've probably been keeping you awake by beating your ass at hearts. Why don't you rest and I'll swing by and check on you later," Janet said. She gave Sylvia a peck on the cheek, then nodded for Sadie to follow her.

"I'm glad your prognosis is good, Mrs. Toth," Sadie said. "And, well, I'm sorry . . . for everything."

Outside the room Janet said, "Can I buy you a cup of coffee?"

"That would be nice," Sadie said, not knowing if it really would be nice or if she was agreeing to a caffeinated verbal abuse session.

They grabbed bad coffee from a vending machine and took it to the end of the hall and out to a terrace where other smokers were huddled against the cold, puffing away.

"I'm sorry to interrupt your visit with your sister. I guess I shouldn't have come," Sadie said, standing to the side a little as the wind whipped across the patio.

Janet lit up and her smoke plumed in Sadie's face.

"Sylvia wasn't exactly thrilled to see me," Sadie went on.

"She's had a lot to handle," Janet said. "She just

buried her son and daughter-in-law, and now she's been shot."

Sadie nodded. "I feel awful."

"You didn't shoot her."

"Yes, but it happened at *my* house."

"Life's too short to blame yourself for things you can't control," Janet said. She sipped her coffee, then took another drag from her smoke and added thoughtfully, "Sylvia told me that you don't believe that Grant killed Trudy." Her gray eyes were unwavering steel as her gaze met Sadie's. "I'd like to know if that comes from evidence or if you're just playing with my sister's emotions."

Sadie had no idea if Sylvia would've told her sister about the ghost thing or not, so she felt her way carefully.

"I thought I owed it to her to explain how I feel and—"

"I worked as a nurse for three decades. I can't tell you the number of times I've seen well-meaning people tell folks on their deathbed that they look great and that everything is going to be hunky-dory. Optimism has its time and place, I guess, but Sylvia doesn't need to get her hopes up."

"I understand your concern, but Sylvia knows I was just expressing my opinion about—"

"She also doesn't need to take up a cause that doesn't exist."

"Yes." Sadie figured if she wanted to complete a sentence around Janet, she'd better make it short.

"Sylvia told me that you don't believe that it was a murder-suicide. That means that either you have proof that you're not sharing with the Seattle police or you're just playing into Sylvia's delusions that Grant was perfect and could do no wrong."

"I've heard nothing but good about Grant. *Could* he do wrong?" Sadie asked.

"Grant and Trudy lived with me during the months they were in Portland." Janet drew in another drag of smoke. "My husband and I are retired, and the house is really too big for just the two of us, so it wasn't inconvenient. Mostly Trudy and Grant did their own thing, of course, but you get to know people when they're living under your roof. During that time I never once saw Grant treat Trudy with anything but love and respect. He worshiped that girl. Plain and simple. It was very hard on him to transplant her to Portland, even though it was only temporary. He knew she wasn't happy there."

"Sounds like he loved her very much."

"He sure did. Maybe too much."

A gust of wind howled across the patio, and they moved into a corner for the protection offered by a jutting of the brick building.

"Is it really possible to love someone too much?" Sadie asked.

Janet appeared to debate her answer before replying.

"Don't get me wrong—Trudy wasn't a bad person, but she was unhappy. She was restless in Portland and hated taking a leave of absence from her job at the school for the deaf. She was able to tutor some deaf children in Portland a couple days a week, but it wasn't enough. You know what they say about idle hands. . . ."

Sadie winced at the foul-tasting coffee and dumped her cup into a nearby trash bin. Janet followed her lead and tossed hers as well.

"So if Grant was at the new store all day, Trudy must've been bored. Plus, she probably missed all her friends in Seattle."

"Hmmph." Janet grunted and flicked the ash off her cigarette. It blew around her feet. "They had their own phone line installed in our house. Trudy had a phone she typed into and would get on it practically the second Grant would leave for the day. In this day and age of computers and gadgets I think it's pretty damn hard to really miss anyone. When she wasn't on that phone, she was on the computer chatting online. One day she left herself logged in on the computer while she went to run some errands. I went into their room just to dust. I wasn't snooping, you understand."

"Of course," Sadie said, but she got the feeling that was *exactly* what Janet had been doing. "Go on."

"Anyway, messages kept popping up on the screen and I couldn't help but read them. They were from an anonymous person but the messages were private. Very private."

"From a lover." Sadie stated it as a fact, not a question.

Janet nodded.

"I confronted her when she got home. She denied it at first, but I didn't let her off the hook. This was my nephew's wife we're talking about. Every time she'd walk away, I was in her face." She shook her head slowly. "It's not easy arguing with a deaf person. She could lip-read fairly well, but when I said stuff she didn't want to hear, she would just turn away or close her eyes." Janet laughed then, a chuckle that turned into a hacking cough. Once she'd recovered, she continued, "Finally, she admitted that she'd been sleeping with someone else when they lived in Seattle. She even confessed that some of her all-day tutoring sessions were actually day trips to Seattle to visit him."

"You must've been angry."

"Furious. I wanted to tell Grant about it, but I knew it would kill him." She smiled sadly at the irony of that. "Trudy begged me not to say anything. At first I said there was no way I'd lie to my own nephew, but then I agreed to keep it quiet as long as she promised to end the affair immediately. She said she would."

She took a last drag on her smoke, then walked over to grind it into a nearby pillar ashtray.

"So she broke it off?" Sadie shouted over another gust of wind that blew forcefully across the terrace.

"She promised that it was over. I have to admit that I didn't believe her right away, but then a small package was couriered to the house. I signed for it, since she was out. When I saw it had a Seattle return address, I was curious, so I opened it and peeked inside. It was a beautiful emerald pendant. There was no note. She never knew I opened it, but when I asked about the package, Trudy said it was a good-bye gift."

"Don't you think that's kind of a strange gift to give to a married woman, since she would have trouble explaining it?" Sadie commented.

"Yes, I sure did, but Trudy was adamant that she'd ended the affair. I assumed that she either returned the necklace or sold it, because I never saw it after that." Janet stuffed her hands into the pockets of her coat. "I thought that was the end of it."

"But it wasn't?"

"Yes and no. A few weeks later she came to me extremely upset. She was pregnant and she didn't think the baby was Grant's."

"Wow!" Sadie blinked in surprise. "That must've been hard."

"Yes. I tried to convince her to have the baby. I knew Grant loved kids and always wanted a houseful. He would've been thrilled and Sylvia would've been over the moon. Although I'm not a fanatic, I'm not pro-choice either. Abortion just seemed wrong."

"And Trudy wanted to end the pregnancy?"

"Yes. She didn't think there was any other way. She had the procedure done and Grant never knew."

"All this time, do you think Grant ever suspected Trudy was having an affair?"

"No." She shook her head. "At least not while they lived in my house. Grant was working his ass off to get that new store up and running and self-sufficient so they could return to Seattle and buy the house she wanted. He was constantly reassuring her that it wouldn't be too much longer." Janet shook her head. "Maybe if it *had* taken longer, things would've been better. I think when they moved back to Seattle, Trudy hooked up with that guy again and this time Grant found out. I'm sure it drove him to do what he did."

"You seem pretty sure he killed Trudy and himself."

"You'd never get Sylvia to admit Grant was capable of such a thing. That's why I don't want you messing with her head." She looked pointedly at Sadie. "But when a man loves a woman as much as Grant loved Trudy, I don't think he can imagine living without her. He was obsessed. It would've killed him to think she'd leave him for someone else."

"A man with nothing left to lose is a man capable of anything," Sadie remarked sadly.

Janet only nodded.

"Sylvia doesn't need the heartache you're offering her," she said. "She doesn't need to fill her head with your pie-in-the-sky hope that things happened differently."

"But if things *did* happen differently, wouldn't it give her comfort?"

"A mother just buried her son, her daughter-in-law, and all of her hopes and dreams. I'm the only family she has left in this world. Nothing you uncover will ever change that, will it?"

"No, but—"

She held up a hand to stop further discussion.

"I've said my piece. I ask that you keep our conversation in confidence and stay away from my sister and let her grieve."

Sadie sat in the hospital parking lot, her head resting on the steering wheel of her car.

"Let it go. Let it go," she mumbled to herself like

a mantra. "You clean up after the dead. No more. No less. You have no business playing detective."

Maybe it was time to take a couple of days off. Even just an afternoon would be great. She still had that gift certificate for a full-body massage that her mother had given her for her birthday. As she turned left on Madison, she realized she could be at the day spa in five minutes.

Buoyed by the idea of spending a couple of hours in a state of self-indulgent bliss, Sadie could feel her body begin to unwind. Even the jerk hugging her bumper couldn't get her riled.

She glared in her rearview mirror and punched the accelerator as she turned onto First Avenue. She was relieved to see the small green car get left behind a slow-moving dump truck. Her grip tightened on the wheel when she thought of the green Toyota whose driver had sprayed her house with bullets.

"There are a thousand green Toyotas in Seattle," she reminded herself. "You can't freak out every time you see a small green car." But her grip didn't relax until she pulled into the spa's lot and made sure that a green car wasn't anywhere nearby.

Stepping through the doors of the spa was like walking into a blissful sanctuary of soothing music, waterfalls, and aromatherapy candles.

Sadie took a deep, cleansing breath and exhaled it slowly as she floated up to the reception desk. She was greeted warmly by an angelic figure in white.

"Welcome. What service do you have an appointment for today?" she asked, her voice as calm and soothing as the surroundings.

"No appointment, but I was hoping for a full-body massage."

"Of course." The young woman tapped her keyboard, glanced at the screen, then looked back up at Sadie. "We've had a cancellation, and I can fit you in a week from tomorrow at eight in the morning."

"A week?" Sadie struggled to keep the whine from her voice. "Nothing today?"

"No and a week from now is good. Often our massage packages are booked a month in advance."

With an exhale of frustration, Sadie halfheartedly agreed to the appointment, then shuffled back to the parking lot. She was a foot from her car when a sharp retort sounded and a spray of pavement dusted her shoes. She looked down in surprise for a split second before she realized she'd narrowly missed being shot.

Bolting to her vehicle, she tore open the door and huddled low on her seat, fumbling to get her keys. A shadow fell across her car and she was sure it was the shooter, who would blow her head off at close range. However, the sound of a motor caused her to glance up. A large linen supply truck had pulled up right next to her car. The driver hopped out his door, rolled up the back of the truck, unloaded supplies onto a dolly, and headed for the spa.

Without thinking, Sadie slowly opened her door and, staying low, opened the passenger door of the truck, climbed inside, and gently closed the door behind her. Crawling on her knees, she made her way to the back and hunkered down between bins of dirty laundry. The driver was back in seconds. He slammed down the rolling back door and climbed behind the wheel. Sadie didn't let him know she was there for fear he'd run the truck up a pole. When he made his next stop, at a medical clinic two miles away, Sadie casually hopped out of the truck after looking in all possible directions for gun-wielding assassins.

Fumbling with her cell phone, she dialed Zack.

"I need you to come get me," she said. "And, if you don't mind, bring your gun."

Only a few minutes passed before Zack showed up. He found her sitting with her back against the wall and watching the door in a far corner of a Subway sandwich shop.

"Spill it," he ordered, grabbing her by the elbow and walking her to his car

She told him everything and swiped tears from her eyes.

"Don't suppose you got the plate number for this green car?"

"No," she admitted, feeling foolish. She sipped some soda and blinked back fresh tears.

They went back to the spa, and Zack circled the lot more than once before pulling up alongside her vehicle.

"Stay," he ordered, flinging open his door and walking around her car. He peered inside and under and finally announced it looked sound.

"Are you okay to drive?"

She nodded, not knowing if she'd ever truly feel okay again.

"I'll follow you."

The excitement wasn't over yet. As soon as she pulled onto her street she could hear the noise of her house alarm, screeching wildly. An SPD car was just pulling up to her driveway. Sadie was certain that pretty soon the neighbors would take up a petition to put her on a dinghy and float her out to sea.

The officers had obviously heard of the drive-by shooting at her house, because they weren't treating this like a routine alarm call. Their weapons were drawn and they were quickly circling the residence.

Once the perimeter was checked, Sadie handed over her keys. While her heart thumped like a hammer in her chest, the cops, joined by Zack, searched the inside of her house. They determined that there was no sign of forced entry and no bogeymen were hiding in closets or under beds.

Sadie punched in the code to stop the shriek of the alarm.

"Your system has a sensitive motion detector. If you set it to indicate you're going out, it'll go off if someone's moving around inside," an officer explained.

"Someone broke in?" Zack asked.

"We think it was most likely your little fuzzy friend." He nodded and Sadie followed his gaze to see Hairy hop by.

"Oh my God, my rabbit set off my alarm?" She laughed in relief.

"It happens all the time," the officer admitted. "Well, it's usually cats or dogs, not bunnies, but the end result is the same. There's a way to set your alarm to ignore smaller movements. You need to check your manual or call your alarm company."

"I will."

Zack walked the officers outside, and no doubt filled them in on what had happened at the spa. Sadie's ears were still ringing from the raucous sound of her alarm.

When Zack returned, he said, "Petrovich will be by in a few minutes. I'll stay until he gets here."

She shook her head. "You don't need to stay."

"I should," he insisted. "Jackie can wait."

"You set up a time to meet with her?"

"Yeah, but we can postpone. It's no big deal."

"You should go. I'll be fine. Like you said, Petrovich will be here in a few minutes. Don't forget, I've got my alarm system and my attack bunny to keep me safe."

He hesitated, but at her insistence he finally left. Sadie walked down the hall to her office. There was one phone message on her machine and she hit PLAY.

"Sadie, it's Egan. Call me."

David Egan owned and operated Scour Power, another Seattle niche cleaning company. They didn't compete for business, but instead shared Seattle's misfortune. Sadie chose to handle the clean of death while Egan's business took care of methamphetamine lab cleanup, marijuana grow-ops, and tidying up non-crime-related squalor.

Egan must've recognized Sadie's number on his phone's incoming display, because he answered instantly.

"Hey, Twisted Sister. Long time no chat."

"How's biz?" Sadie asked.

"Well, you know, the world's a dump. I'm handling a tunnel house right now and there are rats the size of my dog helping me out."

Sadie shuddered. Tunnel houses were what they called the type of human squalor where the person lived in a home shoulder high in clutter and trash that had pathways or tunnels leading from room to room. It still shocked Sadie to realize people actually lived that way.

"You can keep your tunnels," Sadie said with a chuckle.

"And you can keep your brain spatter," he countered. "Which is why I'm calling. I got a call a couple hours ago from some lady needing a suicide clean."

It happened occasionally that someone would look through the Yellow Pages and call Scour Power instead of Scene-2-Clean if they didn't read the fine print of what the company handled. When that happened, usually David and Sadie just redirected the client to the correct company.

"So you told her to call me?" Sadie asked, wondering what was so unusual about this job that required David to call instead of just giving the lady the correct number.

"Actually, I told her I'd call you myself and give you the message."

"Why? Is there something special about this clean?"

"Not really. Her son cut his wrists in the bathtub."

"So why do I have the pleasure of your personal call? This isn't a friend or family, is it?"

"No, nothing like that." He paused. "You know I don't wanna be cleaning your bloody jobs, Sadie."

"And I'm fine letting you handle your disasters." She could feel the big *but* coming.

"But here's the thing—" He sucked in a breath, then let it out. "The woman said she was referred to me by SPD."

"The cops told her to call *you* instead of *me*? Huh. Guess they made a mistake." Sadie tightened her grip on the phone.

"Yeah. Sure."

After a moment to collect her thoughts, Sadie confronted it head-on.

"Look, the two of us have been cleaning the Emerald City for years now, Egan. Anything you've heard that hints that I'm less than honest is flat-out wrong."

"Yeah, I know that," he said emphatically. "Hell, I'd let you mop up after my own next of kin even if their rotting corpses were covered in diamonds, 'cause I know you'd personally shine each and every rock with care before leaving them for me."

Not exactly a pretty visual, but Sadie appreciated the sentiment behind it.

"Thanks."

"The thing is, man, you've got to somehow convince SPD of that. If they're afraid to send the biz your way, well, what choice will I have but to step up to the plate? Neither of us wants that."

David Egan passed along the name and number of the woman who needed the work.

"Thanks for the heads-up about the SPD," Sadie said sincerely. "I appreciate it."

"Forget appreciation. Just fix it."

"I will," she promised before disconnecting.

Sadie got up from her desk, downed the last drops from her coffee mug, then threw it against the wall with such force that it exploded in a thousand tiny shards.

15

Sadie called Shawna Stuart about the call she'd made to Scour Power.

"Mr. Egan said he'd get you to call me," she said. "He said that you specialize in this . . ." She swallowed. "What we need done. So you do this kind of cleaning regularly?"

"Unfortunately, yes," Sadie said. She knew the woman would find little comfort in hearing that her son's method of ending his life was one of the most common. "I can come over now, if that's convenient," Sadie offered gently.

Shawna gave her the address, and as Sadie prepared to leave, Detective Petrovich banged on her door.

"I'm on my way to a job."

"After you tell me about the sniper taking shots at you," he corrected.

She shrugged. "A small green car was on my bumper shortly after I left Pill Hill this morning and I thought I lost him when I cornered onto First. When I came out of my destination on First, somebody took a shot at me as I walked to my car."

"And you took an unexpected ride in a linen delivery van," he said, a smile coaxing the corners of his mouth. "Smart move."

"Yeah, well, I live to scrub another day," she replied tiredly. "So there you have it. Now you tell me

Kent Lasko is skiing, so I got nobody else to point the finger at, but I'm getting tired of dodging bullets. If this guy was a half-decent shot, Zack would be cleaning up his boss's blood."

"I've got the local boys taking a drive by your place on a regular basis."

"Great. I'll be safe as long as they don't get another call at the same time the shooter happens to be ringing my doorbell."

"It's the best I can do. I told Zack you'd be safer staying with him."

She glared at him. "You had no right."

He shrugged. "Then find someone else whose life you'd risk while bunking with them."

"I've got to go." She brushed him off and was soon parking the company truck at the curb in front of a six-story concrete housing project.

Zack called her just as she was preparing her equipment to take it into the building.

"I just wanted to let you know that the Yenkow place is done. I pulled the ionizer, and the restoration company finished the flooring today," Zack said.

"Thanks for taking care of that," she mumbled, checking for supplies like hazmat gear, cleaners, brushes, and bins.

"You sound like you're in a cave," Zack said. "Or in the back of the van. Are you on a job?"

"Yeah. It's a new call," Sadie said. "A slice and soak. No worries. I can handle it on my own."

"You should be at home. Scratch that. You should be at my place."

"Forget it. I've got work to do."

"Then I'll come and help."

"By the looks of this building I'm guessing no insurance and no money. There's no sense in both of us donating our time."

"So you're just going to eat the loss?"

"Probably." Sadie didn't like to work for free, but

there was no way she would walk away from the job and leave a mom to clean up her own son's blood.

"Give me the address."

Zack showed up in time to get the specially fitted shop vac from the van. Sadie was grateful because she knew it would save her a backache later.

The cramped apartment wasn't going to be an easy job. Not because of the clean itself, but because the mom and sister remained in the apartment while the job was being done. This wasn't unusual, but it made things awkward.

They used the deceased's bedroom as their safe zone for supplies and changing. The bathroom itself was tight quarters, particularly with the two of them working the scene. After about five minutes Sadie found herself wishing Zack had stayed home. He was sullen and moody.

They worked side by side in silence, and after all visual blood was removed and the area sanitized, they removed their hazmat suits in the kid's room.

Once stripped back down to her regular clothes, Sadie stretched her limbs and shook off the tightening in her body that came from working in a claustrophobic bathroom for a couple hours.

"I'm going to take another look to make sure we didn't miss anything," Sadie whispered. When family was at a scene, they always kept their voices low.

"You didn't miss anything. You never do," Zack replied tightly. "But you'll check anyway."

And she did. She'd never yet had a customer come back to say, *Hey, you missed a spot.* The sheer horror of that possibility always forced her to be thorough.

"I'll start taking the gear down," Zack said.

Sadie nodded and went to talk with the family.

"We're all done," she told the mother.

"Thank you so much," Shawna replied. She looked too young to be the mother of a teenager and far too young to be burying one. From the looks of the bags under her eyes, though, tragedy was already aging her.

Shawna had another child, a daughter who looked about eight. The girl just sat on a sagging brown sofa and stared at the television, her face eerily bland. Shock. It probably hadn't even hit her that her brother wouldn't be around to tease her anymore.

"Can I get you some tea?" Shawna asked.

"No, thank you," Sadie replied, following the petite woman into her tiny kitchen.

"How much do I owe you?" she asked, grabbing her checkbook from her purse on the counter.

"As I told you earlier, we usually deal with insurance companies for our services."

"And I already told you that I don't have no insurance, so I'll just write you a check." She smiled and brushed her forehead with the back of her hand. "How much?"

Sadie looked down at the floor, which was clean but yellowed with age. As far as businesswomen went, Sadie knew she failed at the money side of things, especially when she was dealing with people who didn't have any.

She handed the woman the invoice. It was modest. She hadn't included her own wage and only a portion of Zack's, but the cost of dumping the waste alone was always staggering.

Shawna nodded at the amount, and her hands trembled a little when she reached for a pen and began carefully writing the amount on a check.

Sadie spoke quietly.

"You know, sometimes we can work something out with families who don't have insurance. In my line of work it's difficult to advertise. It's not like I can take out an ad in the newspaper. Most people would find that very distasteful." Sadie went on quickly. "So sometimes I agree to do a job for free if a client will agree to be a word-of-mouth advocate for Scene-2-Clean."

"What does that mean?" she asked warily.

"It would mean you'd have to tell your family and friends about our services so that, God forbid, if they ever need us, they know who to call."

The woman's eyes brightened with tears.

"You'd do that? Seriously? I know the funeral costs are going to be a lot and—"

Sadie took the invoice from the woman's hands and neatly tore it in two.

"It's none of my business, but you may want to check into grief counseling for your daughter," Sadie said.

"I'll do that," the woman said.

Sadie offered Shawna a business card for a place that specialized in such counseling and also handed her a small stack of Scene-2-Clean cards for her to distribute among her family and friends. Chances were good that she would toss all the cards in the trash as soon as Sadie left the building. Sadie didn't blame her. Nobody wanted trauma-clean business cards hanging around their home as a printed reminder that their son had slit his wrists.

Sadie carried the last loaded bin down to the van and was surprised to find Zack standing there, waiting for her instead of just taking off. He stood with one lean hip against the van, his face partly hidden in evening shadows.

"You didn't need to wait for me," Sadie remarked.

He opened the back door of the truck and took the bin from her arms.

"Did we get paid?" he asked.

"You worked. You'll get paid."

"That's not what I asked."

"It's my company, Zack," she reminded him. "I'll handle things my way."

She faced him, planting her hands on her hips and

staring him down, challenging him to a fight. At least a good rock 'n' roll argument would suck the fear from her gut for a while. Instead, he broke into laughter.

"C'mon, I'll buy you dinner," he said.

They had to drop off the bins at their storage location and then bring the company van home to her garage first. Zack insisted on another search of her home, inside and out, before she hopped into his Mustang. There was a pub nearby that grilled pretty good burgers, and they found a table near the fire, away from the office group that came for happy hour but forgot to go home.

They placed their order with a harried waitress.

"You were pretty quiet tonight," she said. "When we were working the soak."

"The kids are always the hardest. You were quiet, too. I thought maybe you were doing your best not to talk to the deceased since I was there."

"I never saw him. Suicides don't come to me."

"Right. I forgot. Maybe I've been working with you too long, but that makes a weird kind of sense." He said seriously, "You know, whenever we do a teenage suicide, I just want to grab every teen in the state and march them through the cleanup and have them spend a few minutes looking at the scene."

"And then get them to spend an hour looking into the eyes of those left behind."

"Guess the only way to get through these jobs is by telling yourself that if we didn't handle the cleanup, the family would have to."

"Nobody should ever have to clean up their own brother's blood."

When he frowned, Sadie caught her slip.

"I meant their son's blood."

The waitress brought their beers and slid them onto little paper coasters that had silly sayings. Sadie's read, *So many beers, so little time* and Zack's said, *Beauty lies in the hands of the beerholder.*

"Do you want to talk about Brian?" he asked suddenly.

"Not particularly."

"I've been working for you for a year now. You don't often discuss it, but it's kind of like the elephant in the room that nobody talks about. Can I tell you my opinion on the matter?"

"I have a feeling you're going to tell me anyway," Sadie said with a smirk.

"You're right." He sipped his beer. "I know you started this job as a way to heal after your own loss, but maybe five years of this work doesn't heal as much as it just makes you numb. Maybe it's just an anesthetic for what you should be dealing with inside." He poked his own chest with his finger. "In here."

"Thank you, psychiatrist Zack, for your free analysis of my mental state," Sadie sneered.

"Hey, I was only—"

"How about you? When we scrubbed that messy decomp scene last month, the one from that heroin overdose, did it bring back fond memories of your days hooked on Vicodin?"

It was as though she'd punched him in the gut. Anger and pain marched across his face before those feelings morphed into rage. He got to his feet, flicked a twenty on the table, and stormed out of the pub without a word.

"Damn," Sadie muttered and gulped down half her beer.

She'd crossed the line. She knew that she should go after him, but she didn't. Instead she dealt with it by blurring the line she'd crossed with a few more beers and a couple of vodka shooters in short succession. When a taxi driver dropped her at her door just after ten, she barely made it to her bathroom in time to vomit.

The bed was spinning wildly, so she headed for the living room and finally passed out on the sofa while watching Leno. A garbage pail sat on the floor next to her head. When the doorbell rang a couple of hours later, Sadie figured it was probably Zack coming to give her either a piece of his mind or his resignation. She handled it by turning off the power to the television, resuming her prone position on the sofa, and pulling her chenille throw over her head.

Unfortunately, the doorbell would not be silent and its noise was followed by loud knocks that would probably wake the neighbors. Reluctantly, Sadie swung her legs off the sofa, shook away the cobwebs, and headed for the door.

"Who is it?"

"Noel," came the reply.

What the hell? Sadie opened the door and looked into Noel's sheepish face. She couldn't even bring herself to say hello.

"I'm so sorry to wake you, Sadie, but I really need to talk to Dawn."

"Dawn?"

"Yeah, the owner of our house called an hour ago from Australia. She's finally agreed to sell us the place. Best of all, she's agreed to both the price and the terms that we offered."

"Wow, that's awesome news." Sadie rubbed her eyes groggily and tried to make sense of all this by looking at her watch. Nope, it was definitely still the middle of the night.

She looked back up at Noel, who didn't appear the least bit drunk.

"I'm sure Dawn will be thrilled with the news."

"Exactly," he laughed. "That's why I had to come right over. I know you're trying to have a girls' night together, but she isn't answering her cell and I didn't want to leave the news on her voice mail. If you let me in, I won't stay. I'll just give her the great news and be on my way."

Sadie had a sick feeling in the pit of her stomach as Noel stepped inside and began loudly calling out Dawn's name.

"Where is she, in the guest room?" he asked, then shouted, "Hey, Dawn!"

"Um, Noel," Sadie said weakly, "Dawn's not here."

His smile faltered.

He waggled a finger in her face. "Ha! You're such a kidder."

He ran down the hall, throwing the bedroom and bathroom doors open before returning to face Sadie, who still stood at the front door wishing she could disappear.

"Where is she?" he demanded.

"Maybe she's just taking some time to herself—you know, having a little me time," Sadie offered. "Or else she's gone off with Chloe somewhere."

"She said that the two of you were going out for dinner and clubbing as a sister-bonding thing . . ." He took off his glasses and rubbed his eyes before pushing them back up his nose. "Did she cancel at the last minute, or . . ." He examined Sadie's face and winced. "There never was a girls' night out, was there?"

"I'm not really sure. . . . Why don't you have a seat and I'll get you a drink."

Sadie tugged Noel's elbow and led him like a child to her living room, where she pushed him onto her sofa. He sat there, his body stiff and his face twisted in pain. She hurried into the kitchen and poured him a three-finger whiskey and soda and rushed back. She handed the drink to him and he drank it like it was water, then coughed a little before looking up at Sadie with damp eyes.

"She's found someone else."

"Oh no, no, no," Sadie said, and she embraced Noel in an awkward hug. "She's just been working lots and she's probably overwhelmed. Full days at her old job and then putting in extra time training for that new position." She plopped herself down on the sofa right next to him. "I bet she was just so damn tired, she meant to call me and make arrangements for a girls' night out but decided to spend a night with another friend instead, or alone even. She could've gone to Chloe's just to say hi and fell asleep."

His face pulled down into a frown as he put his empty glass on the coffee table.

"She would've told me if she wasn't going out with you."

"Not if it was a last-minute kind of thing. I'm sure in the morning she'll have some goofy explanation that will make us both laugh."

Noel looked down at his hands folded in his lap, and a tear rolled down his cheek.

"Could I have another drink?"

Sadie was more than happy to run off to the kitchen and get him another. While she poured the whiskey, she called Dawn's cell.

"Your fiancé is at my house looking for you," she hissed onto her sister's voice mail.

Sadie brought Noel his drink, and they sat for a moment in silence. When he did begin talking it was mostly to whine that he was losing Dawn. Without her sister there to defend herself, Sadie was left out on a limb as to how to defend her.

When Noel slumped over around four and began snoring loudly, Sadie pulled his legs onto the couch and tried to make him comfortable. She also repositioned the trash bin close to his head. He'd had a number of stiff drinks, and she didn't want to have to bring the sanitizing chemicals in from the garage to clean up his vomit.

Fetching a comforter from the linen closet, she gently draped it over him. He stirred for a moment, mumbled Dawn's name, then fell asleep again. At that moment she really felt sorry for the guy. She also wanted to kill Dawn.

As Sadie looked down at the man mouth-breathing on her sofa, an eerie flash of reality settled over her. She gently removed his glasses and set them on the coffee table. Then she held her breath as she memorized Noel's features—his slight overbite, narrow nose, and shock of blond hair.

Swallowing a lump in her throat, Sadie fought an ever-increasing wave of panic. She ran to her side table and snatched a framed picture of Brian. Her fingers trembled as she walked back and held the photo up next to Noel's face.

They were both blond, of slight build, and about the same age. Other than that, nobody could possibly think they could be related.

"Why did I ever think he looked like Brian?" Sadie murmured aloud.

She felt like a fool. Grief flooded her on a wave of pain so potent it was as if she was hearing of Brian's death for the first time. With a low, animalistic moan, she sank to her knees and sobbed silently into her hands.

Noel began to stir at the sound of her cries, so she found the strength to move. She stumbled into her bedroom and collapsed onto her bed. She squeezed her eyes shut and the agonizing fire of fresh loss seared her chest.

From her bed, Sadie stared at a blank wall for what may have been a couple of hours. Her mind was bent on replaying every moment she'd ever spent with her brother. She recalled her twentieth birthday when he wrote "Happy Birthday" on her car with shaving cream. A few years afterward he'd decided to take her and Dawn on a fishing trip, and he'd laughed at their incompetence. The year he died, both Dawn and Sadie had received Valentine's bouquets from him because they didn't have boyfriends at the time. He'd worried the whole family with his rock-climbing hobby. They'd all been sure he'd take a fall and break his neck.

The memories caused Sadie to whiplash between tears and heart-searing silent grief.

It wasn't yet morning when she heard Noel get up and slip quietly out her front door. She made no attempt to say good-bye. When she heard his car back out of her driveway, she reached for her bedside table and opened the drawer to get out a tissue box. Her hand brushed against her Ruger .22-caliber handgun that she kept in the drawer, and her fingers jerked back as if burned.

She picked up the gun and felt the weight of it in her hand, and the cold, blued-steel barrel shone up at her. She took the gun and the box of ammo and walked both to her closet. She climbed up on a chair and stuffed the Ruger into a shoe box at the very back of the closet.

Her experience told her that suicide wasn't a thunderous, unimaginable roar. It was a seductive whisper that stole the people you loved.

16

The phone rang four times before Sadie picked up the extension on her nightstand.

"God, Sadie, I'm soooo sorry! What did you tell him?" Dawn asked.

"Well, your fiancé showed up on my doorstep expecting that you were here because that's apparently what *you* told him. . . . What the hell *could* I say? Hang on."

Sadie tapped two aspirin from a bottle and swallowed them with water.

Sadie snapped up the phone again and growled, "If you expect me to lie for you, you should at least let me in on it."

"I have no idea why he'd come to your place in the middle of the night," Dawn said in a rush. "I never would've put you in that kind of position if I'd known."

"You never would have, yet you *did*, and that is so not the point! Where were you last night, Dawn?"

She hesitated before blurting, "I was with John."

"John? Who the hell is John?"

"The guy I told you about. Dr. John Irwin, the one who owns the surgical practice. My new job."

"Your new boss?" Sadie asked, dumbfounded.

Dawn began crying softly. "I didn't want Noel to

find out this way. I didn't want to hurt him, really I didn't. Things just kind of happened."

Sadie shook her head slowly from side to side.

"I'll put the coffee on. Come over and we'll talk about it."

"Thanks, but I think I should talk to Noel first. I owe him that much. I'm on my way home to see him."

"Good luck. Call me later."

After she placed the phone back on the cradle, Sadie dressed in sweatpants and a long-sleeved tee. She found her good running shoes far in the back of the front closet and slipped them on. After a few stretches in her foyer, she set her alarm and left her house, stepping outside into the predawn darkness. Her rhythm was fast out of necessity and stress. She was jogging her second mile when the sun peeked out from the horizon and inched up into the first rain-free sky in weeks. The cool air burned her lungs, and sweat traced a line down the center of her back.

She had no idea how long it had been since she'd gone jogging. Certainly months. Maybe even a year. It felt damn good in a pathetic huffing and puffing kind of way.

Back home, she got into the shower and stood under the hot spray. Her body ached with a good fatigue and her head felt clear. In spite of the previous night's lack of sleep and crying jag, she was invigorated.

Sadie felt like she'd finally made a kind of peace with Brian's death. A realization that it was time to move on. For the first time since the fifth anniversary of his death, she even felt hungry. Instead of reaching for her usual morning toast, she made a small stack of pancakes, drowned them in syrup, and inhaled the entire plate.

When Pam came by, she was washing her dishes and in relatively good spirits.

"Oh my God, you're whistling. Did you get laid?"

"No." Sadie laughed at the prospect. "Who the hell would I screw? The last man who kissed me set me up to be arrested for burglary and then hired someone to take a shot at me."

"You're joking, right?"

Sadie didn't reply.

"Well, there's always Zack," Dawn said. "I've seen the way he looks at you."

"Hmmm. Zack." Sadie shook her head, feeling not nearly as relaxed as she had a minute before. "I've got some major sucking up to do. I don't want him to quit."

"This sounds interesting. What did you do? I hope it's something that involves sexual harassment."

"I brought up the fact that he was forced to quit the police force because of an addiction to painkillers."

"Huh. So that's why he's no longer a cop. I always wondered."

"It's not something he's proud of, so of course I threw it in his face and then rubbed his nose in it in a real bitchy manner."

"Wow, when you hit below the belt, you really aim for the balls."

"I didn't mean it."

"Really?"

"Well, he brought up Brian and I lashed out."

"Man, I've taken a few of those shots from you myself."

"It's a sore spot," Sadie admitted.

"And Brian's death isn't hard on the rest of us? I'm tired of you acting like you're the only one in pain."

"Part of me was always hoping I'd get to see Brian. Ask him why he did it." She straightened. "But I'm done with all that. I'm putting it behind me and moving forward."

"This is a lot of deep thinking for so early in the day."

"Yeah, and now I'm off to beg Zack's forgiveness."

"Good luck. Just say you're sorry and if that doesn't work, stick your tongue down his throat."

Sadie agreed to apologizing (not to sticking her tongue down Zack's throat), but she still put it off as long as possible. Once she'd done all her laundry, organized some boxes in the garage, and tackled Hairy's litter box, she knew she couldn't procrastinate any longer.

She could've just picked up the phone, but she figured she owed Zack a face-to-face apology. Besides, she wasn't quite sure he wouldn't just hang up on her.

He lived in a small apartment complex in Bellevue. Sadie parked in the back lot and walked around to use the main entrance. She took the stairs up to the second floor. At Zack's apartment, she noticed his newspaper in the corridor, announcing that he was probably still inside. She picked up the *Seattle Times*, took a deep breath, and rapped louder than necessary on his door.

Sadie was counting on the element of surprise to help her apologize before Zack could get a word in edgewise. When the door opened, she was the one surprised.

"Yes?" asked a tall, slim brunette who was obviously naked beneath a man's bathrobe.

"Oh, I'm—" Sadie gulped. "I'm looking for Zack. Zack Bowman."

"Zack!" the woman shouted over her shoulder. "Someone at the door for you." She turned back to look at Sadie, scrutinizing her openly.

"Sadie, hi!"

His hair was tousled from sleep and his chin dark with stubble. He wore sweatpants but no shirt.

Zack nudged the brunette. "Give us a minute."

Her hips swayed as she sauntered casually away. Zack nodded to Sadie.

"What's up?"

"I owe you an apology," Sadie said humbly.

"Really. Hmmm." He folded his arms across his bare chest. "Did you bring coffee and donuts?"

"Uh, no, I didn't."

He frowned.

"Seems like if you're going to wake someone up to say you're sorry, you should at least bring coffee and donuts. Come back when you've got the goods."

He took the newspaper from her hands and firmly closed the door in her face.

Sadie stood with her mouth hanging open for a number of seconds before she turned and left. Back at her car, she cursed and debated whether or not he was pulling her leg. In the end she decided not to take any chances. Half an hour later she returned, precariously balancing a box of Krispy Kremes, two hot coffees, and a bouquet of spring flowers. The last were an apology for the brunette.

Once outside Zack's apartment again, Sadie kicked the door with her toe, since her hands were full. She wasn't looking forward to having to grovel and plead forgiveness in front of Zack's girlfriend, who was beautiful even though she'd just rolled out of bed.

"You brought this on yourself," she murmured while waiting for the door.

This time when he opened up, his face was clean-shaven, his hair was still damp from the shower, and he was wearing clean jeans and a fresh tee. He eyed her burdened hands and nodded.

"That's better."

"I won't stay long. I don't want to interrupt."

"You're not interrupting. Paula's gone. She had to get to work anyway."

"Oh."

Sadie had never been inside Zack's apartment before. It could only have been described as functional and basic. It was sparsely furnished in neutral colors.

Most of the walls were bare, but at least it was tidy and not a dump.

He didn't seem to know what to do with the flowers, but he eventually found a large jar under his sink, filled it with water, and stuffed them in.

"Those are for Paula," Sadie explained. "For interrupting your, um, date."

"I'll let her know."

Sadie sat down at the kitchen table.

"You know, you've worked for me for a year now and I never even knew you had a girlfriend."

He regarded her with a cool look that offered nothing.

"Not that it's any of my business," she quickly added. "I'm just surprised, that's all." She cleared her throat. "Look, I'm sorry about how I acted last night. I don't blame you for being ticked off. I promise it will never, ever happen again."

"What won't?" he asked, joining her at the table. "Talking? Having a beer together?"

She wrapped her fingers around her coffee.

"No, I don't mean that. I just mean I won't bring up your past . . . you know, stuff . . ." She floundered, felt herself redden, and got the distinct impression he was enjoying her discomfort.

Zack opened his hands palms up.

"Guess all's fair in love and work. I brought up your brother and you just fought back. Rougher than I would've liked, sure, but I probably should've kept my mouth shut."

"I was way out of line."

"Yeah, but I kinda like that about you." He winked.

"You liked me making fun of your addiction?"

"No, I liked you reacting. Showing a little bite about something besides the ghosts you talk to was kind of nice."

He flipped open the box of donuts and grabbed one for himself, then offered them to her.

"I couldn't. I just ate an obscene amount of pancakes."

"You could use some more flesh on your bones. If a man got too close he'd cut himself."

Sadie rankled at his remark but managed to hold back a scathing retort.

Zack placed a donut on a napkin and slid it in front of her.

"Eat."

"What, now you're my mother?"

"Trust me, my thoughts about you being in my apartment aren't maternal."

Rolling her eyes, she picked up the donut and took a bite.

"So we're okay?" she asked.

"Yeah. We're good."

"You're still working for me?"

"I haven't had any better offers today."

"Great. And it won't be weird between us, right?"

"Sadie, it's always been weird." He bit into his donut and washed it down with coffee.

She didn't quite understand if he meant the cleaning of death scenes or the spirit stuff, but she figured it really didn't matter.

"You take on the ugliest job in the world to save families from being traumatized twice," Zack said. "Plus, you hired me when I couldn't get a job cleaning toilets."

"You're cleaning worse stuff now," she joked.

"Yeah, but you never once accused me of being the one to steal the diamond brooch and let you take the fall for it."

She looked stunned.

"Why would I have done that?"

"Because I was the only one besides you and that Kent Lasko creep who had access to the jewelry. Not to mention the fact that you know some of my history before I went into rehab and it isn't pretty. Still, you never once pointed a finger at me."

"Because I knew you'd never do a thing like that." She finished off her donut and licked the icing from her fingers.

He nodded quietly and for a second his eyes were tender.

Then his guard went back up and he joked, "I could sure live without all that ghost shit, but I'm not going anywhere. For now."

She was glad. More than glad.

"Oh, and I met with Jackie," Zack added. "I think she'll be great. Seems to have her head on straight and all that. She's gone back to Texas to get the rest of her stuff but promises to be ready to start in a couple days."

"Thanks for checking her out."

Sadie's phone rang. It was Dawn. She wanted to talk, so they arranged to meet at Sadie's house.

"I've got to go. Family stuff," Sadie said and gave him the brief rundown on Noel's late-night visit and Dawn's cheating.

He whistled. "Sounds like you've had an interesting day already, and it's hardly noon."

"I haven't had any job calls. Maybe we'll get a couple days off."

She got to her feet and stuck out her hand.

"I'm glad we're okay."

"Yeah, so am I," he said, his voice rough as he grabbed her hand softly in his.

Off Sadie went from putting out one fire to watching another slow burn. She'd never seen her sister looking so exhausted.

"So you ended it?" Sadie asked. "Just because you got cold feet and had a fling? Don't you think that's a little drastic?" She felt sorry for Noel.

"He wanted a guarantee that I wouldn't see John again."

"You're kidding. He actually expected his fiancée to stop seeing other guys?"

"Cut the sarcasm. I don't think I can stop seeing John any more than I can stop breathing."

"Cut the drama queen act."

"I'm serious. I've never felt like this before with anyone. Even Noel."

"Are you sure you're not just confusing lust with a bad case of cold feet?"

"But what if it's love?" Dawn shook her head slowly from side to side. "What if it's the real deal? I won't know unless I take the time to find out."

"And you expected Noel to be okay with that?"

"I guess I was hoping for a little space. Some time to work through things. With Noel it was all or nothing and the decision had to be now." Her voice broke. "He moved out, Sadie. He wouldn't even give me a chance to really say how sorry I am. He's staying with a friend and he told me not to even call."

"I'm sorry."

"No you're not. You never liked Noel anyway," Dawn said with sudden fury.

"That's not true."

"Oh come on. Whenever he came around you'd wrinkle up your face like you were disgusted by his presence."

"To tell you the truth, my problem was about the fact that Noel looks so much like Brian. I've dealt with that now."

Dawn's jaw dropped. "Wait a second—Noel doesn't look a thing like Brian. Well, besides the blond hair. Oh and maybe the nose. I guess they're pretty much the same height too. . . . Oh my God! you don't think I subconsciously chose Noel because of Brian?"

"Yes. No. Oh, I don't know." Sadie threw up her hands. "Like I said, this was *my* problem and I've dealt with it."

"I should tell Noel. Even if there's a chance it's true, he has a right to know that maybe all along I—"

"That you chose him to stand in for your dead

brother? Nice. Why stop there? Maybe you can also tell him he was bad in bed. You know, kick him while he's down."

"Maybe you're right."

"I am."

Dawn narrowed her eyes and looked seriously at Sadie.

"You seem awfully sure of yourself today. How are you?" Dawn tapped her chest. "In here."

Sadie knew Dawn was referring to the grief over Brian's suicide.

"Better." Sadie exhaled like she'd been holding her breath for five years. "At least I will be until you tell Mom and Dad the engagement is off."

Dawn cringed. "Please say you'll come with me when I tell them."

Sadie tried to back out, but the truth was, going with Dawn would take her mind off of her own troubles. They stopped at the corner store on their way to visit their parents. Sadie snagged chocolate bars for the two of them for the drive and some low-fat soy ice cream for the parents to help soften the blow.

"I don't think we really need to bring food with us," Dawn said.

"Trust me, I'm getting good at this sort of thing. Treats help."

They'd phoned ahead and found out that Dad's tee-off time wasn't for a couple hours and Mom had a neighbor over but the woman would soon be leaving. They encouraged the girls to come on by for a visit.

Mom greeted them at the door, and while she hugged Sadie she hastily whispered in her ear, "My neighbor thinks you run a cleaning company for Seattle's elite. It's easier than explaining your real job."

Sadie offered her mom a pained look, but in light of the bomb Dawn was about to drop, she let the slight pass without comment. Mom led the way into the kitchen past Dad, who was watching golf on the

TV in the living room. He offered them a limp wave as they walked by—or it could have been a shooing motion that meant don't pause in front of the television.

Marilyn from next door was thrilled to meet Mom's girls and stayed longer because of it. Making small talk was just about killing Sadie, but finally Marilyn looked at her watch and announced she really had to go.

As she got up to leave, she said to Sadie, "I understand your business is really taking off. Your mom tells me you're a real entrepreneur. I'm curious, does your service clean for any Seattle millionaires I've heard of?"

"We pretty much scrape up after everyone eventually," Sadie replied.

Mom quickly ushered her friend out the door, sending Sadie an angry glare from behind Marilyn's back as they went.

"For heaven's sake, Sadie, you don't need to have such an attitude," her mother complained once she was sure Marilyn was out of earshot. "It's not like I could actually tell people what you really do."

Sadie laughed. "Why not, Mom? Do you think none of them will ever die?"

"Hopefully when they do it'll be with some dignity and they won't need your services." She sniffed.

"I give up." Sadie sighed and looked over at her sister. "Dawn has something to tell you. I'm just here for moral support."

Mom's eyes got huge. "Oh my God, you're sick, aren't you? Do you have cancer?" She screamed toward the living room. "Murray, come here, something's wrong. I think Dawn has cancer!"

"What? No! I don't have cancer," shouted Dawn.

Sadie snickered and leaned over to whisper in her sister's ear, "Go with it. If you tell them you're sick, they'll go easier on you."

Dad came into the kitchen and looked at his women.

"What's all the screaming about?"

"Sit down. Dawn has something important to tell us," Mom said and she clasped her hands over her mouth. "Oh my God, you're pregnant!"

"No!" Dawn took a deep breath and blurted, "Noel and I broke up." Then for clarification or conscience-easing she added, "I was the one who ended it."

Dad nodded. "Okay. As long as you're happy." He got up to leave, but Mom shot him the original Novak death glare, so he sat his ass back down.

"Why did you break up? He seemed like such a nice boy," Mom whined.

"He's thirty-something years old, Mom. Hardly a boy," Sadie said.

In a big rush Dawn blurted, "I've met someone else. His name's John. I might be in love."

Mom looked like she'd been slapped. You could've heard a pin drop. Then she began to sob, huge crocodile tears leaking from her eyes.

"It could be worse," Sadie said. "She could have cancer."

"That's not funny," Mom snarled, and she began to cry in earnest. "We were going to have such a beautiful wedding!" she wailed.

Dawn rushed to comfort her while Sadie and Dad just sat there looking uncomfortable. Sadie got up and got everyone some of the soy ice cream she'd brought.

Dad ate one spoonful and pushed it away.

"It tastes like melted Styrofoam. Put some whipped cream and chocolate sauce on it and maybe it'll be okay."

Sadie ignored him. When it looked like Mom's tears would never end, she said loudly, "Did Dawn mention that John's a doctor?"

Mom grabbed a napkin and dabbed a little at her eyes. "Really?"

Dawn nodded.

"Will he pay for half the wedding?" Dad asked.

"We've just started dating," Dawn said. "But when, or if, the time comes then, yes, I'm sure he wouldn't mind paying for half."

"I'm good," Dad announced. He got up and walked back into the living room to resume his position in front of the television.

For Sadie and Dawn it wasn't that easy. It took a promise of lunch the following week and a promise of an outlet mall shopping venture to finally extricate themselves from their mother's vortex.

Once back in Dawn's car, Sadie sank into the passenger seat and let out a low whistle.

"All things considered, that went better than I thought it would."

Dawn agreed, and on the return trip Sadie listened while her sister went on about her new job. Sadie peppered her with questions about the so-called new love of her life, but she didn't offer any digs. If she analyzed it she'd have to admit that she was glad— and, yes, possibly jealous—to see the sparkle in Dawn's eyes.

"By the way, did you know that Zack has a girlfriend?" Sadie asked casually. She took a long drink from the water bottle she'd snagged from her parents' fridge.

"I don't know about a girlfriend, but I know he occasionally dates a woman named Paula."

"How come you know this and I'm in the dark?"

"Noel and I ran into them one time at a restaurant and Zack introduced us." She looked pointedly at Sadie. "Unlike you, the man has a life."

Sadie thought about that for a minute and decided to change the subject.

"You know, I just thought of a big drawback about canceling your engagement," Sadie said.

"What's that?" Dawn pulled up to the curb in front of Sadie's house.

"Once you and Noel moved in together, Mom stopped asking me when I planned on settling down with a good man and making babies. Now it's just a matter of time before I have to start screening my calls again."

Dawn laughed, but Sadie wasn't joking.

"Seriously, Dawn, I sat up with your crying ex-fiancé last night and stood by your side while you dropped the bomb on Mom and Dad today. You owe me."

"Fine. If Mom starts in on you about finding a husband and popping out babies, I'll tell her to lay off."

"And?"

"And maybe I'd hint that I'm thinking about kids."

"Deal." Sadie leaned in and embraced her sister in a strong hug.

"Seriously, though," Dawn began. "You could do worse than to hook up with a nice guy. Hell, you don't even go anywhere to meet men. Live ones, that is."

"Not true. I had a dinner date with a man just last week." Sadie opened the car door and climbed out.

"Wait a second. You can't just leave me hanging here," Dawn called. "Tell me about this guy."

"There's not a lot to tell. He turned out to be a jerk." As Sadie said it she couldn't help but think of Grant and how much he loved Trudy. "I think all the good ones are dead, married, or both."

Sadie closed the car door, ending any further questions. The clouds had gathered in a tight knot of gray, and fat drops began to plop onto her head as she dug out her keys and jogged up to the front door.

Once inside, she kicked off her shoes and ran to deactivate the alarm. Hairy bounded around the corner, his nails click-clacking on the hardwood, and his back legs skidded comically as he rushed to say hello.

"Who says I need a dog." Sadie grinned, bent, and rubbed his fuzzy head. "Let me dump this water bottle in the recycle bin and I'll get you some yogurt treats."

She kept the recycle bin on her deck just outside her back door. As she walked through the kitchen, Hairy happily hopped behind her. When she reached the door, she gently pushed Hairy away with the side of her foot before she opened it. She didn't want him to hop through to the yard with hopes of munching on grass.

"Wait," she instructed him.

As she opened the door, Sadie glanced up from Hairy's soft face and straight into Kent Lasko's murderous glare.

17

A shocked screech burned her throat as she tried to slam the door shut, but Kent's foot shot out and stopped it from closing.

"I heard about what's going on. I had to see you," he said. "Please, just listen to me."

"Get the hell off my porch! I'm calling the cops," Sadie threatened, trying to keep fear from her voice.

"I just want to talk. I'll stay right here—you don't even have to let me inside."

He didn't have a weapon that Sadie could see, but that didn't mean he wasn't hiding one inside his jacket. Her mind raced. She knew that by the time she could get to the phone or to her closet for her gun he could easily slit her throat or shoot her.

"Okay, go ahead and talk," she answered, surprised at how calm her voice sounded. Her breath came in and out in adrenaline-laced gasps. "I'll give you two minutes. You can start by telling me why you lied about going to Tahoe."

"I'm sorry about that, but I have a real good reason for asking my friend to cover for me."

He relaxed a bit and even offered her a deceptively sexy smile.

"You're looking good, by the way."

"Start talking," she barked.

"First of all, I don't know why you told the cops

that I put a diamond pin in your coat when we went to dinner. I didn't do that. That's not exactly the best way to end a date with a woman when you're hoping for another."

He had the audacity to wink.

"Are you actually flirting with me? After you slit my tires and shot Mrs. Toth?"

"What?!" He jerked backward, as if surprised, and his foot slid out of the way.

Sadie abruptly turned and shouldered him hard so that he stumbled backward at least a foot. Hurriedly she tried to close the door, but just as quickly, Kent snaked his hand out to stop her and she slammed the door on his fingers, making a sickening crack.

"Argh!" he screamed. "My fingers! You're breaking them!"

He tugged and finally yanked his hand free. Sadie successfully forced the door the rest of the way closed and speedily bolted it.

Her heart pounded as she raced to get the phone at the other end of the kitchen. She was dialing 911 while Kent hopped around and cursed outside on her deck.

"Nine-one-one. What's your emergency?"

"I've got a man trying to break into my house," Sadie panted into the phone. She rattled off the address and promised to stay on the line.

"The cops are on their way!" she screamed for Kent's benefit.

He leaned against the door.

"I'm sorry, Sadie," he called out. "That's all I wanted to say. I'm just sorry you got mixed up in all this. You've been in the wrong place at the wrong time. I'm sorry."

"You should tell that to Sylvia Toth!" Sadie screeched, her voice warbling with emotion. "Hell, you should send your apologies to Trudy and Grant too, you no good, backstabbing, mentally defective, lying son of a bitch!"

She heard his footsteps as he walked down the stairs of her deck and toward the back lane. When she was sure he'd gone, she slumped onto the linoleum and began to cry, her sobs coming in strangled gasps.

The sirens came, but not fast enough.

"He's gone," she told the officer when she opened her front door. "He was at my back door when I came home and he tried to force his way inside when I went to put a bottle in my recycle box. He took off when I told him I'd called the cops."

"Did he hurt you?"

"No. I was able to slam the door on him. I've no doubt he would've killed me if he'd had the chance."

"You know the man?" the officer asked.

"Yes. Kent Lasko," Sadie said. She pointed to her door frame. "You can tell Detective Petrovich he admitted to having his friend lie for him. He wasn't in Tahoe skiing."

"Petrovich is on his way, and we've got vehicles searching the area for this guy," the officer assured her. "You just need to calm yourself and stay put."

"As if I'm going anywhere," Sadie mumbled to herself as the officer left to make his calls. She took a seat on her sofa and stared blankly at the wall. She stared so hard her eyes began to burn.

"I should probably paint this place," she said, as if seeing the pale walls for the first time. "Or move."

When the officer returned from a look at the deck, he sat down in the chair next to the sofa.

"Kent killed Trudy and Grant Toth and made it look like a murder-suicide," she told him. I don't know how he did it, but he did it. There's got to be a way to make the evidence tell the truth."

He tapped his notepad with the tip of his pen and frowned. "We've got cars all over the neighborhood looking for this man, but you say you didn't see his car?"

"No. He could've parked far away or maybe he was on foot. He used a green Toyota when he was after me before."

"That's what Petrovich said. Our guys are looking for him either on foot or in a green Toyota. I'm sure we'll find him."

Sadie sighed and blinked back tears as she focused on the feature wall of her living room.

"I'm thinking green, but nothing too dark. Maybe a light seafoam color."

"Excuse me?"

"Paint."

"Ma'am, are you all right? Do you need medical attention?"

"Maybe I need a vacation. I don't think I can wait until next week for a massage."

"You know, my brother takes rescue dogs. You should consider one for protection."

"I've got a rabbit. Hairy and I have agreed a dog wouldn't be a good idea."

"Even a well-trained dog would be tempted by the taste of rabbit," he admitted. "But you could always keep your bunny locked in a cage or in a separate room."

Sadie watched as Hairy hopped over to his little basket and hunkered down with Mini-Hairy.

"I don't think keeping Hairy locked up would be good for either of us."

He handed her his brother's business card.

Sadie looked down at the card and smiled. "Kalvin Newton. Huh. I went to school with a Kalvin Newton, except he spelled Kalvin with a C." She looked up. "Thanks for the card. I promise to give serious thought to the dog thing."

Petrovich arrived but didn't talk to her until he'd spoken with the officers searching the neighborhood, and even then he wasn't much help. They hadn't found Kent Lasko and by now he could've been anywhere. Kent's brother, Christian, had been at his house alone, but he claimed he hadn't seen Kent for days and appeared genuinely shocked that his brother wasn't off skiing in Tahoe.

After Petrovich and all the other cops had gone, Sadie double-checked all her windows and doors and set the alarm as Petrovich had insisted. Then she had a lengthy discussion with Zack on the phone and promised not to leave her house. There was no danger of that. She was exhausted. Even though it was midafternoon, she climbed into bed, pulled the covers up to her chin, and began reading a romance novel that had been waiting on her nightstand for months.

She nodded off and was enjoying an erotic dream involving a blond with washboard abs and a penchant for whipped cream when the phone rang. She pulled a pillow over her head and tried to go back to sleep, but a woman's voice echoed through the house through the speaker on the answering machine.

"Sadie, it's Maeva. Pick up the phone. I know you're there." Pause. "If you don't pick up I'll keep calling every five minutes until you do."

With an exasperated sigh, Sadie flung the pillow off her face and snatched the phone.

"Why don't you use your evil ESP on someone else?" Sadie demanded.

"That wasn't ESP. I drove by your house an hour ago and all these cops were around. What's up?"

"Someone tried to break in. Now I'm going back to sleep."

"How can you fall asleep after someone just broke into your place?"

"He never got inside. It was Kent Lasko. He was lurking in my backyard and wanted to talk."

"Good for you for calling the cops. Did you find out first why he killed Trudy and Grant?"

"No, I didn't," Sadie said evenly. "Since he probably would've killed me, I didn't invite the man in for tea."

"Don't get grumpy."

"I've had a rough day. I'm going back to sleep, where I'm hoping to find a muscled man-slut waiting to service me."

"Fine, but I'd like you to help me communicate with Grant again. He keeps interrupting every séance I have, but his messages are so jumbled they don't make sense. Will you help?"

"I'm not in a helping kind of mood."

"But you could uncover some clue that would help prove Kent Lasko's guilty and put him in jail."

Sadie considered this.

"You know, Maeva, I'm just not overly in touch with my inner Nancy Drew. If you're able to uncover some clue that will put this all together, go for it. I'm just going to mind my own business and maybe get a dog."

"Hairy would hate it if you got a dog."

"I'm hanging up now," Sadie said, and she did.

Regardless of her attempts, the Adonis of Sadie's dreams was gone for good. After tossing and turning for a while, she ignored her promise to Zack. She knew one place she could go and still be safe. She headed for the mall for some retail therapy.

After an hour of wandering she'd only managed to eat some greasy fries and hadn't found a damn thing that interested her. However, she did feel safe among the throngs of shoppers.

She walked into a small lingerie shop all decked out in Valentine's Day splendor, but it only made her feel old and alone. Besides, she'd been considering a simple bra; she wasn't aiming for one in hot pink with sparkly hearts, thank you very much. She thought of asking the perky clerk for help, but her tolerance for perky was low these days. Instead, she abruptly whirled, walked out of the shop—and bumped directly into Christian Lasko.

"Ah, jeez," he grumbled.

He tried to keep his head down and walk around her. Unfortunately, Sadie had the same idea and when she stepped to one side he did the same, and when he reversed directions she matched his. It was as if they couldn't get away from each other.

"Stop!" Sadie shouted, attracting unnecessary attention from shoppers walking by. "I don't want to see you any more than you want to see me." She pointed to her left. "I'm going in that direction. Feel free to go the opposite way."

He nodded abruptly and took one step to the right. Then Sadie had second thoughts and grabbed him by the arm.

"By the way, tell your crazy brother to stay the hell away from me and my house. Tell him I'm getting a pit bull."

"Sure. Whatever."

He tried to yank his arm free of her grip, but Sadie held him fast.

"And tell him that I'm working on proof that he killed both Trudy and Grant and I'm not going to give up until he's in jail."

"You're crazy. Leave my brother alone or you'll regret it," Christian hissed, but he looked around furtively and he was obviously afraid.

He freed his arm from Sadie's grasp and broke into a run, nearly capsizing a middle-aged woman leaving the lingerie shop with an armload of purchases.

Sadie found it strangely empowering to strike fear into the heart of somebody after spending so much time lately scared herself.

Instead of leaving the mall, she spotted a mega sportswear store and decided it was her new destination. Even though her muscles were already starting to ache from her morning jog, it was a good kind of soreness. Maybe some new running clothes would bolster her enthusiasm.

She walked inside the store, where rock 'n' roll played loudly over the speakers and neon signs blinked sales slogans. She casually looked through the racks in the running section.

"Can I help you?" a pimply young man asked from behind her.

"Just looking for something to wear for jogging," Sadie remarked. She pulled a long-sleeved emerald green tee from the rack.

"Oh, you don't want that," he said, taking the item from her and hanging it back up. "Let me show you our new and exciting running wear."

Sadie was pretty sure that the new and exciting clothes would have a huge price tag, but she was curious, so she followed him just the same.

"Run-Tec has just come out with this new line specifically for joggers. It's made of textured microfiber. That means the fabric is breathable, and it actually lifts moisture away from your body."

"Yeah, but is it bulletproof?" Sadie asked sarcastically.

The clerk laughed politely and reached for a shirt on the shelf in front of them.

Sadie took the dark red shirt he held out and searched for the tag. "Fifty dollars for a shirt?" She handed it back to him. "I don't think so."

"There's a twenty-dollar rebate if you join Run-Tec's mailing list on their online store."

She looked skeptical. "Twenty dollars just for signing up online? How would that work? I sign up and then I'm spammed to death?"

He shook his head. "No, you just need to sign up for their newsletter that comes once a month."

"I'm not interested."

"It's really informative. It gives tips for working out, but it also offers coupons and rebates. So if you buy this shirt and enter the code you get on your receipt, they'll mail you your twenty-dollar rebate, plus you'll be able to download coupons from the site immediately. As a matter of fact, if you buy this shirt you'll get a coupon to buy the matching running shorts for half price. It's a steal. Everyone's snapping them up."

"And the coupon is good for all stores?" she asked.

"Sure, any sports store that carries the Run-Tec line. But," he quickly added, "we carry the largest selection of running wear in the city, so of course we should be your first choice."

Sadie eyed the rack.

"I kind of like the yellow one. Do you have it in a medium?"

He checked, but extra-small and extra-large seemed to be the only options for the bright yellow shirt for ladies, although if she wanted the basic men's design, he had her size in that color.

Sadie declined the yellow and tried on the red. It fit like a glove and she had to admit that spending fifty bucks on a running shirt would be strong motivation to get jogging on a more regular basis.

She left the mall feeling somewhat sated by both her run-in with Christian Lasko and her new sportswear purchase. However, when she got home and took that fifty-dollar shirt out of the bag, it didn't look nearly as impressive.

Pam was equally disappointed.

"It feels like it's made out of some new age plastic," she said, feeling it between her thumb and forefinger. "If you got near an open flame it would probably shrink-wrap you."

"It's microfiber blended with spandex," Sadie informed her. "And it's breathable. All the cool joggers are wearing them."

"Hmmm. Well, download the coupons. If you can balance cool with frugal it may be worth it."

"Good idea."

Sadie powered up the computer in her office, waited a couple of minutes for all the icons to pop up, and soon was inputting the Web site address shown on her receipt. With a click of her mouse and a few strokes of the keyboard, she was signed in to the online community and was printing off a colorful array of coupons and a lengthy newsletter, no doubt going through a few dollars' worth of ink from her color printer in the process.

As the newsletter chugged out of the printer, Pam began reading the pages and appeared deep in thought.

"Wow, selling sportswear is a huge moneymaking racket. I wonder what will happen to Grant Toth's store now that he's dead," Pam murmured.

Sadie blinked at her friend in surprise. "You know, I totally forgot that he was in that business." She snatched up the coupon from her desk. "Maybe I'll go down and see if they carry the Run-Tec line. I can make use of my coupon and check out Grant's store at the same time."

She looked up the store's address in the phone book. It was at the other end of Seattle, but because it gave her something to do, she didn't hesitate to drive there. The small sportswear store was in a strip mall, squeezed between a Subway sandwich shop and a Kinko's. Inside she found the place clean but without the bright lights and rock 'n' roll of the mall megastore.

"If I can be of any help, just holler," a young woman called from behind the counter.

"As a matter of fact," Sadie began, walking up to the desk, "I've got this coupon for the Run-Tec line and was hoping to see your selection of shorts."

Sadie held out the paper, and the young woman flinched as if repulsed by it.

"I'm sorry, but we don't carry that line. Never have and never will."

She reached behind the counter and handed Sadie

a buff-colored sheet with bold lettering proclaiming, "Saving the World One Child at a Time."

"This is a list of clothing lines that are known for using child labor. You'll notice that Run-Tec is at the top of that list. As an ethically run business, we've chosen to educate our clients and not carry Run-Tec products."

"Oh!" Sadie felt immediately guilty. "I had no idea."

"Most people don't, which is why when the owner started this store he made sure that all his employees were informed about ethical business practices so they could spread the word to the clientele."

"You're talking about Grant Toth?"

"Yes. He's the owner. Do you, I mean, did you know him?"

"I've done work for his mother," Sadie said truthfully. "What's going to happen to the stores now that he's gone?"

"We don't know," she admitted sadly. "Grant's lawyer called the store manager and told him that Grant's mother would inherit the business. We hope she'll consider keeping the stores open."

Sadie couldn't imagine Sylvia Toth running a sportswear store.

"I'll show you our alternative to Run-Tec," the clerk offered. "You'll find our line less expensive and with all of the same great features, just not made by some child in a Bangladesh sweatshop."

She showed Sadie some very attractive running outfits, but most of them were in bland blacks, whites, and beiges.

"I really like the bright colors that the Run-Tec line has," Sadie admitted, then quickly held up her hand. "Not that I'm going to put someone into slavery just so I can have a bright yellow shirt."

"Well, we don't carry any shirts in yellow, but I can show you this same style in a bright blue or red."

Sadie walked out of the store having spent a small fortune in guilt money, but at least she was now fully equipped from the top of her head to new running shoes for her feet. She'd have to make another trip to the mall to return her Run-Tec shirt, but that could wait for another day.

When she got home, she returned to her den and noticed the computer was still open to Run-Tec's home page. Splashed across the screen were photos of the shirt she'd bought at the mall. The largest one showed the same shirt in yellow. She had a sudden tickle of remembrance that led to an epiphany.

Before she could stop herself, she dialed Detective Petrovich. She wasn't able to reach him and instead got his voice mail.

"This is Sadie Novak. I've got an important question about the Toth case. Please call me as soon as you get this message."

She nervously tried to keep herself busy. She even cleaned behind the TV, admonishing Hairy for the few little raisin-type poops he'd accidentally left there instead of in his litter box. Next she fed the rabbit and played a half hour of solitaire before Petrovich called back.

"You said that the bloody clothing found in the Toth hamper was running clothes, right?" Sadie asked.

"Yes," he said impatiently. "Look, I don't know why you're so hung up on this, but my job didn't end at the Toth house or even at your house. I'm working another case right now."

"Did you or did you not say that the shirt was one of those fancy running shirts in bright yellow?"

"I did." He sighed. "Why?"

"Well, I've got news for you. Grant didn't own a yellow running shirt and he would *never* have owned a yellow running shirt," she announced triumphantly.

"So the guy hated yellow. Big deal."

"It's not the color. If you'll check you'll find that the bloody shirt was made by a company called Run-Tec."

"So what?"

"Grant was ethically opposed to Run-Tec."

She could almost hear him rolling his eyes.

"For God's sake . . ."

"Listen to me!" she shouted. "He wouldn't wear something made by Run-Tec because he believed them to be an unethical manufacturer. Even though it's the largest-selling sports brand in the country, Grant refused to have that line in his stores because they supported child labor. His employees are trained to give out handouts opposing that company!"

There was a pause.

"So what? It doesn't mean a damn thing. Hell, maybe he wore it to make a point. Getting the yellow shirt soaked in his wife's blood could've been a way for him to make a global statement about how he felt about that Run-Tec company."

Sadie said quietly, "But you've said all along you never believed this was a premeditated act. A crime of passion, you called it, right? What you're saying now is that he dressed in clothes he found reprehensible to make an ethical statement. If that was true, he never would've stuffed those clothes into a hamper instead of being caught wearing them, right?"

Petrovich was quiet for a moment.

"Plus, when I had dinner with Kent he admitted to going into a sports megastore and spending a fortune on running clothes."

"Fine. It's a stretch, but I'll get the clothes from evidence and see what I can find out. I'm not promising anything, okay?"

"That's all I ask," Sadie said and thanked him.

She felt like she was onto something, and she couldn't stand just sitting around the house. She decided to go back to the mall and return the red shirt.

By the time she got to the mall, she'd decided not to return the shirt after all but instead to exchange it.

"Let me get this straight," the same pimply man who'd waited on her earlier said. "You want to exchange this shirt for the men's style in yellow."

"Yes."

He went and got her the other shirt.

"Are you sure?"

"Yes." Sadie took the shirt to the counter.

"Don't you want to try it on?" he called after her. "The men's style is a looser fit."

"That's okay."

Instead of heading home, she drove to the hospital to visit Sylvia Toth. There was a chance that being shot at had convinced Mrs. Toth to be open to Sadie's ideas. Then again, it could've just convinced the woman to get a restraining order. Sadie might soon find herself being hauled down to the police station. Again.

18

Sadie drove straight to the hospital. She got out of the elevator and walked hurriedly into Sylvia's room, where she found a middle-aged man asleep in the bed where Sylvia had been.

"She's gone," Sadie murmured in surprise.

On her way out she stopped at the front desk.

"Excuse me. I'm looking for Sylvia Toth. She was in room five-ten."

The duty nurse thumbed through the charts and looked up.

"Mrs. Toth was discharged this morning."

Sadie had been hoping against hope that Sylvia's sister, Janet, wouldn't be in the hospital room, but she knew now that she would have to face her. Regardless, it had to be done.

Sadie got into the elevator and was alone, except for a man whose rib cage was spread wide open to expose his organs beneath.

"I hate hospitals," Sadie grumbled. To the man she said, "Heart surgery?"

His eyes grew wide.

"How'd you know?"

"Lucky guess."

On the ride down in the elevator, Sadie dealt with the heart surgery ghost but got little satisfaction from helping him go over. She was too worried about Sylvia Toth.

When she reached Sylvia Toth's townhome, she snatched the shopping bag from the passenger seat and composed herself as she strode to the front door. She rang the bell and held her breath as footsteps sounded on the other side.

The door opened and Janet stood there, looking not at all thrilled to see Sadie.

"I thought we had an agreement that you'd stay away from my sister," she spat angrily.

"This will only take a second. I just have a question regarding Grant's clothing." She held up the shopping bag.

"His clothing? You've got to be kidding."

"I think the bloody clothes found in Grant's hamper may have been from the Run-Tec line, and I suspect Grant would never have worn that line, so—"

"Wait a second." Janet held up her hand. "You *think* the clothes *may have been*, and you *suspect* Grant wouldn't have worn them? Listen to yourself!" She shook her head. "I'm sorry, but you're going to have to play detective with someone else's loved one. I'm not interested."

"Who's at the door?" Sylvia Toth's weak voice called from down the hall.

"A salesperson who's just leaving," Janet answered over her shoulder. Then to Sadie she hissed, "Get out of here and don't come back. If you come around again, I'll call the police."

Sadie was left standing outside holding her shopping bag. A few icy raindrops fell on her cheeks like sloppy tears.

As she started her car, she felt sullen and morose. She'd been so stupid to think that she, a glorified cleaning lady, could break a murder case wide open using a jogging shirt as evidence. She would have laughed at herself, but she didn't have any energy left for even a smile.

Back home she dressed in her non-Run-Tec jogging

clothes purchased from Grant's store. She carefully activated the house alarm the way she'd been told and slipped a spare house key into a small zippered pocket in the lining of her new shorts.

She stayed on the main roads and constantly looked over her shoulder. She didn't make it nearly the distance she had before. This time her sore muscles screamed in protest at such abuse, so she spent the last quarter mile walking, contemplating, and generally berating herself for letting the Toth situation take over her life.

When she stepped back into her house, she quickstepped to the keypad and turned off the alarm. Then she went in search of the phone. She'd decided to call Petrovich and let him know that she was done with the entire Toth thing. She was sure it would make his day.

Her answering machine blinked that it had one message and when she hit PLAY, it was Petrovich's voice that came out the speaker.

"Call me," he said.

Great minds think alike. She dialed the number he'd left and while she waited for him to pick up, she prepared her speech announcing that she was backing off.

"The shirt in the evidence bag was a yellow Run-Tec shirt, like you said," he barked, seemingly annoyed at the idea. "I went to Grant Toth's store, and you're right. Run-Tec is not something Grant would've been caught wearing, probably dead or alive."

"Good—but I've been thinking and it was probably like you said," she replied. "He wore it to make a point. Maybe he didn't even buy it. There's a good chance that he got tons of promotional freebies given to him and if he got it for free, he might've brought it home and worn it."

"Maybe," Detective Petrovich agreed. "The pants in the hamper were regular fleece-lined jogging pants in a size medium. A style that anybody would've worn to exercise."

"Sure, and just because he wore the Run-Tec shirt because he got it for free, that doesn't mean he'd go out of his way to sign up on their Web site to get the coupon for the discounted matching shorts," Sadie reasoned.

"What do you mean, matching shorts?"

"Nothing," Sadie replied, tired of the whole thing. "I'm done with this, Dean. I've been a pain in the ass and I've way overstepped my bounds."

"You were doing what you thought was right, although why on earth you picked this case to fixate on is beyond me," he said, half joking.

She couldn't exactly blurt out that it was because of Trudy's messages. Instead, she said, "I'm going to concentrate on clearing my name the old-fashioned way, with good old-fashioned hard work. What happened with the diamond pin and Sylvia Toth being shot was an unfortunate side effect of my not keeping my nose where it belongs."

"I'm reopening the case, Sadie."

"What?" She stopped short of drinking the water she'd just pulled from her fridge.

"That shirt stuff makes sense, and I'm not going to be able to sleep until I've answered some of the questions you've brought up and made sure the shooting and the tire slashing aren't tied in with the Toth house."

"Sounds like I've given you an extra load of work," Sadie said apologetically.

"Better you pointing it out than it being picked up by some reporter a year down the pike. Anyway, it won't hurt to do some more digging into the whole Run-Tec lead, and then, hopefully, we can put this baby to rest."

"Good."

"And that doesn't mean we're not still looking for

Kent Lasko or whoever banged off those bullets in your direction. Keep yourself safe."

"I'm trying."

After she hung up, Sadie showered, then made herself a salad and shared a handful of it with Hairy.

She checked her e-mails and found a couple tired old jokes forwarded to her from Dawn and a Run-Tec advertisement that smacked of the spam the store clerk had promised she wouldn't receive.

Sadie hit DELETE, then thought better of it and clicked on the e-mail folder that held all her recently deleted e-mails and found it.

When she opened the message it shouted in bold blue and red letters that they were having a WILD WACKY SALE! It demanded to know if she, Sadie Novak, had downloaded her coupon for half off the running shorts and did she know that, as a valued member of the Run-Tec online team, she could look forward to specials offered only to online members.

Sadie couldn't help but wonder how many people fell for the store clerk encouraging them to sign up on this Web site.

She clicked the link at the bottom of the e-mail and it brought her to the Run-Tec site. It took her ten minutes to locate an area on the site where she could discontinue her Run-Tec membership. Even then, she doubted she'd be removed permanently from the mailing list.

"Probably people still get e-mails long after they've died," she muttered to herself.

She made a mental note to ask Petrovich if he could find out if Kent was on their client list. If Kent Lasko wore Run-Tec clothing, that would've annoyed Grant. Then again, it would've angered him a helluva lot more to find out his friend was screwing his wife. Probably Kent couldn't face Grant. That's why he was shopping at the sports megastore in the mall instead of supporting his best friend's sportswear shop.

She frowned, switched her e-mail off, and opened FreeCell instead. While she clicked on cards she found her mind drifting again to Kent Lasko in a bright yellow running shirt.

"Damn."

To take her mind off Kent she dialed Dawn's number at work.

"Feel like getting together for a bite after work?"

"Sure, except John and I were going to go out for Chinese. But, hey, I'll just tell him I'm going out with my big sister instead."

"That's all right. I don't want you to cancel your plans," Sadie said, then added, "I could always join you, unless—"

"That would be great!"

"Good. I'd like to meet this guy who stole my sister's heart."

It gave her a reason to turn off the computer and focus on getting ready for their dinner instead of on the Toths. She changed into dark pants and a gray sweater. After applying some blush and lipstick, she felt human.

John turned out to be a nice enough guy. Certainly not Sadie's type, but he looked at Dawn like she was the best thing since biscotti met coffee, and Dawn seemed to reflect the same sentiments. They enjoyed their meals at a small Asian restaurant where John ordered for everyone. Sadie thought that was a little arrogant, but even she had to admit that he made great choices—she'd have to run twenty miles to burn off all the calories she consumed.

Sadie left them to enjoy dessert alone while gazing lovingly into each other's eyes. John had turned down her offer to pay, not even allowing her to leave the tip.

On her drive back home, Sadie passed one of the numerous local parks where joggers wound up and down paths and between trees, oblivious to the rain. She slowed to a stop at a crosswalk and two women jogged in front of her car, the reflective bands on their jogging gear glinting in the glow of streetlamps and car headlights.

As much as she tried to keep the thought from her head, every man she saw reminded her of Kent Lasko, all geared up to murder his lover and her husband.

She found herself desperately wanting to break into his house and search his dresser for the matching shorts. Obviously that would not be a great career move, since she would undoubtedly be caught either by the police and end up in jail or by Kent and end up dead.

She realized that just because the bloody shirt in the hamper was a yellow Run-Tec, that didn't prove Kent owned the exact same shirt.

"Forget it," she admonished herself out loud. "Think of something else."

An older, overweight man passed Sadie's car, walking his dog on the sidewalk. He reminded her a lot of her uncle Larry. Suddenly she knew exactly who *would* possibly know about Kent's jogging wear, and she couldn't resist cranking the steering wheel to turn her car around.

Her first stop was Ralph's Meats. He had the best garlic sausage in the Emerald City. She bought an entire coil of the good stuff, plus a large wedge of Gorgonzola.

Zack called her as she was steering her car into the Laskos' neighborhood.

"Just wanted to give you a heads-up that the police are on the scene of multiple gunshot victims found in Magnolia," he said.

"It'll take them a few days to work the scene, but we'll no doubt get the call—that is, if they're still willing to refer business to us," she said dryly.

"They will," he said with more confidence than she felt. "What are you up to?"

"Just some final checking into a few details on a little matter," she said vaguely.

"But you're not playing detective, right?"

"Nope," she said. "I just got tired of hiding out at home. I went to the store for sausage and Gorgonzola."

"That stuff'll kill you."

"Yeah, but I'm back jogging, so I can handle it. Gotta go."

Sadie parked her car one block down and half a block over from the Lasko residence. She grabbed a Mariners baseball cap she kept in the trunk and yanked it down on her head, then walked up the street in the misty drizzle carrying her bag of goodies.

She knew she was taking a risk. Kent or Christian could come driving down the street at any moment and spot her—but it was dark, she was wearing dark clothing, and she was betting they wouldn't expect to see her hoofing it up their street alone.

A squirrel darted out of a spruce tree and cut quickly across her path, and Sadie thought her heart would fly out of her chest. She made a few promises to God and the saints and then turned to walk up the sidewalk that led to the house belonging to Kent Lasko's nosy neighbor.

She rang the bell, and an eerie feeling crept over her when she realized she was probably being appraised through the peephole in the door. Finally the door opened a crack, and he spoke to her from behind the chain.

"What do you want? Tired of peeping in my neighbor's window?"

"Actually I'm here to see you, Mr. um . . ."

"Eckert. Rudy Eckert. What do you want?"

"Well, Mr. Eckert, I've been trying to put together a block watch committee for our neighborhood, and it's not been going that great. Then I remembered what you said about being the captain of your block watch, so I figured you'd be the perfect person to help me out."

There was a pause; she wondered whether Mr. Eckert bought her excuse.

"Hang on," he said and closed the door.

A minute later he reappeared.

"Everything you want to know about the program you'll find in here." He thrust a glossy brochure through the crack in the door.

Sadie took it and looked it over. It was a pamphlet on the Seattle Block Watch program.

"This is great, but I've already got this information. What I was hoping for was some one-on-one time with a successful block captain like yourself."

"Why should I miss watching *American Idol* to talk to you?"

Time to pull out the big artillery.

"I brought garlic sausage and Gorgonzola."

He closed the door, unhooked the chain, and opened it wide.

"Come on in."

Sadie had never met an old man who could resist smelly meat and moldy cheese.

Mr. Eckert wasn't going to win any awards for housekeeping. She was betting that Mrs. Eckert had either passed on or given up. He led her into the kitchen, snatched the bag from her hands, and dumped the cheese and sausage on the counter.

Sadie lifted a stack of newspapers from a chair at the kitchen table, put the papers on the floor, and took a seat.

He brought the sausage and cheese to the table on a cutting board with a huge knife in his hand and proceeded to slice pieces of cheese and saw off hunks of sausage. Stabbing the pieces of food with the tip of his knife, he popped them into his mouth.

"You always walk around with sausage and cheese?" he asked around a mouthful.

"No, but my mama always taught me to never call on someone empty-handed."

He pointed the knife in her direction. "Your mama is a smart woman."

Sadie felt only marginally guilty watching Mr. Eckert consume a year's worth of cholesterol at one sitting. Once he'd had his fill, he stuffed what was left into a Ziploc bag and quickly put it in the fridge, as if he was afraid she'd ask to keep the leftovers.

Then he took a large red binder off his kitchen counter and brought it to the table.

"Lots of people will try and tell you that block watch is only keeping an eye on your neighbors and reporting suspicious behavior."

"And it's not?"

"No. It's much more." He grabbed a toothpick from a small container and began picking his teeth and sucking the food off. "Take you, for example. I bet one of your neighbors had a break-in and that's why you decided to start a block watch."

"Actually, it was me who had the break-in."

"Aha!" He pointed the toothpick at her. "This is how it always starts. People wait to be broken into and then they put things in place to stop it." He shook his head as if this was the biggest crime of all. "But it's not too late. You need to be extra vigilant now, because they will be back."

"The burglars?"

"Yes. They know you have insurance and they'll wait until you file your claim, replace all your property, and then boom!" He slammed a fist on the table, making Sadie jump. "They come back and steal from you again."

"Wow."

Sadie really didn't want to stay here all night. She needed to move this conversation back in the right direction.

"So tell me, Mr. Eckert, how do you do it? How do you keep tabs on everyone on the street?"

"With this." He patted his red binder lovingly. "Everything I see and hear on this street goes into this book."

Now we're getting somewhere!

"Do you mind if I take a look at that?" Sadie asked, snaking her hand out to grab it.

Mr. Eckert clutched it against his chest.

"There's lots of personal stuff in here." He flipped the binder open and slid his finger down a page. "This entry, for example. Last Tuesday morning at six, Miss Yakamoto in the bungalow at the corner kissed her new boyfriend good-bye on the front porch."

"And you wrote that down?" Sadie could barely contain her smile.

"Of course, and it's not because I give a donkey's arse who she's fooling around with. It's because if I know who belongs on the street, then it's easier for me to spot the impostors and the would-be burglars." He flipped to the next page. "See here." He flashed her the page briefly. "That was the time I caught you spying in Kent's windows."

"Right." Sadie nodded thoughtfully. "It must be really hard to keep track of everyone, though. For example, if Kent Lasko went jogging at odd hours, how could you possibly mark it down every single time? You're human and you need your sleep."

"Sure, but not as much as I used to. I've got problems with my bowels and I'm up every hour like a newborn baby."

That was entirely too much information.

"I see. So you've probably never seen Kent jogging. Or anyone else," she quickly added. "If they do it during those times when you're in bed or, um, indisposed."

"Only saw Kent jog a couple times, with his brother. Christian can run like the wind, but it didn't really look like Kent's thing, even though he was wearing all those bright running duds like Christian. Kent likes to ski, though. He's got a buddy who has a condo in Tahoe, and he goes there a couple times a year."

Damn. So much for that idea.

"Now old Mr. Diago across the lane has taken up jogging recently." Mr. Eckert got to his feet and opened his kitchen window blinds. "He's a fatty, but he won't be for long 'cause he's been sticking to a regular schedule. See?"

Sadie got to her feet and politely looked where Mr. Eckert was pointing. She saw a dark blur of a large person exiting a back gate across the lane. When the person got closer, Mr. Eckert's motion detector flood-lights came on and illuminated his entire backyard and parking pad.

Sadie drew in a sharp intake of breath.

"Mr. Eckert, is that your car?"

"Of course it's my car. It's in my driveway, isn't it?"

"Does it have some rust on the driver's door?"

"Sure, but it still runs like a top."

"You know, a green Toyota like that one drove by my house and shot at me. Put a lady in the hospital."

"It sure as hell wasn't my car," he said indignantly. "It hasn't left that spot in ages except to get the tires rotated."

"Are you sure?"

"Of course I'm sure. I wouldn't've let Christian take it to the garage for a tire rotation, but he offered since he had a coupon to get it done for free and didn't need his own tires done. I figured what the hell. The tires don't look no different to me, though."

Sadie swallowed nervously. If Christian had the car, Kent had access to it. The hairs on the back of her neck stood up, and she felt a sudden need to snuggle with Hairy.

"Well, thank you for your time, Mr. Eckert," she said. "I can see I have lots to learn before I can hope to be captain of my block watch."

"Wait just a second. Let me show you my highlighting system." He flipped the binder open to the last few entries, privacy be damned. "See how I've highlighted some in yellow, a few in green, and a couple in pink?"

"Yes," Sadie said with barely passing interest.

"It helps me to keep track of the hours people are at work."

"Why would you want to know that?"

He looked at her like she was crazy.

"Jeez, you do have lots to learn." He shook his head. "Well, if I know who's at work at what time, I know when I should be keeping a special watch on their house. The thieves always wait for people to go to work. So those working normal nine-to-five jobs I've got highlighted in yellow, those working night shift are in green, and the oddball hours, unemployed or retired are all highlighted in pink."

"Right." Sadie nodded. "So how would you keep track of the Laskos next door for example? Christian works nights, and since Kent is a Realtor, his hours can't be regular."

"Yes, that's why I've got them here. See?" He pointed to *K. Lasko* highlighted in green and *K. Lasko* highlighted in pink.

"So you've highlighted Kent in green and pink, meaning that he works nights and odd hours?"

He shook his head. "No I've got Kent in pink because he works odd hours, but his brother is green because he works nights as a janitor at a school."

"Oh, I was confused because you labeled them both with the first initial K."

"Their names both do start with K," he explained. "Kristian spells his name with a K as well."

"Are you sure?" She felt a little dizzy.

"Of course I'm sure," he snapped. "Sometimes the stupid postie drops their mail at my house and I have to walk it over. All Kristian's mail has his name spelled with a K."

"And you said he's janitor at a school?"

"Yeah but not a regular kind. A special one somewhere."

"A school for the deaf maybe?"

"Yeah, that's it."

Sadie's head swam with the information. "I've got a headache. I really should go."

He walked her to the door.

"I'd be happy to walk you through the hazards of surveillance next week. You can bring some corned beef next time. Sausage gives me the burps." He belched as if making a point.

She shook his hand, thanked him for his time, and promised to stay in touch.

As she quick-walked back to her car, Sadie was aware of every person out for an evening stroll and every shadow. Her heartbeat raced whenever she passed a shrub close to the sidewalk where someone could be hiding. She jogged the last half block and peered inside the backseat of her car before opening the door, climbing behind the wheel, and locking the doors.

She turned the key in the ignition and didn't take a breath until she'd floored the accelerator and was two blocks away.

When she stopped at a red light half a mile away, she dialed Zack's number.

"Did you know that Kent Lasko's brother, Kristian, spells his name with a K?" she asked.

"And this is important why?" he asked.

Sadie heard a woman's voice in the background before Zack covered the phone with his hand.

"It's important because Trudy tried to send me a message spelling the name of the person who killed her and only got out the letter K and I've been thinking all along that she meant Kent."

"So now you're thinking Kristian killed her?"

"Yes. Maybe."

"Well, as long as you're sure." He chuckled.

"Look, Kristian is a jogger and whoever killed Trudy wore a Run-Tec shirt."

"How do you know Kent isn't a jogger?"

The pitch of her voice rose. "Because the captain of the block watch told me that Kent doesn't jog as much as his brother, and, trust me, this guy would know."

"Calm down. You sound hysterical."

"Besides, Kristian also worked as a janitor at a school for the deaf!"

She heard Paula, or whoever, talking to Zack in the background, and her grip on the steering wheel tightened.

"Okay, you're right. It's probably nonsense," she said, suddenly anxious to be off the phone.

"Maybe not nonsense, but you might be jumping to conclusions. Share what you know with Petrovich and I'll call you later, okay? I've got another call coming in."

Sadie told him that was fine and then she pulled into a 7-Eleven and bought herself a large Slurpee and a chocolate bar.

By the time she got home, she was feeling both mildly sated by the excess sugar and a whole lot embarrassed about calling Zack. He was right. She was jumping to conclusions. What she needed to do was think things through calmly, and then, if it still sounded plausible, she'd call Petrovich with the details.

She walked into her house and hustled to turn off her alarm after she dead-bolted the front door. Then she went to toss her Slurpee cup in the kitchen trash. Hairy came skidding across the linoleum, and as Sadie bent down to greet him she noticed movement out by her back door. Her breath caught in her throat, but fear turned to laughter when she saw that the movement was caused by Maeva standing on her back deck, her eyes wide and a stupid smile on her face.

"You sure are persistent," Sadie said as she opened the door.

Her mind registered her fatal mistake even before Maeva cried out, "I'm so sorry, Sadie!"

Kristian Lasko shoved Maeva through the door ahead of him, a revolver pressed to the back of her head.

His eyes were wild with rage.

"If you scream," he whispered, "I'll blow her head off."

19

Sadie leapt backward and stumbled, but Kristian grabbed her by the front of her shirt and pressed the muzzle of the gun roughly to her cheek.

"Not one word," he said icily.

Hairy, being the pillar of support to his mistress that he always was, hopped out the open door to his freedom. Sadie had no time to be concerned for her pet because Kristian's eyes never left hers as he kicked the back door closed with his foot and reached behind him to lock it tight.

"Let Maeva go. She's got nothing to do with this."

"Like hell," Kristian barked. "She's been sitting out there in her car watching you. You would've been better off getting that guy who works for you to play bodyguard rather than using your wimpy friend."

"I should've warned you," Maeva said, her eyes pained.

"You did it. You killed Trudy and Grant," Sadie said, focusing on Kristian's hard eyes.

She grimaced as he roughly grabbed her upper arm and forced the two of them out of the kitchen and down the hall. He kept one hand clamped on Sadie's arm and the other pointing a gun at Maeva.

"I never killed Grant," Kristian said. "God, the guy was such a wuss. I was still in the house after things went bad with Trudy. When I heard him come home

I hid in the upstairs closet. He came into the bedroom, saw his wife, and totally lost it. I thought I'd have to kill him before he dialed nine-one-one, but instead he just cried like a baby and went downstairs and blew his head off." Kristian shook his head in disbelief. "So I showered, put on some of Grant's clothes, and got the hell out of there."

"But why did you kill Trudy? Didn't you love her?" Maeva asked him.

"Damn straight I loved her. And she loved *me*, not him," Kristian snarled. "That's why I gave her my mother's necklace. My own mother's necklace!" he shouted. "I was going to marry the bitch, but she got cold feet, so I went over there to reason with her. When she told me she'd had the abortion I just couldn't take it! Do you believe that bitch? After all I went through to learn sign language. I'd even traded with another dude at the janitorial service so that I could clean the school she worked at, and those people are pigs, I tell you."

He waved the gun at them.

"Now get on the bed!" he shouted.

The two women took a seat side by side on the edge of the bed.

"So Kent broke into the house afterward to get the necklace and cover up for you. Nice brother," Sadie sneered. "Covering your ass even for murder."

"He only went to get the necklace because he didn't want to tarnish Trudy's reputation. He never knew I had anything to do with what happened because he believed me when I told him I'd broken it off with her last year. He just figured Grant had lost his mind when he discovered the affair." He chuckled maniacally. "You know it just about killed Kent to have to lie and tell you he was the one that was screwing Trudy. Saint Kent." He shook his head slowly. "And everything would've been fine except the moron just grabbed everything, including that damn fancy pin."

He walked to the window and yanked the blinds down. "But you!"

He whirled on Sadie, and with a furious growl he slammed the butt of the gun down on her head.

She moaned in agony and swayed as spots danced in front of her eyes.

"You were the reason Kent lied about a trip to Tahoe. He just went down to Portland because he knew the aunt suspected something with Trudy. He wanted to find out from the aunt if I'd ended it with Trudy when I said I did. Guess he was suspicious, thanks to you. But it was a waste of time, since the old biddy was here staying with Sylvia. When Kent got back, he heard about Grant's mom being shot and he figured it had to be me."

"Because it was you," Sadie said. "How could you do that?"

"It's your fault!" he shouted. "Kent called and begged me to turn myself in. Said he couldn't turn me in, blood being thicker than water and all that." He rolled his eyes. "Well, he doesn't have to worry. I'm cleaning up what I started. You'll both be dead. Another tragic murder-suicide."

"You can't do that," Maeva cried.

Kristian threw his hands up toward the ceiling and started pacing. "It's not my fault. Blame your friend." He whirled on Sadie and waved the gun in her face. "And don't think I didn't warn you. I tried, but you just wouldn't back off. Slashed your tires, fired a few rounds at you. But damned if you don't just keep on coming back for more. Well, you'll get more," he spat.

Sadie's head ached, but she tried to focus on finding something, anything, to grab and use as a weapon. If he'd leave them alone for a second she could get her gun from the closet and use it.

"I don't think the front door is locked," Maeva blurted suddenly, as if reading Sadie's mind.

"I don't remember locking it," Sadie added, hoping he would go check.

"It's locked." He smiled wildly. "And you don't need to get me out of the room to get the gun down from the top shelf of the closet. As a matter of fact, I'll get it down for you. It'll sure make things easier."

"You were watching me," Sadie whispered in disbelief.

"Yeah, and when I saw you had a gun of your own I knew how to solve things. You're depressed after cleaning up blood and stuff. Nobody would ever question it if you went off the deep end and killed yourself after taking out your friend here."

Abruptly, Maeva closed her eyes and began to hum *The Wizard of Oz* tune.

Oh God, she's trying to summon the dead!

Sadie swallowed, but the lump of terror in her throat remained. Suddenly the room temperature began to plummet. Maeva kept on humming, and Kristian looked at her like she was a pesky insect.

"What the hell's wrong with her?"

He didn't seem to expect an answer because he turned and walked to the closet, then opened the door and felt around on the top shelf with one hand while never taking his eyes off Sadie and Maeva.

"I'm getting your gun, and this time you'll follow through. You'll kill your friend and then yourself."

He didn't appear to notice that his breath came out in a white cloud.

"Why would I kill my friend and myself if you'll just shoot me anyway?" Sadie asked, hoping to keep him talking.

He turned to face her and as he did, a box lifted off the closet shelf behind him. The box levitated and moved slowly just outside of Kristian's peripheral vision.

"You'll do it because there are worse ways to die

than a precisely aimed bullet. In your line of work I would think that you would know that. I'm not above slowly dissecting one of you while the other one watches."

Sadie looked into his dead eyes and knew he was telling the truth.

Maeva kept on humming, and when Kristian began searching the closet shelf again, Sadie knew the gun was no longer there. She saw that the shoe box with her Ruger was now beside her feet, partially protruding from under the bed.

Kristian was getting increasingly frustrated.

"Where the hell is it?" he snarled, tossing down a stack of folded sweaters.

"It's—it's behind the photo box," Sadie said, just needing him to turn around briefly. "Use the chair."

Maeva's humming had stopped, and Sadie could feel the anger radiating from her.

Finally Kristian took his eyes off them long enough to stand on the chair and move a large box of photos on the closet shelf. Sadie bent swiftly and her fingers snaked to the floor. She snapped the lid off the shoe box and snagged the gun.

When she lifted her hand, Kristian was just turning around. He fired a shot. It missed Sadie and took out a portion of her mattress.

There was more shooting and the sound of breaking glass. Sadie could hear screams and knew one was her own. She watched as part of Kristian's skull exploded and a spray of blood and bone fragments hit her wall before he slid down to become a heap on the floor.

Sadie stared down at the gun in her hand, momentarily perplexed. She didn't remember pulling the trigger. Someone was calling her name. It took seconds for the voice to register as Zack's. She turned and looked through the shattered remains of her bedroom window to see Zack's face, as pale as her own felt.

She turned to Maeva and screamed when she saw the psychic had fallen back onto the bed. Blood oozed from her side.

"I'm okay," Maeva said, wincing as she spoke. "Go open the door for the cops."

As if in a trance, Sadie ran down the hall, passing Pam to open the front door. Behind Zack came Detective Petrovich.

The detective had a fearsome look in his eyes that would've been more believable had he not been carrying Hairy tucked tenderly under one arm.

Sadie rushed back to Maeva's side.

"It isn't bad. Just a scratch," Maeva said, but she groaned a little as she sat up.

"Just relax," Sadie said, trying not to look at what was left of Kristian Lasko.

"It was Grant who came," Maeva said, a small smile playing on her lips. "I felt his presence, and the minute I started humming it was like he'd been waiting around you all the time for a chance to get back at that guy. He whisked that gun to us like a pro." She chuckled.

"He sure did." Sadie smiled back. "I hope he's at rest now."

"Who? What are you talking about?" Petrovich demanded.

"Nothing," Maeva and Sadie shouted simultaneously.

"He *is* resting," Maeva whispered to Sadie. "He's with Trudy now."

"You got it right," Sadie whispered back. "You said you saw brushes, mops, and buckets. Kristian's a janitor. You were right."

"Of course I was right," Maeva said indignantly.

Maeva's wound was superficial, but the ambulance took her to the hospital, where she got a few stitches. After the strobe lights of the police cruisers stopped illuminating her yard, Sadie began to piece it all together.

"It was Kent who called you, wasn't it?" she asked Zack. "He finally decided to give up his brother instead of protecting him."

"Actually, Maeva was the one who called," he replied. "She got my number off a business card you gave her. She called me up and said that Grant told her it was Kristian who killed Trudy. Grant killed himself, Sadie. The suicide part of the evidence was right."

"That's why I couldn't see Grant. He really did kill himself." Sadie put a hand to her throbbing head. "And Kristian borrowed his neighbor's car and used it to try and shoot me, but he hit Mrs. Toth instead. And he had it again when I was at the spa."

"We would've gotten here sooner, but Petrovich pulled Kent over a block away. It took a while to figure out that he'd just been following Kristian, trying to stop him. Kent knew that if you kept looking at him you'd find out he was really covering for his brother. Maybe that's why he came over to talk to you." He blew out a long breath. "It's a good thing Grant filled Maeva in. She headed right over here to keep an eye on you until I could get here."

"Remind me to send that woman flowers," Sadie said. "Or diamonds. Maybe both."

"I screwed up." He shook his head slowly. "I should've taken you more seriously and called it in right away when you called me about Kristian," he admitted, his lips in a tight line. "I was almost too late."

"It's not your fault. Hell, you rescued me. And Maeva. Oh, and Hairy." Sadie clasped her fingers tightly in her lap because they'd yet to stop trembling. She glanced around her house sadly. "I never realized my next job would be my own place."

"Not a chance," Zack said. "This one's on me. You

and Hairy can stay with me. When the cops are done here, I'll do the cleanup. Jackie called and said she'll be back in town tomorrow, so she can help. It'll be her first job with Scene-2-Clean, so we can both judge how well she does."

"I don't think that's such a good idea."

"We'll never know if she's any good unless we see her at work."

"I'm not talking about Jackie doing the cleaning. I'm talking about staying at your place. *That's* not a good idea."

"My sofa is a helluva lot more comfortable than yours."

She met his eyes. His sofa might be comfortable, but they both knew it didn't have the restraints required to keep her from his bed.

20

Zack insisted on taking the sofa and giving Sadie his bed. She felt warm and safe as she crawled under his covers, surrounding herself with his scent. Shock and exhaustion overcame her, and it wasn't long before she fell into a dreamless sleep.

When she woke up she called to check on Maeva.

"I told you it was only a scratch. I doubt I'll even have a scar to show for my troubles," Maeva said over the phone. "Oh, and don't think I've forgotten my promise to you."

"What promise is that?"

"I told you I'd try and put you in touch with Brian, and I will. As soon as you're ready."

"Thanks," Sadie said, "but I think I'll pass. At least for now."

"Are you sure?"

"Yeah. I'm not so sure that even matters anymore. It can't change anything. Besides, there's some other, more important stuff I've been putting off." Sadie glanced up at Pam, who'd popped in at Zack's place. "I'll call you in a few days so I can take you out for a thanks-for-saving-my-life fancy dinner."

"Great. I like steak and lobster."

Sadie put down the phone and smiled wearily up at Pam.

"I've got a great day planned to help us forget all

our troubles," Pam said, clapping her hands together with excitement.

Sadie listened quietly while Pam described their itinerary.

"We're going to start by giving each other complete manicures and pedicures. Afterward, we'll do each other's hair while we watch a really stupid comedy. You can send Zack to the video store to get one."

Sadie just looked at her best friend forlornly.

"We need to spend some girlfriend time, all right. I'll get Zack's keys. We're long overdue for a field trip."

Zack figured she was still too shaken to drive, so she and Pam road in the backseat while he took the wheel. Pam was a chatterbox, cracking jokes about Zack and his cute ass. She was trying her best to get Sadie to giggle, but laughter wasn't the order of the day.

Sadie kept her eyes forward, her gaze occasionally connecting with Zack's in the rearview mirror.

Finally Zack steered his Mustang between wrought-iron gates and up a narrow, winding lane. At the top of the hill, he stopped at the exact location that Sadie instructed.

"Stay here," Sadie told Zack. "I don't think this'll take long."

Sadie climbed out and held the door for Pam. The two of them walked slowly across the belt of green grass between the grave markers. The sun peeked out from behind the thinning clouds and warmed Sadie's face as they walked.

"Why are we here?" Pam asked, her eyes wary and her smile faltering.

"Remember when we went for that spa weekend on Vancouver Island?" Sadie asked.

"Sure. It was positively divine. I've never felt that pampered in my life. Remember the boy toys who served drinks in the bar?" She winked.

"Your back was sure bothering you on that trip,"

Sadie reminded her. "You'd taken enough painkillers to knock out a horse. You could barely get out of bed most of the weekend."

"Well, yeah, my back always hurts."

"True." Sadie nodded. "It got so bad that when we got back to Seattle I had to take you to the hospital."

"That's right." Pam nodded. "My God, those kidney stones were awful!"

"Not kidney stones." Sadie had stopped walking now and looked at Pam sadly. "They performed some tests, then exploratory surgery. Your belly was filled with cancer. The doctors suspected it had spread rapidly from your ovaries. There was nothing they could do but close you back up."

"No, that's not right." She looked worried and perplexed. "It wasn't cancer. It was kidney stones and—"

"Pam, you've been my best friend for so very long. You always let me lean on you."

"And I've leaned on you. It worked both ways."

"No. I've let you down." The tears blurred Sadie's vision, but she didn't wipe them away when they coursed down her cheeks. "I've just needed you so damned much that I forgot what *you* needed. I didn't want to lose you."

"Don't be silly. This is what friends do, Sadie. We're there for each other."

"It's time, Pam."

"I don't know what you mean."

"Yes you do."

Sadie took a deep breath and pointed to the grave marker at her feet, which read PAMELA LAWRENCE, BORN MAY 3, 1967, WENT TO BE WITH GOD NOVEMBER 5, 2005.

Pam shook her head vehemently. "No."

Sadie swallowed the lump in her throat and turned to face her friend. She put her hands on Pam's shoulders and fought the icy revulsion that crept through her fingers.

"You're dead, Pam. You died of ovarian cancer two years ago. I stayed by your side until your spirit left your body. You've been by my side ever since." Sadie's voice cracked. "It's time for you to go."

"I don't want to," Pam whimpered.

"It's time."

"I don't even know how . . ."

"Let go. Let go of your life. Let go of me."

Sadie released her friend's shoulders and watched as Pam's spirit knelt on the ground beside her own grave marker. Pam traced the outline of the engraved words with the tip of her finger, and slowly her shape began to fade.

"Good-bye," Pam whispered, looking beseechingly up at Sadie.

Finally Pam's essence shimmered around the edges and vanished altogether.

Sadie covered her face with her hands and swallowed a sob. With a deep breath, she turned around, aware that Zack was watching her, leaning casually up against his car. Sadie walked toward him and didn't look back.

Turn the page for a preview
of the next Ghost Dusters Mystery.
Coming from Obsidian in December 2008.

When she walked in, Sadie expected the sickening stench of ammonia that proclaimed the outwardly tidy bungalow a clandestine meth lab. She did *not* expect to be confronted by a vicious Rottweiler preparing to rip her to shreds. A step backward and Sadie found herself pinned against the screen door that had snapped shut behind her.

"Easy, boy," Sadie said, although it was doubtful the dog could hear her muffled voice behind her respirator.

The dog snarled, snapped, and inched forward. Thick ropes of saliva dangled from his yellow teeth.

Sadie's knees shook as she grappled behind her back for the door latch. The sleeve of her disposable hazmat suit snagged and caught on the splintered door frame. *Damn!* She tugged hard and stumbled when her arm came free. The dog lunged.

Sadie shielded her face with her arms and braced for the pain of teeth sinking into her flesh but felt only a mild shudder of revulsion. She looked around and realized the dog had sailed right through her to drop to the ground outside the door.

Sadie put a hand to her heart and blew out a relieved breath as she stepped outside. She pulled off her respirator and watched the confused dog as he attempted to right himself. Sadie now noticed the other side of his body. A large strip of flesh hung from his rear flank. Through the fatal wound, she could see the knee-high grass and weeds that covered the acreage behind the house.

"Hey, Fido, you're dead." Sadie chuckled.

When the mutilated canine charged again, snapping and snarling, Sadie merely closed her eyes and prepared for the skin-crawling disgust that flooded through her whenever the spirits of the dead touched her body.

"Talking to ghosts again?" Zack asked as he came around the corner of the house carrying a stack of rubber medical waste bins.

"A dog," she replied, rubbing her hand over her short-cropped hair.

"A ghost dog?" Zack grinned, put down the bins, and straightened to his near six feet.

"Yeah and he scared the hell out of me."

"Riiight. The lady who mops blood, guts, and meth while talking to ghosts is afraid of a dead puppy."

"He's a big Rotty, not a cuddly puppy." She fanned her face with her hand.

"Dogs scare you but dealing with human spirits is, apparently, a walk in the park." The lines around his dark eyes crinkled with amusement.

"I forgot the cops had to shoot a guard dog when they raided this place."

"It happens. The dog was probably trained to protect the house. Guess you can't fault a businessman for protecting his assets."

"You can if that business is crystal meth."

He nodded in agreement and wiped sweat from his forehead.

"Man, it's hot."

Sadie reached to help him with a couple of the bins. Zack went for them at the same time and their hands touched. They both jerked their fingers away as if they'd been singed. With an awkward smile, Zack hurriedly picked up the containers and walked toward the back door.

Sadie watched as the dog leapt in the air in a desperate attempt to tackle Zack.

"Oh give it up," Sadie muttered.

The Rottweiler skidded to a halt. He tilted his head at Sadie in a look of comical bewilderment. The poor thing had no idea why his attempts to ward them off were futile. Sadie was at a loss about how to explain to a dead dog that he was, in fact, dead.

She fell into step behind Zack and walked up the back steps with him. Pausing while Zack got out his disposable hazmat suit, they chatted about the estimated time involved in cleaning the meth lab.

Suddenly, they both glanced across the grassy field toward the sound of a vehicle kicking up gravel.

"There's a dirt road beyond that tree line." Zack pointed across the scrub of grass and tall cedars that edged the back of the property. "Nothing else down that road. Somebody must've made a wrong turn."

Sadie was about to say something but stopped when she heard another sound.

"What?" Zack asked.

Sadie strained to listen, then shook her head.

"Nothing." She prepared to slip on her headgear. "I think I'll stop by the other scene later today to see how Jackie's doing." When Zack gave her a skeptical look, she added, "I'm not checking up on her."

"Yes, you are." He held up his hands in a stopping motion. "That's all right. Scene-2-Clean is your company. You have every right to make sure your employee's doing a decent job on the first scene she's worked alone."

"I don't want her to think I don't trust her. It's just—" She stopped.

There was that sound again. Turning, Sadie stared a couple dozen feet away, across the weed-choked yard to an old wooden garden shed. A warm wind fingered the tall grass and a crow cawed from the top of a monkey puzzle tree.

"That's funny. I keep thinking I hear a—" She broke off and turned to Zack.

The look on his face said he heard it, too.

When the noise came again, Sadie realized it was definitely the muffled, keening cry of a newborn baby.

"There's a baby in that shed," Sadie said, already down the steps and walking toward the building.

Zack caught up and stopped her with a hand on her arm.

"Before the Seattle police released this property to us for cleaning, they would've cleared the outbuildings," Zack said, his voice tight. "Whoever's in there showed up since then. They could've been dropped off by the car we just heard."

"Some methhead could be holed-up with her baby waiting for this place to reopen for business," Sadie said. "We'd better go tell her to do her shopping elsewhere."

Again, Zack put a hand on her arm.

"We?"

Sadie nodded. "Yeah. We."

She determinedly shrugged off his hand and walked toward the shed. Zack started after her, the two of them stamping down the tall dry grass as they angled across the yard. They stopped when they were a couple feet away. Sadie wiped the sweat from the back of her neck. The sun was rising, and it was promising to reach into the eighties by noon.

"Get back," Zack hissed in her ear and pulled something from the waistband of his jeans.

Sadie's eyes grew wide.

"Since when do you carry a gun when we work a scene?"

"Since you decided to let Scene-2-Clean mop up meth labs instead of just trauma cleans."

"Helping out Scour Power is temporary. Just until Egan gets back."

"Then this is temporary, too." He indicated his gun.

The infant's cries cut into their discussion.

"Just step aside, Sadie, and let me do my job."

Her back straightened.

"You're not a cop anymore, Zack. I shouldn't have to remind you that you work for *me*."

He rolled his eyes.

"Are we going to have a pissing contest right here and now?"

"Well, no, because you have better equipment for that."

"Fine. Go ahead," he whispered, stepping aside and indicating the door with his hand. "The person with that baby is probably a paranoid tweeker out of her mind from withdrawal and hoping to trade her baby for a dot of crystal."

Sadie cringed.

"Okay, I guess you *do* have more training in this sort of thing."

"You think?"

The baby's cries sounded frantic.

"Don't just stand there, Mr. Macho." She nodded. "Do your thing."

"Stay outside until I tell you it's safe." His jaw tightened and his dark eyes hardened into bullets.

"Just hurry up."

Plastering his back to the wall of the windowless building, Zack slipped into cop mode like it hadn't been a couple of years since he'd turned in his badge. Using both hands to hold his gun in ready position, he called out, "I'm armed! Throw down your weapons and come out with your hands up or I'll come in shooting!"

"That's a little extreme," Sadie whispered to his back.

"Shut up."

There was no answering shuffle of movement or voices from within. The only sound was the muted wail of a baby. Sadie had a chilling visual of a drug-crazed lunatic holding the newborn. She nudged Zack's back with her finger.

"Go already."

In one quick movement, Zack booted open the thin door. Splinters of dry wood fluttered in the air. He disappeared inside and Sadie heard him suck in a gasp and blow out a loud curse.

She hurried into the building. Her eyes took a few seconds to adjust to the dim interior. The smell hit her first—a peculiar barnyard scent. Her bewildered gaze went to Zack, then zoomed in on what had captured his look of disgust. On the opposite side of the ten-by-ten space was a makeshift bench, and on it lay the body of a goat. The eviscerated animal was on its side, its pale tongue protruding between lifeless lips.

Sadie noticed a tiny fist rise up from behind the animal carcass and she took a step forward.

"Don't go any closer," Zack warned. "We need to call this in. The carcass could be booby-trapped."

"A booby-trapped goat?" Sadie raised her eyebrows at him.

"Hey, it's a baby beside a mutilated goat. You explain it."

Sadie could only shake her head. There was no explaining it but she knew what had to be done. She crossed the dirt floor, swallowed nervously, then shoved the animal aside to get at the tiny infant wedged snugly between the goat and wall. With rapid movement, Sadie scooped the baby boy from his dismal hiding place and noted the infant's umbilical cord had been tied with twine. She unzipped her hazmat suit and pulled the sobbing child to her chest. He curled against the hard buttons of her shirt and his vulnerable body, tacky with blood and vernix, vibrated against her.

About the Author

Wendy Roberts lives in Surrey, British Columbia, along with her husband and four children. She is currently at work on her next novel. You can visit her at www.wendyroberts.com.